Praise for Gigi Pandian's Jaya Jones Treasure Hunt Mysteries

# ARTIFACT

"Pandian's new series may well captivate a generation of readers, combining the suspenseful, mysterious and romantic."

— 4 stars from *Romantic Times* Book Reviews

"If Indiana Jones had a sister, it would definitely be historian Jaya Jones."

— *Suspense Magazine*

"How wonderful to see a young, new writer who harks back to the Golden Age of mystery fiction. *Artifact* is witty, clever, and twisty... Do you like Agatha Christie? Elizabeth Peters? Then you're going to love Gigi Pandian."

— Aaron Elkins,
Edgar Award-Winning Author of the
Gideon Oliver "Skeleton Detective" Mysteries

"Fans of Elizabeth Peters will adore following along with Jaya Jones and a cast of quirky characters as they pursue a fabled treasure."

— *New York Times* Bestselling Author Juliet Blackwell,
Author of the Art Lover's Mystery Series (written as Hailey Lind)

"In her fast-paced and entertaining debut novel, Gigi Pandian brings readers into a world full of mystery and history...As with classics in the genre, this first book in the Jaya Jones series will appeal to readers who enjoy delving into a complex puzzle."

— ForeWord Reviews

"Elizabeth Peters' Vicky Bliss mysteries were fun romantic capers with unexpected twists. Gigi Pandian offers that same exotic world of treasure hunts, foreign lands, and a touch of romance. I miss Vicky Bliss. But, now we're all lucky to have Jaya Jones' treasure hunts. I hope *Artifact* is just the first of Gigi Pandian's skillfully written capers."

— Lesa's Book Critiques

"Masterfully plotted."

— Midwest Book Review

"*Artifact* is a jewel of an adventure, and Jaya Jones is a plucky heroine to treasure."

—Avery Aames,
Nationally Bestselling Author of A Cheese Shop Mystery Series

"Pandian is an adept storyteller. *Artifact* has it all—castles in the mist and caves at midnight; archeologists and fairies; hidden treasures and a bit of magic as well. Taking us on a journey from San Francisco to London to Scotland, Pandian weaves a mystery with all the elements of a good puzzle."

— Camille Minichino,
Author of the Periodic Table Mysteries

"*Artifact* is a treasure...a page-turning, suspenseful story."

— Penny Warner, Author of *How to Host a Killer Party*

# ARTIFACT

# The Jaya Jones Treasure Hunt Mystery Series
## by Gigi Pandian

### Novels

ARTIFACT (#1)
PIRATE VISHNU (#2)
(*February 2014*)

### Novellas

FOOL'S GOLD (prequel to ARTIFACT)
(in OTHER PEOPLE'S BAGGAGE)

# ARTIFACT

A JAYA JONES TREASURE HUNT MYSTERY

# GIGI PANDIAN

HENERY PRESS

ARTIFACT
A Jaya Jones Treasure Hunt Mystery
Part of the Henery Press Mystery Collection

First Edition
Trade paperback edition | August 2013

Henery Press
www.henerypress.com

This is a work of fiction. Any references to historical events, real people, or real locales are used fictitiously. Other names, characters, places, and incidents are the product of the author's imagination, and any resemblance to actual events or locales or persons, living or dead, is entirely coincidental.

*56023616  3/15*

ISBN-13: 978-1-938383-68-7

Printed in the United States of America

*To James.*

# ACKNOWLEDGMENTS

So many thanks are in order. I'm especially grateful to the following people who helped make this book possible:

The Pens Fatales, the best writers group a gal could have—especially Julie and Sophie, who I'm fortunate to count as both mentors and friends, and Martha, who never fails to show me how to get things done. My early readers, Emberly Nesbitt, Brian Selfon, Carol Fairweather, and Janet Bolin, for their encouragement as I learned to craft a mystery. The Sisters in Crime Guppies, who taught me so much about this crazy business, including what great people mystery writers can be. Members of the Northern California Chapter of Sisters in Crime, for their ongoing support and friendship.

The Malice Domestic Grants Committee, for seeing the potential in this book and giving me the push I needed to take my writing seriously. My agent, Jill Marsal, for taking a chance on me and believing in this book. My editor, Ramona DeFelice Long, for helping me execute my ideas and turn this book into what I knew it could be, and copyeditor extraordinaire Nancy Adams. Historians Taymiya Zaman of the University of San Francisco and Joanna Williams of UC Berkeley, who helped me bring history alive. And Henery Press, especially Kendel Flaum, for believing in me and Jaya.

The doctors and nurses at Kaiser Permanente in Oakland, for saving my life so I could live to see this book come to fruition. My partner in crime, Diane Vallere, without whom I never would have gotten this far. My parents, for being the most supportive parents on the planet and for never doubting I would succeed—even though they knew firsthand how difficult it is to write a good book. And James, for always believing in me.

# CHAPTER 1

The door of the house swung open before I had a chance to knock. It was almost midnight. The woman in front of me was fully dressed and held a cup of coffee in her hand, which I hoped for her sake was decaffeinated. Her face was in shadow as she stood in the door frame of the San Francisco Victorian, but the dim porch light must have illuminated all of me down to my toes, for I heard her breath catch.

"Is that blood on your shoe?" Nadia asked.

I glanced down at my shoes. I admit they were stilettos tonight. I always wear heels of some sort for the added height.

"Your note said a package had been delivered for me?"

"You are bloodied," she said in her thick Russian accent. "Yet you speak of mail." She turned her back to me and gestured with her free arm, ushering me inside the house along with the large tabla drum case slung over my shoulder.

I didn't resist my inquisitive landlady as much as I normally would have. I like my independence. The news I had received earlier that day had thrown me off balance. Without meaning to, I found myself following her inside, setting my tabla case in the corner, and sitting down on the stiff sofa.

"It was one of those helpful men, no?" she asked, handing me a box of tissues. "I knew it! One of those nice fellows this city is full of, who offer to help you carry your drum case when you are out at a 'gig.' One of them was too insistent, eh?"

"Nadia—"

"You could not resist putting him in his place. Stomping on his innocent foot with your treacherous heel as he valiantly offered to help ease your burden." She swept her arm through the air in front of her. "You drew blood, and it splashed up from the tip of your heel onto the cuff of his Dockers and the top of your high-heeled shoe."

My eyes widened as I imagined the vivid scene. Just because there had been one teeny-tiny, well-justified incident ages ago....And where had Nadia learned her English? All I was certain of was that the cup of coffee that hadn't left her hand was definitely not decaffeinated.

"Really, I—"

"Yes, yes," she said, tucking a loose lock of her gray-blonde hair behind her ear as she found her stride. "I understand, Jaya. You are not helpless. Not at all. But you must see that your drum case is almost as big as you are! It is only natural that a man would want to exert his alpha side when he sees you."

Nadia's fanciful story would have amused me if it hadn't been for the shock from which I was still reeling. Nadia opened her mouth to continue, but I cut in more forcefully this time.

"It's chicken tikka masala," I said.

"What?"

"The Indian curry."

"Yes, I know what tikka masala is."

"It's *sauce* on my shoe."

"Not blood?"

"Not blood."

I lifted up my shoe to prove my point, then wiped off the sauce with the tissue. It wasn't even blood red. A dark orange burnt sienna was more like it.

Nadia frowned, deepening the wrinkles on her face.

"Sauce," she repeated. "Then I cannot give you a lecture about how someone might press charges one of these days."

"If I did defend myself as you suggested, I'd hardly get arrested."

"You would not make as much of a sympathetic defendant as you think. You can bat those thick eyelashes as much as you like, but your innocent Indian girl act does not go far once you open your mouth...." She trailed off, giving me an odd look. "Your mouth. You have not used it as usual tonight. You are far too quiet, letting me talk on and on. Something is wrong."

I sighed. Nadia knows me better than most people. I reached inside my messenger bag to show her the source of my dismay. I'd read the article at least a dozen times that day. I had even brought it with me when I left my apartment to play a set of tabla music at the Tandoori Palace restaurant earlier that evening, so I knew the article had to be in my bag somewhere.

It was a small story. Only one short paragraph. Rupert Chadwick, age twenty-nine, was killed when his car lost control on a winding coastal road in Scotland. Rupert's family was important enough that the news was reported in the papers and spotted by an acquaintance who alerted me. A simple enough story. It would have been of little consequence to the reporter who had written the blurb. Not to me, though. Rupert and I had once been lovers.

I felt Nadia's intense gaze as I searched for the piece of paper in my bag. If I hadn't known better, I could have sworn that she perceived the depth of my uncharacteristically sentimental weakness. That she knew how I wondered, perhaps for the first time, if I loved Rupert.

I found the printout at the bottom of my bag. As I handed the paper to Nadia, she placed a small package in my hand.

It was a padded envelope with a bulging center. The stamps were foreign. British. Nothing unusual there. I'm a historian, so my work often involves corresponding with people and institutions in foreign countries. I didn't normally receive work-related packages at home, but I was glad to turn my attention to something other than Rupert.

The return address caught my eye. There was no name listed. No university or institute either. Instead, the address of an inn in Scotland had been written by hand. I stared at the address. The address itself wasn't familiar. Yet there was something....

"Jaya?" Nadia said.

I realized it wasn't the first time she had said it.

"You knew him well?" she asked.

I gave a slight shrug. "It was over a year ago."

Nadia nodded, then disappeared through the kitchen door.

As I waited, I turned over the curious package. *Scotland.* It had to be a coincidence.

I tugged at the edge. It didn't budge. Strong tape reinforced all the sides. The person who sent the parcel had taken no chances. At least I didn't have any fingernails to break. I pulled at a puckered section of tape until it gave way. A folded handkerchief of bright white cloth fell onto my lap. I shook the package to make sure there was nothing else inside, then opened the bundle.

A band of thick gold appeared beneath the folds of cotton. The piece of jewelry had been damaged and was missing several pieces of whatever had once been inlaid in the gold. That wasn't surprising. The piece was old. Old enough to evoke a feeling of centuries past. Jewelry isn't my expertise, but when you study history, you get a sense of how things change over time. I knew I wasn't holding something created during my lifetime.

As I turned over the piece, I saw more than gold. A solitary stone of the deepest red sparkled in my hand. The rough-cut gemstone dwarfed the thick gold frame. Even in the dim living room light of a midnight conversation, the huge ruby absorbed the light, seeming to breathe it in and out before my eyes. At that moment I understood the preciousness of jewels. I would have sworn this was no piece of costume jewelry.

*This was real.*

I ran my fingertips over the ruby stone, and along the rest of the piece. Based on its size, I guessed it was an anklet. A few granules of dirt stuck to my skin. I raised my fingers to my nose and sniffed. The dirt was what it looked like. Soil. Not dust.

Before I had a chance to think about what to do next, I heard the door to the kitchen creak open. I wiped the dirt from my fingers onto the handkerchief, then quickly covered up the anklet and eased it back into the package.

As the cloth slipped out of my fingers, I saw something that nearly made me drop the bundle. Initials were embroidered on the handkerchief: RCC. Rupert Cedric Chadwick.

My heart was beating far too quickly as Nadia placed a tray on the coffee table.

"I found some gin," she said. She poured generous shots from a Gordon's bottle into two ice-filled tumblers that were on the tray next to some sticky Russian pastries.

"Drink," she said. "It is...restorative."

Nadia's English is perfect, if formal, yet sometimes I could tell she felt there was no proper translation for a Russian word she wanted to use, and it would give her momentary pause before she spoke. She lifted one of the glasses, still frowning as if she hadn't expressed what she meant to.

I took the other glass, hoping my hands weren't shaking too obviously. Nadia didn't seem to notice. Her lips puckered as the gin touched her mouth.

"Wouldn't you rather be drinking vodka?" I asked. Damn. My voice sounded shaky as well.

"Jaya," she said, shaking her head. "You of all people should know not to stereotype a person based on where they are from."

"But you do like vodka."

"It is true. I think I will have some."

She disappeared into the kitchen again. I was tempted to look at the anklet and Rupert's handkerchief again, but I instead opted for steadying my nerves. I took a large gulp of gin. It was the right choice. Nadia returned almost immediately with a bottle of some sort of vodka I had never seen before, and a small glass with no ice.

After pouring herself a straight shot and refreshing my gin, she raised her glass and made a toast, offering her sympathy.

I appreciated the thought, though honestly I can't remember a single thing she said. My mind was spinning elsewhere. An old lover was dead before his thirtieth birthday. A ruby anklet rested in my lap inside his handkerchief. The package had been sent to me from Scotland, where said old lover was recently killed in a car wreck.

A feeling of helpless confusion spread through me. In spite of what Hollywood movies suggest, it's not commonplace for historians to receive mysterious packages containing jewel-encrusted artifacts previously in the possession of recently deceased archaeologists.

"Upsetting news," I said, then downed the last of my drink. Nadia could invent a wild story out of my hastily eaten dinner. There was no way I was going to tell her I was holding a ruby from a dead man. Without meeting her gaze, I opened my bag and put the package inside.

"Now that I've shared the news about Rupert's tragic death with someone," I said, "I think I'd like to be alone."

I got up and pulled my drum case over my shoulder. I'll grant Nadia that the instrument case does look rather sizable next to my not quite five-foot frame. It's not light, but I'm used to handling it.

"One last thing," Nadia said as I headed toward the door. "He was here again."

I stopped walking. The only he I could conjure up in my mind at the moment was Rupert.

"The lurking fellow," Nadia continued, taking the opportunity to press one of her homemade Russian pastries into my hand. "I should have called the police."

"You mean Miles?" I asked. The last person I needed to see that night was the neighborhood poet who had developed a crush on me. "He's harmless," I added, then stepped through the front door into the night.

I polished off the pastry as I reached the top of the stairs at the side of the house that led to my attic apartment. I have a good appetite to start with, and it grows even larger when I need to keep a clear head, such as when I happen to have a ruby in the bag bouncing against my hip.

I kicked off my shoes and set down the tabla case, then closed the door behind me with the ball of my bare foot. Before sitting down to examine the package, I turned around and locked the door. I didn't believe Miles was anything to worry about, but it couldn't hurt.

I removed the anklet from its package and set it down on top of a relatively stable stack of journals on my coffee table. My hands were still shaking as I found a flashlight to inspect the piece more carefully. It looked every bit as real under the brighter light. The dirt was also more prevalent than I had previously noticed. The style was more obvious, too. As the exquisite gold design and the jagged ruby shone in the light, I thought of India. I was relatively certain my impression wasn't merely because it was the country of my birth. I left India when I was a child, so my gut reactions are more American and Western than anything else.

The anklet hadn't been sent from India, though. I looked more closely at the packaging itself. I ran my index finger across my name and down to my address. My body froze. I knew why the package had triggered a feeling of familiarity. I recognized the handwriting. My address had been written by Rupert himself.

The writing had been scrawled sloppily with a thick pen, as if it had been addressed in a hurry. The funny swirl of the "S" in San Francisco stirred a memory. Rupert could never resist adding small flourishes to the various aspects of his life.

My head spun, and it wasn't from the gin. Rupert would never simply hand over something so valuable. I knew him well enough to know that with certainty.

Rupert had a classy enough upbringing that he had monogrammed handkerchiefs in the twenty-first century. Along with his breeding went a sense of entitlement. He wouldn't give something like this anklet to someone else. Not under any circumstances. Not even to me.

I scrambled to my desk and grabbed a pair of scissors. I cut along the edges of the padded envelope, snipping away at the package until it lay flat. With the excessive taping of the package, a small sheet of lined notebook paper had stuck to an inside corner. The edge tore in my haste to remove it. There it was. My explanation lay on the coffee table in front of me.

I smoothed out the wrinkled paper and read the handwritten note.

> *Jaya, love. I'm sending this artifact to you for safe-keeping. And for your help. I'm onto something. But somebody knows it. It's not safe for me to hang onto this at the moment. You'll know what to do. Ring me on my mobile and I'll explain everything. You're the only one I can trust. xox Rupert*

I turned over the mangled package. The postmark confirmed my creeping suspicion. The day Rupert had mailed me the package that wasn't safe for him to keep was the same day as his accident.

It no longer seemed believable that Rupert had accidentally lost control of his car as the press reported. And I was the only one who knew it.

Me, and whoever killed him.

# CHAPTER 2

*"Our paths will cross again someday."*

I woke up in semi-darkness with those words in my mind. They were the last words Rupert had said to me. I was leaving London, having finished the research for my doctorate. At the time, I thought it was a romantic way to end an affair. Quite unlike me to think such a thing, really. I don't need anyone, romantically or otherwise. That's something I learned a long time ago, when I saw what my mother's death did to my father. Life with Rupert was an exciting rush, nothing more. Yet it pained me more than I thought it would to realize our paths would not cross again.

I wiped away the single tear that rolled down my cheek. Sitting up in my bed, I grew nervous as I looked around the shadows of the studio apartment. Nothing was different, yet I was uneasy. It wasn't the memory. I had the strongest impression that something had woken me up.

A hint of light seeped through a window, suggesting either sunlight filtered through morning fog, or the beam of a streetlight in an otherwise dark sky. The clock informed me it wasn't quite six o'clock. It was August, so it would be the day's first rays of sunlight trying to fight their way through the summertime fog.

I'm not the type to stay in bed and drive myself crazy. I threw back the covers and looked through the peephole in the door. Then out both windows. Nothing. I rubbed my temples and looked absently out my front window.

Why had Rupert thought I could help him? I study trade routes and military skirmishes of the British East India Company. Not ancient Indian jewels. I gripped the window sill until my knuckles turned white. It wasn't as if the note mattered now anyway.

I pulled on an oversized sweater—oversized for me at least—and made my way to the kitchen in search of coffee. All my dishes were in the sink. I selected the least filthy mug I could find, which turned out to be one bearing the logo of the British Library in London. Great.

After washing the mug, I filled it with several spoonfuls of instant coffee and sugar while waiting for water to boil. I like the real thing better, but there was plenty more time in the day.

I stepped onto the small landing outside my door, eager to feel cool air on my face. Summer in San Francisco is unlike the season in the rest of California. Fog enveloped me as I sat down on the top step, and I watched the wisps of steam from my coffee blend into the fog gently blowing around me.

In the light of day, I couldn't deny the truth. Rupert was of the treasure-hunter school of archaeologists. Not the scholarly branch. That mentality was what made him so exciting. And also so infuriating. He had a tendency to jump to tenuous conclusions based on local rumors or vague references in forgotten academic texts. During the time I had known him, the ideas he pursued had always resulted in wild-goose chases. Except this time. This ruby anklet was real. Could it really have gotten him killed? Or was I going crazy?

Murders from the annals of history are one thing. India under British rule was full of unnatural deaths. A present-day suspicious death is quite another beast. If Rupert had truly been murdered on the other side of the world, what could I possibly do about it?

I was distracted from the problem by a movement I caught out of the corner of my eye. I turned my head, but it was gone.

It was probably only a cat, I told myself. But when I sensed it again, it was accompanied by the sound of creaking from below.

That would have to be one fat cat climbing up the twisty wooden stairway.

I poked my head over the ledge and caught a glimpse of unkempt auburn hair and delicate wire-rimmed glasses. As if I needed more help to get my day off to a bad start, it was my poet stalker.

"I thought I saw you," Miles said as he reached the stairway landing below me.

The stairs are barely visible from the sidewalk and accessed through a narrow gate along the side of the house. I could have pointed out that he would have had to come through the gate with the sole purpose of finding me. I decided against it. As I'd said to Nadia, I didn't think Miles was anything to worry about. I wasn't convinced enough to smile at him, but I did nod an acknowledgment.

"I thought you might be up already," he continued, proceeding up a few more stairs until he was eye level with me. "We poetic souls rarely sleep well. Coffee?" He thrust out a hand-painted thermos in front of my face.

I declined the offer, indicating my own mug and its remains. Miles pulled back his outstretched arm. For a moment he stood there, awkward and quiet. He took a deep breath, his eyes fixed on the empty space next to me on the top step. "May I?"

"Sure," I said, after only a moment's hesitation.

If a stalker is someone who stakes out your house to determine when you're home, then yeah, Miles is technically a stalker. A better assessment is that he's a harmless poet who lives down the street and has nothing better to do than walk around the neighborhood to find inspiration for his poetry.

Miles was in his usual army camouflage gear, which always seemed to me a strange thing for a pacifist to wear. Sticking out of one of his oversized pockets was his beaten-up poetry notebook. He set down the thermos and rubbed his ink-stained hands together in the crisp morning air.

"You were out playing a tabla gig last night, huh?" he asked.

"You do realize it's not cool for you to follow my every move."

"But you're a fellow artist in the neighborhood."

"Did you come around here earlier?"

"What, today?" A blush spread across his face. "Did you have a dream about me?"

I rolled my eyes. "What brings you around this morning?"

"We poets need to stick together."

"I'm not a poet," I said. "As I've told you. Several times."

"But you *are*," he said. "Don't you see? You played your tabla at the cafe that one time, while that guy read his poems. That makes you a poet."

The rhythmic drumming sounds of the tabla do make for a nice accompaniment to various types of performances and can create a poetic melody on their own, but I didn't think "that one time" with "that one guy" made me much of anything Miles wanted me to be. Playing the tabla for people is my release. My escape. Not my real life.

"I was thinking," he continued slowly, "I have something I wrote. I read it at open mic last week already, but if you would accompany me next time, it would be so much better. Here, I can show you." He pulled out the mangled notebook sticking out of his pocket.

"Maybe later."

"Oh, okay. But I wish you'd at least come see me read sometime, even if you don't want to play. Nobody else gets me except for you."

"I don't think I get much of anything these days." I leaned back onto my elbows. *Why on earth had Rupert thought I would know what to do with the anklet?*

"That's okay. What fun would it be if life was easy?" He looked over my face for a few moments. "It's in your soul, you know. You get things. You know how to piece together all that history stuff. I know it's not easy. It's the same with poetry. It's all a puzzle until it's pieced together. You see through what's on the surface."

I nearly knocked over the mug I'd set down next to my elbow. Was I really receiving sage advice from my stalker? Miles is a few years younger than me, in his mid-twenties. I realized I didn't know if he even had a job, since I'd only ever seen him at neighborhood coffee houses or in front of my own house. But the man had a point. I did see something that nobody else did. Nobody else would believe Rupert's car accident might not have been an accident.

"Earth to Jaya." Miles scratched his scruffy head. "You okay?"

"You were right," I said, standing up. "I do see something that nobody else does."

"You mean you'll do open mic with me?"

"No," I said. "Something even better."

I slipped inside my apartment, leaving a stunned Miles on the landing. I grabbed my phone and dialed Rupert's number from memory. He had to have realized I'd have a different cell phone back in the U.S. without his number saved. The arrogant bastard had known I'd remember it.

As soon as I finished punching in the number, I wondered what I would say to whoever answered the phone. Presumably it would be his best friend Knox or his father. *Do you happen to know why Rupert sent me a precious Indian artifact? Oh, and by the way, there's a possibility his death wasn't an accident.* Not the smoothest way to start a conversation.

I never had the opportunity to figure it out. My call was met with an automated message. "The subscriber you are trying to reach is currently unavailable," the recording of a woman with a refined English accent told me. Of course. A cell phone wouldn't necessarily survive a fatal car accident any better than a person.

There had to be someone else I could call. Even though it was early here, six o'clock in the morning in San Francisco meant it was two in the afternoon in England.

If anyone knew what Rupert had been up to with the anklet, it would be Knox Bailey. Where Rupert went with a pseudo-scholarly scheme, Knox would follow. Knox had once been an archaeology graduate student along with Rupert, but had dropped out. Knox claimed it was because he didn't want to settle on a single project for a dissertation, but I knew from Rupert that Knox had been caught plagiarizing and was discreetly asked to leave.

I didn't have Knox's phone number, so I was considering what to say in an email when the last line of Rupert's note flashed into my mind.

*You're the only one I can trust.*

My stomach clenched and my head throbbed. Rupert had no longer trusted his best friend. Who could *I* trust?

# CHAPTER 3

"What's the matter with you?" Sanjay's groggy voice asked through the receiver.

"You sleep with your phone under your pillow?" I asked, surprised he picked up the phone after one ring.

"Pocket. Must've fallen asleep practicing my new act."

"You're asleep in a trunk?"

"Escape shaft." Sanjay yawned. "There's a set of pillows here to cushion my landing."

Sanjay is a magician. He's also my music partner. We play sets at the Tandoori Palace two nights a week, entertaining diners with his sitar and my tabla. It's not a real job for either of us, but it's fun. The rest of the week I'm buried in history books or with my students at the university, and Sanjay is a successful stage magician who goes by the moniker "The Hindi Houdini" and sells out entire seasons at a winery theater just north of San Francisco. In spite of his accomplishments in the magical field, Sanjay is one of the worst sitar players in this hemisphere. He's like a brother to me, so I pretend I don't notice when his fingers hit the wrong strings and we fill the restaurant with sounds reminiscent of a screaming monkey. He makes up for it in other ways, such as the fact that he's the only person I knew I could call upon with no hesitation at this early hour.

"Are you at the theater or in your studio at home?" I asked.

"Studio. Why?"

"Can you meet me at my place in twenty minutes?"

"Are you okay?" he asked.

"Sort of. Are you coming?"

After hanging up with Sanjay, I looked out the peephole of my door. Miles was gone. Good. I needed some sustenance to think while I waited for Sanjay. I didn't have to look in my fridge to know there was nothing in it.

The Coffee to the People cafe was full of people who were surprisingly cheery for the early hour. I had no idea there was a secret population in my laid-back neighborhood who woke up by six in the morning. I ordered a muffin for Sanjay and got myself a scrambled-egg bagel sandwich with crunchy peanut butter instead of cheese. The morning staff don't know me as well as the afternoon staff, so the woman behind the counter raised a pierced eyebrow before ringing up my order.

I walked the few blocks back to my apartment while I ate. I barely tasted the food, I was so distracted thinking about Rupert and the ruby anklet. When I reached my front door, I forgot about both. My door was ajar.

I didn't think I'd been absentminded enough to forget to lock up. It's not the sort of thing you do when living in San Francisco. Had I been so distraught about Rupert's death that I'd acted so stupidly? Only one way to find out.

Without thinking, I gave the door a hard shove. It didn't swing open in the lightning-fast motion I had anticipated. Unfortunately, I was still holding the paper bag containing Sanjay's now-squished muffin. As the door swung slowly open, I stayed on the landing, ready to toss a banana nut muffin at the burglar before running down the stairs.

Since the apartment is a studio, I could see ninety percent of it from where I stood. Dressed in an impeccably tailored suit and a custom-made bowler hat, Sanjay sat on the couch with his elbows resting on his knees while he looked at the screen of his phone. He looked up at me as I stepped into the apartment.

"I hate it when you do that," I said, closing the door.

"Let myself into your apartment? Since when have you hated that?"

"I know it goes with the territory, that being friends with a magician means one must accept his ability to let himself into or out of any building he'd like. But today was a bad day for you to do it. How did you get here so quickly, anyway?"

"I supposed you'd slap me if I said magic."

"Definitely."

"In that case," Sanjay said, "I was already dressed, and it's too early for there to be much rush hour traffic. What's in your hand?"

I tossed Sanjay the paper bag containing his smashed muffin.

"What would you do," I said, "if I told you someone had just been killed, that I was the only one who knew it might be murder, and that I now have the ruby he was killed over?"

"You brought me here after I slept less than four hours to tell me a new plot idea for my stage show? Couldn't it wait? A ruby is good, though. Those always look great under the stage lights."

I pulled the ruby anklet out of my bag and held it in my hand in front of Sanjay's face. He swore. At least I'm pretty sure that's what he did. He spoke the words under his breath in Punjabi. I'm half Tamil, so I don't speak any Punjabi. But I know Sanjay.

"You're serious?" he said. "Please don't tell me you're serious. Where did you get that thing?"

"I told you. From someone who was killed." I hesitated. "It was Rupert."

"The guy you knew in London? I thought you hated that guy. You said he was an immature ass."

"He was. But that doesn't mean I wanted him dead. And that's not the point."

Sanjay took the anklet from my hand, keeping it in its hand-kerchief cushion. "You have to go to the police with this, Jaya."

"If it was that easy I wouldn't have woken you up." I scooted Sanjay over on the couch so I could sit down next to him, then told him everything I knew about Rupert's death in Scotland, the ruby anklet, and Rupert's note. I wouldn't say I felt a weight lifted as the story poured out of me, but it did feel better to confide in someone.

When I finished speaking, Sanjay handed the anklet and handkerchief back to me and sat in silence. He took off his bowler hat and ran his fingers around the rim. I half expected the answer to my problems to pop out of it. It's the stage prop he's most attached to. I've seen everything from a bouquet of flowers to a baby goat emerge from that hat (though Sanjay swears the goat was never actually inside the hat). He wears it offstage so much that I suspect it's a security blanket of sorts.

"The timing of his death *could* have been a coincidence," he said. "Or more likely, he was driving while distracted about this ruby, which is what made him crash. That's got to be it."

"Really? He was so upset he drove off a cliff? You're no help."

Sanjay began typing on his phone.

"What are you doing?" I asked.

"Googling this anklet."

"Wait, do you recognize it? Is it famous?"

"No, but how hard could it be to find?" Sanjay frowned. "Oh...besides 'ruby,' what do you think I should type?"

An Internet search to identify the anklet didn't go far. As much as I hated to admit it, I was going to need more than Sanjay's help. I needed someone who knew about the history of Indian jewelry. I had a couple of ideas about who I could ask, but I wasn't sure I wanted to bring anyone else into this. I knew nothing about the anklet's history.

What if I was a conspirator in a theft from the Louvre or some other renowned museum? Though I didn't think Rupert would have turned to a life of crime, I wasn't nearly as certain of that conviction as I'd have liked.

While Sanjay was typing random search terms into his phone, I grabbed my laptop to look for online articles about museum jewelry thefts in the news. Just in case.

My news search wasn't any more fruitful than Sanjay's. I did, however, learn that there were a surprisingly large number of unsolved museum thefts I wasn't previously aware of. The folks at Interpol certainly had their work cut out for them. It was also clear they meant business. I glanced uneasily at the anklet.

"I have to show this to someone who can identify it," I said.

"If you're not going to take it to the police, there's no way you should show it to anyone else."

Sanjay was right. It might not be a good idea to show the anklet itself to anyone while I asked my innocent questions. Not even the man I had in mind.

"I have to do *something*," I said.

"Where's your camera?"

"Sanjay, you're brilliant." I found my camera in a desk drawer. "Hold this." I took the anklet out of the handkerchief and handed it to Sanjay. He held up his hands before I could place it in them.

"After what you've told me," he said, "I don't want to get my fingerprints on that thing."

"They're already on it."

"Nope. I only touched the wrapping."

"Fine," I said, throwing the handkerchief at him. "Use this, then. But I need it in your hand so I can take a photo that shows how big it is."

"Make sure you don't get my face in the photo."

I snapped a photo of Sanjay's hand holding the thick gold band with the ruby stone, and printed out a copy on my squeaky printer.

I was ready.

# CHAPTER 4

Professor Michael Wells, right across the bay in Berkeley, was an old family friend. I grew up in Berkeley after leaving India, and my hippie father knew just about everyone there, it seemed to me at the time. My father taught sitar music lessons out of our house, and the Indian instrument was quite popular in Berkeley. Most people didn't stick with sitar lessons for long, since there's a steep learning curve. But lots of people tried it. Michael was a graduate student at Berkeley who used to come around the house for lessons when I was a kid. Now he's a professor of South Asian art history.

It was late enough that I was betting Michael would be heading into the office, even if he wasn't teaching summer term. He'd always been a workaholic. I'm not being judgmental when I say that. If it hadn't been for the mystery Rupert had thrust upon me, I would be heading to my own office. Even though it was summer, I needed to work on a research paper. I only started my tenure-track job a year ago, and I wouldn't keep it long if I didn't keep up my publishing.

My car was parked on a side street only two blocks away from my apartment, so I was on the Bay Bridge within ten minutes. I turned up the volume on the stereo, blasting modern tabla beats out the windows of my vintage silver Mercedes-Benz roadster. The gears screeched as I accelerated. The old car needed more servicing than I could afford, but I couldn't bear to part with it. The car had been left to me by an old friend of my father's who thought of me like a daughter. Shortly before he died, I moved back to the Bay Area for a teaching job in San Francisco. He was the one who put me in touch with my landlady, Nadia. He knew her from when she sold medical marijuana.

When Nadia first converted her attic into the freestanding room that's now my apartment, she did it to grow marijuana plants in the space. The Russian free spirit had come to San Francisco in the 1960s and never left. Her pot-growing business was quite successful, and she found herself most dedicated to medical marijuana. Nadia hated waste, so after she retired from the business she turned the space into an apartment.

I drove around several side streets on the south side of the Berkeley campus before I squeezed the car into a semi-legal parking space right off Telegraph Avenue. I stopped to buy myself a double espresso and gave my change to a homeless man with a "Starvin' Like Marvin" sign before I stepped onto the grounds of the sprawling campus.

Walking through Sproul Plaza, I was reminded of one of my first childhood impressions of my new home in the United States. When I moved to Berkeley, Sproul Plaza was no longer the hotbed of political activity that it had been in the 1960s, but I remembered the plaza well because I learned to ride a bike there.

I found Michael in his office, staring at his computer screen with his brows drawn together. He didn't notice me until I knocked.

"Jaya, is that you?" He pulled off his reading glasses and greeted me with a hug. "It's been a while, hasn't it?"

"It's been a busy year. You know how it is when starting out as a first-year professor."

"Right," he said, glancing back at his computer. "Yes, of course."

"I can tell you're busy, and this isn't actually a social visit. I need some help identifying a piece of old jewelry from India."

"Lane Peters."

"What?"

"A graduate student here," Michael said. "He's the best person to talk to about Indian jewelry."

"I thought that you could take a quick look—"

"Lane Peters is your man," Michael said, cutting me off.

"—at a photograph," I finished. "It'll just take a minute."

"If Lane can't help you, why don't you email this photo of yours to me?"

Before I could give a proper answer or farewell, I found myself back in the hallway.

It had been almost a year since I'd seen Michael. We attended an exhibit at the San Francisco Asian Art Museum shortly after I moved back to the Bay Area, and he dropped me off at home afterwards even though I lived well out of his way. At the time he'd been a really nice guy, an older version of the carefree young man I'd known when I was a kid. I heard he'd recently divorced. He must not have taken it well.

I shook off the rejection and followed the labyrinthine hallway in the direction Michael had pointed. I found Lane's office in the midst of a stark basement hallway of identical doors. They were all closed. Not the most social bunch.

I knocked on the door and heard a squeaking chair and faint footsteps. The door swung in a few inches. A lanky man with a lit cigarette in his hand looked out at me through the slit. He watched me for a few moments as smoke curled up from the cigarette. It didn't look as if the highly esteemed Lane Peters was going to say anything or invite me in.

"Michael Wells sent me to you," I said.

"Ah." He pulled open the door, revealing one of the smallest offices I'd ever seen. Once I stepped inside, he closed the door and expertly maneuvered the small space to return to the chair behind his desk. Piles of faded books filled the office. Most of them were stacked on the sole bookshelf, with the overflow on the desk as well as two stacks on the floor. A small plastic fan hummed from the edge of the desk, and a small folding chair rested against the wall.

Lane Peters' attire matched the office. He wore thick horn-rimmed glasses, baggy cargo pants, and a similarly loose-fitting dress shirt. Silky hair between blond and brown obscured his eyes, which might have been hazel. I glanced up at the smoke detector not far above his head in the closet-sized office.

"It's disabled," he said, stubbing out his cigarette in what I guessed was an ashtray, although my view was blocked by a stack of books. With a quick jerk of his head, he motioned for me to sit in the folding chair. "How can I help you...?"

"Jaya Jones," I said.

I caught him subtly glance down toward my unadorned ring finger as I unfolded the chair. He was smoother than most, and the obfuscation was aided by his hair and glasses. I still noticed the action. It's a common one after hearing my surname. At least he didn't ask me outright. I think that's why I answered the unspoken question.

"It's not a married name," I said. "Only my mother was Indian. My dad is American. Blonder than you are."

My short stature and dark hair and eyes come from my mother, but my features are more like my father's. Especially my large eyes and full mouth, both of which I've always thought were slightly oversized for my face. My brother is over a foot taller than me at a full six feet, with delicate green eyes, black hair naturally flecked with copper highlights, and skin several shades darker than mine. In one sense we're exact opposites, yet next to each other you can tell we're related.

Lane acknowledged my answer with only a flicker of his eyes. I felt a minor lurch in my stomach. I was probably hungry. I'd eaten breakfast early, after all. Plus I was nervous about the situation. That was all.

"How can I help you?" he asked, picking up a pencil and twirling it between his fingers absentmindedly. His deep voice was polite but reserved.

I took the photo out of my bag and set it down on the desk.

"I'm trying to identify this piece of jewelry," I began. But he wasn't listening to me. He was staring at the photograph.

His lips parted. The pencil dropped out of his hand and rolled across the desk until a book stopped it from dropping onto the floor. He didn't seem to notice. He ran his fingers through his hair, pulling it away from his face. I hoped he was as preoccupied as he appeared to be so that he didn't hear my involuntary intake of breath.

I could see his whole face clearly now. The chameleon shade of his hazel eyes seemed to change in the light as I watched him. Prominent cheek bones rested under his glasses. Their striking structure was diminished by the thick frames, but they were noticeable nonetheless. He had a face of elegant angles, and it was impossible not to see how handsome he was.

It was a few moments before he recovered himself enough to speak. I can't say I minded the time he took.

"Where did you get this?" he asked, releasing his hair so it fell back over the sides of his face. He folded his hands in a forced effort to appear composed.

"Does it matter?" I asked. "You obviously recognized the anklet."

"It's a bracelet."

"What?"

"It's a bracelet. Maybe an armlet. But not an anklet."

"But the size—"

"You can tell because it's made of gold," he said, pointing at the photograph. "It's Indian. In India gold is considered pure, while the foot is impure. People wear silver on their feet instead."

I should have realized that myself. The Indian notion of the impurity of feet applies elsewhere. With the tabla, you need to make sure your feet don't touch the instrument when you sit down cross-legged with the pair of drums.

"You can identify the *bracelet*, then."

He didn't respond immediately.

"I could see that you recognized it," I said, trying not to lose my patience.

"Well...."

"You clearly recognized something about it."

"It's not that simple."

"Why not?"

"Because," he said, "the piece in your photograph isn't supposed to exist."

# CHAPTER 5

A few minutes later the center of Lane's desk was cleared off except for the photo, and we were drinking stale coffee he had retrieved from the department lounge. Or at least I was drinking it. Lane was so absorbed in the photo he forgot about his.

I know the annoyance of being interrupted while contemplating your research. Letting the gears in your mind turn over facts that don't mean much until you've put them together to create meaning out of them. I forced myself to sit back and sip my coffee to give Lane time to think.

"If the bracelet in this photograph is real," he said, tapping on the edge of the photo, "then this is a really big deal."

"I got that," I said. "You were going to tell me why."

"Where did you find this?"

"It's from a friend."

He stared at me, waiting for more.

"Someone gave it to me," I said. "I don't know where it came from. I came to see Michael to figure that out. Why is it such a big deal?"

"Like I said before," he said slowly, holding my gaze as he spoke. "It's apocryphal. It doesn't actually exist."

"Then how did you recognize it?"

"It only exists as an *idea*," Lane said. "In artwork."

"You've seen this bracelet in artwork," I repeated dumbly.

"It's very distinctive. This cut of the ruby, and the setting...."

He trailed off, his gaze drawn back to the photograph.

I cleared my throat after a few seconds of silence. He looked back up at me with an arched eyebrow.

"Artists sometimes take liberties in artistic renderings like paintings and sculptures," he said. "I'm talking specifically about Indian royal court paintings here, where artists were hired to depict the life of royal families in India. It's called Selective Realism."

"You mean making someone more or less attractive depending on if the painter liked them or not. Like how artists made Richard III look like a hunchback."

"Sort of," he said. "But it's more than that. Sometimes paintings were purposefully misleading representations to show symbols of wealth. Or the painter thought his painting looked more aesthetically pleasing than the scene that existed in front of him. Who was going to argue with the result?"

"But surely there are ways to tell what's a true representation and what's not. Other historical documents—"

"Of course," Lane said. "There are lots of other historical sources to shed light on what's real versus what was the artist's imagination. Portraits are often fairly accurate. And there are other records that are used to determine historical accuracy. For example, Jahangir, a Mughal ruler in the early 1600s—"

"I know who Jahangir is. He played a role in helping establish the East India Company, granting them trading privileges in exchange for prestigious European goods." I paused as Lane's expression changed. Was he surprised I knew so much about Indian history?

"I'm not here for an Indian history lesson," I said. I tapped my finger on the photograph. "Right now I'm interested in this piece."

"I'm going somewhere with this." Lane paused to take a sip of coffee, his expression unreadable as he looked across the desk at me. "Jahangir had all sorts of fanciful paintings commissioned that showed his power. One famous painting shows King James of England and a Turkish emperor both visiting Jahangir's court."

"They did?"

"No," Lane said. "That's the point. It never happened. It's *painted* like that. And the piece in your photo. I know I've seen it—the intact version—in a painting before."

"That Jahangir commissioned."

"Possibly." He shifted in his chair. "I'm not sure. Definitely a Mughal painting, though. I think. Look, this isn't something I come across every day. But I've studied this subject." He indicated the books around us. "I suspect the photo you've got shows something that popped up in multiple paintings—before disappearing."

"It *was* stolen," I mumbled mostly to myself.

"I don't mean 'disappeared' in that sense. When something like this happens, the prevailing theory is that the artist who painted it died or was no longer painting in a particular place. There's an account of some grand pieces of jewelry ceasing to be represented in a court's artwork."

"And the painter?"

"Indian artists weren't always as well documented as European artists. Some Mughal emperors, like Akbar, were interested in their artists receiving credit for their work. Elsewhere, though, many paintings are unattributed. Meaning there's no way of actually proving that particular theory. But since the jewelry depicted didn't show up again, that's the popular understanding. Rather than that the jewelry actually existed."

"But that's a theory based on *no evidence*."

"Personally I thought it was most likely the gold was melted down," Lane said. "It was, and still is, quite common in India for new techniques and styles to replace traditional ones. Unfortunately, but understandably, they use the existing materials they have on hand. That's one of the biggest problems of studying the art history of such malleable forms. But if that was the case, it was odd that the distinctive gemstones never resurfaced. They should have. If they existed. Which is why the theory embracing Selective Realism doesn't seem like such a stretch."

"When did it disappear?"

"Centuries ago. Long before the advent of photography. That's why it's amazing you—" He stopped abruptly.

"What?"

He didn't answer.

"What is it?"

"I was wondering," he said slowly, "if it's possible to fake a photo this good."

"You're kidding."

"I know it *looks* real. But it would prove established belief wrong. That creates a huge motivation to fake something like this."

I glanced uneasily at the messenger bag at my feet.

"It's not a fake," I said.

"How do you know? Photoshop is really good these days."

"Trust me."

"No offense," he said as though he meant the opposite, "but I'm guessing you don't have a trained eye, since you came here for help."

"Okay, then don't trust me. Treat it as a hypothetical exercise."

He sat perfectly still as he looked at me coldly. "I don't have time for hypothetical exercises."

"Then believe me when I tell you it's real."

"I don't know what you expect to learn from whatever game you're playing."

"I'm not—"

Lane stood up without warning and squeezed around the desk. He leaned across me and pulled the office door open, leaving his hand firmly planted on the doorknob. "Thanks for stopping by."

"It's not a game," I said. I made no attempt to leave.

He loomed above me, his expression blank. I swiveled in the folding chair and kicked the door shut. It threw him off balance. He nearly fell, but caught himself on the desk and glared at me.

"What if I told you I have it?" I said. "That I was given the bracelet."

"You can't be serious." Lane sat down on the edge of the desk and gaped at me. "You're *serious?*"

I picked up my bag and extracted Rupert's handkerchief. I opened the folds and held it out in front of him. Even in the bad florescent lighting, the uncut ruby shone beautifully.

He didn't presume I'd let him touch it, but he leaned in closer. When he looked up, I saw the awe in his eyes.

"You can't expect me to believe," he said, "that your friend casually handed this to you without any explanation."

"I never said that," I said. "It did belong to a friend who gave it to me. But I don't know where he got it. He's dead, so I can't ask him."

"And the rest?"

"It only had the one ruby when I got it."

"No, I mean the other pieces of the collection. The full treasure. He didn't leave the rest to you as well?"

I stared openmouthed at Lane. He must have thought the bracelet had been left to me as part of an estate in a will. There was more? My normally expressive vocal chords didn't want to cooperate. I swallowed and shook my head.

"A treasure?" I whispered.

Rupert had certainly gotten himself into one big mess.

# CHAPTER 6

"Your friend wasn't a maharaja, was he?" Lane asked.

A day ago I would have thought it was a joke if someone had asked me if I was friends with a maharaja. I wasn't laughing now.

"It's the real deal, then?"

"It certainly is."

The chair squeaked beneath me as I took a deep breath and looked up at the ceiling.

"He was English," I said. "Killed in a car wreck in Scotland. I don't know how he got the bracelet, except that I'm sure it wasn't a family heirloom. I don't know anything else. I had to start somewhere, so here I am."

I wasn't lying. Not really. Concealing certain facts isn't quite the same thing.

"I don't know any more off the top of my head," Lane said.

"But I thought..." I trailed off as a sickening sensation washed over me. "From what you said before, I thought you knew more."

What I really thought was that there was no way I would have shown him the bracelet if I thought he didn't have anything else he could tell me.

My mouth went dry. What had I done? *Someone now knew I had the bracelet.* That was exactly what I had wanted to avoid. Why hadn't I listened to Sanjay?

"Don't worry," I said, trying to appear casual even as I found it difficult to speak. "You've been a tremendous help already. I owe you one. Let me know if you ever want a free dinner at the Tandoori Palace restaurant in the city." I covered the bracelet and stood up.

"Wait a sec," he said, scrambling to his feet as well. "I can still help fill in the missing pieces. I just have to look up a few things."

We stood close to each other in the cramped space in front of the desk. I had to arch my neck to look him in the eye.

"That's really okay," I said. "With what you've told me, I can take it from here."

"But you won't know what to look for."

"I know how to do archival research," I said. "I'm a historian." That threw him off.

"Oh," he said after a beat. "You mean you're a history major in one of Michael's classes."

"I have a doctorate," I said, more icily than I intended. Since I've only been teaching for a year, I get mistaken for a coed more often than I'd like.

"You're a *professor*?"

"A damn good one."

"Dr. Jones," he said thoughtfully.

"Yeah." I sighed.

"At least you're not an archaeologist," he said, smiling.

I reached for the doorknob.

"Wait." Lane reached out a long arm in a gesture to stop me. "As a historian, you know how research works. You know how much easier it is to dig into something if you already know some facts about what you're looking for."

I lowered my hand from the doorknob.

"In your field," Lane said, "what's your expertise?"

"The early foundations of British India. The British East India Company in its various incarnations. You know, trading power, military power, its dissolution when rule was assumed directly from the British Crown."

"So I bet you could tell me all about pirates on the high seas, but you couldn't even identify this piece as a bracelet."

"If you have further tips, don't hold back."

"You know the intangible nature of doing research like this. Even if I could tell you more about where to look, that narrows things down from a thousand haystacks to maybe a hundred. With my background, it would be easier for me to find something. I wouldn't mind doing a bit more research."

Whatever historical origins Lane might be able to find, I needed them to lead to the more recent origins of where Rupert had gotten his hands on it. And now that Lane had told me of a larger treasure somewhere out there, I had a feeling I needed to work quickly. The idea of extra help was tempting.

"I know a few things I can check out right away," he added.

"Why are you so interested in helping me?"

"Can't you tell? This is a really big deal in Indian art history. Something like this could make my career. I can help you, so I'd like to be a part of it."

I stood there feeling helpless and indecisive, two emotions I rarely encounter. What was I doing? I scribbled my cell phone number and email address on a piece of paper.

"Call me as soon as you find anything," I said.

We headed out of the building together. Lane said he would get started at the university's library right away. As we passed Michael's office, I stuck my head inside to thank him for putting me in touch with Lane, then hurried back to my car, anxious to get the bracelet out of my hands. A safe deposit box seemed the safest place. The fact that I didn't have a safe deposit box wasn't going to stop me. I drove straight to my bank and opened one.

Feeling much better without the priceless artifact on my person, I whipped the car around a sputtering VW Beetle and headed to my own university's library.

Lane was right that he was much more likely to come across relevant information. That didn't mean I couldn't try. I'd go crazy if

I sat at home waiting. I was thinking about Rupert too much already. In those spare moments when I didn't have something else to focus on, I wondered what could have been.

I hadn't thought too much about Rupert in the past year. I'm good at staying busy and pushing inconvenient thoughts from my mind. Rupert's mysterious death was stirring up feelings I hadn't realized were so close to the surface. Feelings that I wasn't even certain I had. God, I needed somebody else's history to throw myself into. I sped through Golden Gate Park and floored the car toward the library.

The librarian I often worked with was on vacation, so I got some assistance from a new librarian before settling into a corner table with a heap of references for Mughal art and jewelry. I sighed as I looked at the long list, then got down to work.


Several hours into my research, my stomach was growling, I was dying of thirst, and I still hadn't managed to find a single thing I thought might be helpful. My least favorite thing about libraries is their policy on no food or drink.

I wasn't getting anywhere, so I decided to call it a day. I drove home with vigorous bhangra beats blasting on my speakers and a Big Gulp balanced between my knees. As I pulled into a parking space only a block from my apartment, my thoughts turned back to Lane. I hoped he'd been more successful than I had. I needed something—anything—that would point me in the direction of the ruby bracelet's modern history.

Nadia stood on the porch in front of the house, an icepack held to her head.

"Jaya!" Nadia called out when she saw me. "You have been robbed!"

# CHAPTER 7

Nadia held the icepack to the back of her head with one hand and a shot of vodka in the other.

"Are you sure that's a good idea?" I asked, pointing at the vodka. "You might have a concussion."

She narrowed her eyes. "You want to hear what happened with the burglar, yes?"

I shut my mouth. I needed to know if the unthinkable had happened. If Rupert's troubles had followed the bracelet across the Atlantic.

"I heard a crash from your apartment," she said. "I was worried, so I went upstairs to check. A strong man knocked me down."

Nadia paused to drink the shot of vodka. She shook her head as she placed the empty shot glass on the railing of the porch. "He was too fast for me to see his face. I only have a sense of his build."

"You sure you don't want me to take you to the hospital?"

"People in this country are soft. There is no problem with my head. Only with your door. We will get you a new one. Let us go upstairs to see if I was fast enough or if he has stolen anything."

On the walk upstairs, I found myself hoping something was missing. That would mean it was a random burglary. Otherwise it would mean Rupert's murder was jumping into my life 5,000 miles away and Nadia was lucky to only have a bump on the head.

It *could* have been coincidental timing, after all. The Haight-Ashbury area was the home of free love in the '60s, and while the liveliness of the neighborhood has endured, it's not known for its safety. I would have been happy to find a few of my belongings missing if it meant this was a random break-in that had nothing to do with the ruby bracelet.

The digital camera I'd used that morning was in plain sight on the kitchen table, next to the music player I used when I went running. This wasn't looking like the standard burglary I was hoping for. But I was relieved to see my tabla case. I would have been devastated to lose those drums.

My body tensed as I spotted the one object that was out of place. Aside from the door, there was only one thing leaving evidence of the burglar's presence. My jewelry box from Goa had been smashed. The contents were spilled across the bed.

I sat down on the edge of the bed and closed my eyes. My body shook as I took a few deep breaths in an attempt to calm myself. A jewelry box was exactly where someone looking for the ruby bracelet could have expected I would put a piece of jewelry I now had in my possession.

"What is missing?" Nadia asked.

"Nothing."

"Good. Then we do not call the police."

"Shouldn't we still—"

"The lurking fellow!" Nadia exclaimed, making a hand gesture that caused the icepack to fly out of her hand and hit the wall. "Why did I not think of it? Poets do this kind of thing for the love of a woman." She pointed a finger at me. "You should have gotten a restraining order."

The idea of *Miles* breaking into my apartment hadn't occurred to me. I considered the idea, but it was hard to believe the pacifist would knock down a retiree.

"Miles couldn't have done this," I said. "He's more likely to harm himself than anyone else. Like accidentally stepping in front of a car or walking into a tree while writing in his notebook."

"I will interrogate him the next time he comes back."

"Nadia," I began, but she had already scooped up the ice pack and was headed out the door.

Instead of following her, I contemplated whether or not I should call the police. Nothing had been stolen, and Nadia didn't want to tell them about her injury.

I fell back onto the bed and stared at the ceiling for guidance. As the bedsprings jostled underneath me, I realized one more important thing I hadn't checked on. I rolled over and poked my head under the bed, looking for the packaging in which the bracelet had been sent. It was still there.

In my relief, something clicked in my mind. I had ignored a crucial piece of information. *The return address.* Rupert had written an address not for a private residence, but for the Fog & Thistle Inn.

My cell phone rang, causing me to drop the package. Lane's voice greeted me.

"I'm done following up on those leads," he said. "I've found some things at the library I thought you'd like to hear about."

An idea I didn't like flashed into my mind. "Where are you?" I asked.

"Right outside Doe. Why?"

The caller ID on my phone gave a Berkeley area code. But if Lane was calling from his cell phone, he wasn't necessarily at the library like he said. He could be in San Francisco half a block away.

"How long would it take you to get to San Francisco?" I asked.

"Don't you want to hear—"

"It would be easier if we talked in person," I said. "Don't you think?"

I gave him directions to my place. Of course I was curious to hear what he'd found. But there was something I was even more curious about. Since Nadia had gotten a sense of the build of the attempted robber, it wouldn't hurt to have her take a look at Lane. The graduate student had been awfully interested in the ruby bracelet.

To avoid either screaming or pacing a hole through my floor while I waited for Lane, I looked up the Fog & Thistle Inn, which turned out to be a small pub with a few rooms for rent in the lower Highlands of Scotland. It didn't have its own website, but was listed on a local tourism page and on a blog of an avid hiker. It wasn't too far from the famous Dunnottar Castle ruins.

More searching explained what Rupert had been doing there. An archaeological dig for Pictish standing stones was taking place less than a mile from the inn. Professor Malcolm Alpin from the University of St. Andrews had put together a thorough website about the expedition.

He was seeking additional funding for the project, which explained the abundance of information. That was fine with me. It told me what I needed to know. The site included a photograph of a man next to a Pictish standing stone. That man was Knox Bailey, Rupert's best friend.

Neither Rupert nor Knox had been academically interested in the Picts when I knew them. The Picts were the long-ago barbarian painted people of Scotland, as Professor Malcolm Alpin's website reminded me in great detail. They left standing stones across Scotland, with carvings in their primitive language. A newly discovered cluster of standing stones in this region of eastern Scotland provided the impetus for this dig.

I was fairly certain the Picts did not possess any hidden treasures that would have attracted Rupert and Knox. And an Indian bracelet had nothing to do with the Picts. *What were they up to?*

I slammed the laptop shut and headed down the stairs to see how Nadia was doing. I heard her voice before I rounded the corner of the house.

"Now is not a good time for a visit," Nadia was saying. "Jaya has been burglarized. No, there is no need to worry for her. She knows jiu-jitsu. You would not think it of someone so small, no?"

Enrolling me in jiu-jitsu classes was one of the rare practical things my dad had ever done. When he realized I wasn't going to make it to five feet tall, he drove me around in his old VW bus to all the martial arts classes he could find in Berkeley and Oakland. Jiujitsu was the one that stuck.

I hurried around the corner of the house. A floppy mess of dark blond hair attached to a long-limbed body stood on the sidewalk in front of the house. It was Lane. His hands were tucked into the pockets of a jacket in the crisp late afternoon air.

"I suppose you've already told Lane about my magic messenger bag, too?" I asked as I reached them.

"She mocks me," Nadia said. "After all I do for her. Does she tell you what a good landlady I am? I saw a magnifying glass in that bag of hers once. A *magnifying glass*! As if she were that Sherlock Holmes."

"What's strange about that?" I asked. "Original texts can be hard to decipher. Don't all historians carry one around with them?"

They didn't answer.

"Well, they should."

"I was telling your friend it is a bad time for a visit," Nadia said.

"It's okay," I said. "I asked him to come. Lane is helping me with some research."

"A house call," Nadia murmured, shaking Lane's outstretched hand. "How nice."

"You didn't tell me you just had a break-in," Lane said to me. "We didn't have to do this right now."

"I don't want to dwell on it. I'm glad you got here so quickly."

"I lucked out catching BART right away."

Nadia sniffed her right hand with a curious expression on her face. Her eyes lit up. "You have Gauloises cigarettes?" Her eyes crinkled as he nodded. "Could I impose on you?"

"My pleasure," he said, handing her a cigarette from the pack in his jacket pocket.

"I thought you quit smoking, Nadia," I said.

"These are too good to pass up."

"I'll meet you upstairs in a minute, Lane. My apartment is up the stairs around the side of the house. I need to ask Nadia one more thing about fixing my door."

"*Spassiba*," Nadia said as she waved goodbye to Lane.

"*Nyezashto*."

"I have already called a good locksmith," Nadia said. "You think I would not act so quickly?"

"That's not what I wanted to ask you about."

"But you said—"

I ran to the side of the house to make sure Lane was on his way up to my apartment. Peeking through an opening between the wooden slats of the side gate, I waited until he started up the stairs before returning to Nadia's side.

"Could he have been the burglar?" I asked Nadia, keeping my voice quiet.

"This man Lane? No. Too tall. But why would your friend—"

"Thanks, Nadia." I felt my muscles relax. "That's all I needed to know."

Nadia inhaled deeply from one of the shortest cigarette butts I have ever seen between someone's fingers, then stubbed out the remains in the flower pot next to her.

"I will never understand Americans," she said. She shook her head and went into her house.

Upstairs, Lane hadn't gone past my doorway. He scanned the studio, running a hand through his hair as he looked over the chaotic space. Maybe I should have done the dishes.

"Do you need help putting things back together?" he asked.

"You don't like the path of carpet that winds between all the books?" It's true that I don't use the most conventional system of organizing an apartment. But I know where every single one of the books is located, as well as the ones in my university office. Being a historian, I have to do much of my research on paper.

I pointed to the broken jewelry box. "That's the only thing the burglar touched."

"Did he get it?"

Lane Peters wasn't slow. I'll give him that much credit. "You planning on telling me what's really going on now?" he asked.

He leaned into the frame of the doorway rather than stepping inside. There was something about him I couldn't gauge. He slouched almost lazily in the doorway, yet at the same time held himself with an air of confidence. I couldn't remotely guess his age. Maybe that's what was jarring about him. He looked both young and old. A worldly air about him balanced out what would otherwise have been a gangly figure.

"If you're up for a little walk," I said, grabbing a scarf from the back of my couch, "I know a good place where we can talk."

# CHAPTER 8

"Who goes first?" I asked as we walked down the street.

"That would be you," Lane said. "I'm the one who's been misled."

"I didn't mislead you."

"No?" Lane stopped at the street corner and looked at me. His hazel eyes grew dark as his lids narrowed.

"Not on purpose." I looked away and kept walking. Lane caught up with me easily.

"You failed to correct my natural assumptions," he said.

"Would you have in my position? It sounds crazy, doesn't it?"

"I don't even know what *it is* that's supposed to sound crazy," Lane reminded me. "Except I'm guessing the bracelet wasn't left to you in a will. Or if it was, then a very contested one."

I didn't answer right away.

"Maybe this was a bad idea," Lane said, stopping again. "You're not going to tell me what's going on."

I stopped and faced him. "You said you found something. I need to know what."

"Why? What's going on?"

"Here," I said, rummaging through my bag. I pressed Rupert's note and the newspaper article into his hands. "This is how I got the bracelet. The note was in the package. He and I were...He's my ex-boyfriend. He is—*was*—an archaeologist." I explained about the dig in Scotland where Rupert had been when he sent the package.

Lane read the note and the article in silence. He handed them back to me without a word, then started walking again.

"What do you think?" I asked.

"I don't know yet," he said. "I'm thinking." He pulled out one of his cigarettes and walked on in silence.

"You call that a *little* walk?" Lane said more than a short time later when we arrived at Zeitgeist, a biker bar à la San Francisco. Motorcycles out front, bicycles along the fence in the beer garden. He hadn't said another word for the rest of the walk.

"Too much for you? You should get out of that stuffy little office more."

"I don't know how you do it in those heels."

We ordered drinks at the bar, then took them through to the back beer garden's wooden tables and benches.

Lane quickly scanned the garden. It was only half-full. He led the way to a table in the back corner and sat down, facing outward. I sat on the other side of the table and tucked my legs underneath me.

I took a gulp of my Bloody Mary. I felt like I needed some vegetables.

"This car crash," Lane said. "You don't think it was accidental. Why?"

"Are you hungry?" I asked, avoiding the question. "We could order some burgers." Even though I'd told him what was going on, I wasn't quite ready to share everything. When I thought about what I would say next, that I thought Rupert had been murdered, it sounded too crazy to say out loud to someone I'd met only that day.

"What I *am* is not hungry," Lane said.

"Right."

"Jaya?"

"Mm?" I took another sip of my drink. He couldn't expect me to talk with a mouthful of tomato juice.

The hum of voices around us was starting to pick up. Pieces of conversations about bad bosses, new restaurants, and trips to Lake Tahoe blended together. I looked around at the tables. A stocky man drinking a beer by himself caught my eye, then looked quickly away.

"The car crash," Lane said again.

"I know it sounds crazy," I blurted out. "But with the package he sent to me the very same day—"

"The note isn't dated."

"There was a postmark," I said. "Between the timing of when he was killed, what you told me about the bracelet, and now the break-in...."

"You think he was murdered."

"I knew you'd think it was insane."

"I didn't say that," Lane said. "Quite the contrary. I was wondering why you were so calm at your apartment and walking down here in the wide open. You believe someone is after the ruby treasure, has broken into your apartment, and that a murderer is on the loose. What I think is that you should be taking this more seriously."

I believe I gasped. Hearing him state the implications so clearly and calmly made the situation all too real. I untucked my legs so my feet were firmly on the ground.

"But why go after me?" I asked. "Rupert was involved in something that got him murdered. But even if someone is after the bracelet—and I'm still not totally convinced the break-in was more than a coincidence—"

"You're too intelligent to believe in this degree of coincidence."

"You really believe there's a murderer on the loose? *Here?*"

I said it a bit too loudly. Two people at a nearby table stopped their conversation mid-sentence and tried to look at us without turning their heads completely around. I ignored their terrible attempt at subtle eavesdropping.

"Not just one," Lane said.

If I didn't gasp again, I'm fairly certain that at the very least my mouth was gaping open more than was attractive.

Lane had spoken at a more appropriate volume for the discussion of murder. The eavesdroppers returned to their own conversation. I, on the other hand, returned to my drink and polished off the last of it.

"You can't think the same guy who killed your ex was sneaking around your apartment," he said. "We're in another country. On the other side of the world."

"*Now* who's the one being contradictory? You're the one who went on and on about an apocryphal treasure existing. That sounds like a big enough deal for someone to hop on a flight. You can't have it both ways any more than I can."

"I'm not," he said, calmly taking a sip of his drink. "I figured it was a conspiracy."

As he said it, it dawned on me that he had purposefully selected a seat in the farthest corner of the garden. He had sat down first, facing outward. Although he'd been paying attention to me, I had the sense that whenever his hair fell over his eyes he was watching what was going on beyond me. He suspected something like this since he arrived at my apartment.

"But this can't be a conspiracy," I said.

"Why not?"

"This is *my life.*"

Lane did not look as if he accepted my impeccable logic.

"You know something else," I said breathlessly.

He blinked at me, startled.

"You said you found out something this afternoon. That's why you believe me."

"I have one last question for you first," he said. "So we can make sense of this."

"Fine."

"Why did your ex send this to you?" Lane asked.

"You read the note."

"I didn't think the East India Company exported jewelry."

"They didn't. But he sent me the priceless—is it priceless?"

"I'm sure it's worth a hell of a lot."

I swallowed hard. "He sent me the bracelet to get it safely out of the way. That much is clear. He was right that he could trust me. He was rushing to mail the package to me, and he thought he could fill me in when I called him. He must have equated my research on one aspect of Indian history to another. Sometimes I'd tell him some of my more romantic discoveries that weren't exactly relevant to my work. Like how before organized British rule began in 1858, British men in India were free to marry Indian woman, which many of them did."

"That doesn't sound especially relevant to Mughal jewelry."

"It's not. But since I know more about Indian history than Rupert did, maybe he thought I could help him identify the ruby piece. He was wrong."

"If he wanted your help with the bracelet itself," Lane said, "it wouldn't have been only to identify it. He needed help finding the rest of the treasure."

"What makes you think he didn't already have it?"

"It was dangerous for him to have one piece, so it would have been dangerous for him to have all of them. All the evidence you have points to the fact that he didn't have any other pieces."

"So the treasure is out there somewhere?"

"Hidden for centuries."

"My brain hurts," I said inelegantly.

"Then you prefer the simpler explanation of why he sent the ruby bracelet to you?"

"Which is?"

"You really didn't think of it?"

"*What?*" I scowled at him.

"He wanted you back in his life."

"There are a lot easier ways to get back together with someone than sending them a priceless—I know, I know—valuable artifact."

"Think about it," Lane said. "I've never heard of anyone sending an expensive piece of jewelry to an ex-girlfriend without an ulterior motive. Even under the circumstances, there's some symbolism there."

I swore. The couple from the nearby table looked over at us again. Evidently they were not suited to city life.

I curled my arms together on the table and rested my head. "I need a hamburger," I said, my voice muffled by my sleeve.

"Don't you want to know what I found?" Lane asked.

"No."

I only play tabla at the Tandoori Palace a couple nights a week, so I didn't have to be anywhere else that evening. I had time. It was my turn to call the shots.

"I want you to order me a cheeseburger," I said. "Well done. Extra cheese. With fries." I fished some cash out of my bag and handed the crinkled bills to him.

The sun was starting its initial descent into the horizon, and the garden was filling up. Soon it would be loud enough that we could scream about murder without being overheard. Long shadows stretched across the tables. People rolled their bikes into the enclosed space, and friends raised their voices in greeting. The solitary stocky man who had caught my eye earlier was no longer at his table.

My heart skipped a beat. I looked around, trying to remember what he looked like. Surely if he was a burglar/assassin, he would stick around to finish the job. Unless he thought he'd been made. In a conspiracy, he'd have a back-up he could call.

Lane set a fresh Bloody Mary on the table. I jumped in my seat.

"You're welcome," he said. "I didn't think you were the jumpy type."

"You were the one telling me conspirators are on the loose against me. You've got me seeing bad guys everywhere."

"It's one theory."

"What did you find today?"

His face lit up as he smiled. "I was right, Jaya," he said. "I found it."

# CHAPTER 9

"The treasure is there," Lane said. "In a Mughal painting. I wasn't just convincing myself that your piece fit with the story. The whole set is really there."

"That's all? Your big news of the day is that *you weren't wrong* about what you told me this morning?"

He frowned. "I thought you'd see what a big deal it is. It's true that your piece is from the collection that disappeared."

"I already believed you."

"Oh."

I was saved by the barbeque chef calling out my order. I sprang up to get it. I stopped to apply generous portions of condiments, and by the time I sat back down Lane had his burger as well.

"What exactly did you find?" I asked.

"I found where it existed before disappearing."

"Where? Can I see the painting?"

"I didn't find the painting itself," he said. "Is that honey on your fries?"

"Here I was thinking you cared about this great discovery."

"A reference," he said. "An article referencing some exquisite ruby jewelry that has to be your set. The description fits. Even the timing fits. It was used as an example of Selective Realism to show how something was included in paintings that never really existed. The author was assuming the jewelry was fake, but it describes your bracelet perfectly."

"That's the problem with scholars," I said. "Everyone thinks they have everything figured out without any real proof. Both our fields are filled with some of the most speculative nonsense without facts to back up a hypothesis. If people had done their research properly, there wouldn't be this *mythical* treasure that got Rupert killed. It would already have been in a museum." I consoled myself with my burger.

"I'm sure your tenure committee loves you," Lane said.

"Now that I have this ruby bracelet, who says I need tenure?"

Lane looked across the table at me with an enigmatic expression. I rather thought it resembled respect.

"I'm joking," I said through a mouthful. "I know it's not mine for the keeping."

"You'll figure it out," he said. His gaze lingered on my face. I thought I detected the briefest glance past me, but it was only the slightest flicker of his eyes.

I felt a chill run through me as a breeze swept by. I readjusted the scarf around my neck.

"You aren't smoking," I said.

"You're terribly observant."

"Why am I freezing out here if you didn't even want to smoke?"

"Oh," Lane said, starting to pull off his jacket. "Do you want my coat?"

I waved off the offer.

"I only smoke when I need to think," he said.

"What else was in the shoddy article you found?"

"How much do you know about the Mughals' cultural pursuits?"

"They were Muslims from central Asia," I said, "They arrived in India before the British, and many of them were important in granting concessions to the British for trade. Not just Jahangir, although he was the first, right at the height of the Mughal Empire before their decline."

"And their art?"

"You know I don't know anything about their jewelry," I said. "I do know a little about Mughal architecture. Like Shah Jahan's romantic story of the Taj Mahal. The supposedly great love story of how the Taj Mahal was built for his wife. How this ambitious and war-hungry leader, who bankrupted the masses to build extravagant palaces, loved his wife so much that he built her a lavish tomb after she died giving birth to their fourteenth child—or was it the fifteenth? Something like that. Just because his jail of choice was to be imprisoned in a tower overlooking the Taj Mahal tomb after his pious son overthrew him, it's supposed to be a romantic story. It never sounded very romantic to me."

"Interesting take. But that's not the point I was getting at. He also had treasures like his Peacock Throne of gold. So did lots of other Mughal rulers. His son was Jahangir."

"And lineage is important because—?"

"Not the lineage, but the huge significance of art in various Mughal courts over time. They left us a wealth of paintings. Several Mughal rulers were great patrons of the arts. They commissioned huge numbers of paintings involving large numbers of people. And those people were often wearing important jewels.

"You have to understand there are far too many of these paintings to be covered in the texts at one library, no matter how good, that doesn't specialize in Indian art. There are well over a thousand paintings in the multiple volumes that make up an epic story painted during Akbar's rule. And that's just one of many. Even specialty books can only include so many examples. That's why I couldn't find the painting itself, only the article. But the article did also give me a very good idea of where to start looking for some of the paintings that featured this set."

"In the early 1600s?" I asked.

"Yeah, that's when—"

"When it still existed in paintings," I said sadly. "Not where it went when it really disappeared. Or where it reappeared."

"Not at first, of course—"

"No," I said. "I should have realized it couldn't be pieced together so quickly. It's been gone for centuries. I don't know what I was thinking. I appreciate your help."

"You're not trying to put me off again."

"I do appreciate what you've done," I said. "Truly. But you've spent most of the day researching, and you've gotten up to the seventeenth century. You can keep the photo of the bracelet and keep moving forward on your research. I'm sure you'll write a great article proving all those scholars wrong and make your career. I don't have time to keep up this slow pace. I need to figure out what happened *this week*, before it's too late. I know it sounds strange coming from a historian. But there's a murderer out there. I don't have time for slow and steady research."

Night had fallen without me noticing. The outdoor lights clicked on around us. I glanced around. I didn't see anyone suspicious.

"Since you don't have your ex to fill in the blanks," Lane said, "what did you have in mind?"

The streaks of outdoor lighting accentuated his features. His cheekbones formed shadows down his face, and his eyes seemed especially large behind his glasses.

"I've got some frequent flyer miles," I said. "I'm going to use them. I'm going where Rupert was when he was killed. A Pictish dig in the Highlands of Scotland."

With a slight pang of some emotion I wasn't used to feeling, I stood up to leave. Lane didn't try to stop me as I departed.

# CHAPTER 10

*What was I thinking?*

My latest research paper wasn't going to write itself, and it was already months later than I'd hoped to have it finished. I wasn't teaching over summer session specifically so I could catch up on my research that I hadn't had time to do during the school year with a first-year assistant professor's teaching load. The university had hired two of us with specialties in South Asian history. In this economy, it looked like only one of us would be getting tenure. I loved my new home in San Francisco. I didn't want to leave.

But I couldn't let Rupert's murder remain an "accidental death" and his murderer run away with this treasure. I pushed my selfish concerns about tenure aside.

That night, after catching a cab home, I cashed in some airline miles to buy a one-way ticket on the next available flight to London, leaving the following afternoon.

I printed out another copy of the photograph of the bracelet before I realized how tired I was. Now that I'd formed a plan of action, the adrenaline of the day was wearing off. Sanjay had left me several texts and a voicemail message, but I didn't have the energy to get back to him that night.

As promised, Nadia fixed my door. The door frame was reinforced, and there was an extra dead bolt. I wouldn't say I felt good about whatever lay beyond that door, but at least I felt safe inside my apartment. I fell asleep as soon as my head hit the pillow.

\* \* \*

In the morning I called Sanjay back.

"You're insane," he said after I told him my plan. "You can't just leave the country later today in search of a murderer and a treasure."

"Why not? I'm not teaching summer session. Besides, you do things like that all the time."

"That's different," he said. "That's when I find a historic piece of magic memorabilia. I can't go around calling myself The Hindi Houdini without real props owned by Houdini, now can I?"

"You're impossible to argue with, Sanjay."

"Which is why you're going to call me every day to let me know you're okay. My next season of shows is starting soon, otherwise I'd go with you myself."

"Who said I need help? The break-in is nothing to worry about."

Sanjay made choking noises on the other end of the line. "You had a break-in?"

Damn. I'd forgotten he didn't know about the burglary. Everything was happening so fast.

After I calmed Sanjay down and promised to keep him up to date, he grudgingly assured me it was no problem for him to play on his own until I got back.

He said it would give him an opportunity to try some new things. After I hung up, I wondered if he meant more than music. Restaurant-goers might find themselves watching flowers magically grow from sitar strings before I returned.

I wasted much of the morning searching for my passport. I know where all of the books in my apartment are located, but not so much when it comes to everything else. The rest of the morning was spent assuring Nadia I wasn't taking an unplanned vacation because I was worried about staying at the house. I wasn't left with much time to pack.

My phone beeped that I'd missed a message. It was my brother, Mahilan. Speaking Hindi. The problem was, I don't speak Hindi. Well, not very well. I remember bits and pieces of the various local languages from my childhood, which included our mother's Tamil and widespread Hindi, but I'm far from fluent in either. Mahilan is older and remembers more of the languages. Recently he had begun speaking with me only in Hindi.

This new Hindi phase is the fault of his latest girlfriend, whose parents are Hindi speakers. Mahilan is serious about her and thinks they might start a family. He's brushing up on his Hindi and insists it will be easier for their kids to be bilingual if I speak it, too.

Luckily my Hindi is passable enough that I was able to squeak through my higher education language requirements. Most of my research consists of English-language documents, thanks to thorough British colonization of India. The few non-English documents I need, I can spend the time to translate. I didn't have time to decipher Mahilan's message that afternoon. He would try me again if it was important.

I called a cab to save time. I hadn't quite finished packing when I heard what I thought would be the cabbie knocking at the door. I realized my mistake after I opened the door. It was Miles.

He was outfitted in black cargo pants, black combat boots, and a black t-shirt. The words "je t'aime" were written in blue pen across his left forearm.

"I heard you were robbed," he said. "Do you...I thought, maybe, you might want to talk about it?"

I froze where I was, holding the door. I had encouraged him the day before. Could it have been enough encouragement to give him fanatical ideas about getting inside my apartment?

My brain hurt again. Two days ago my life had made sense. Sure, it wasn't perfect. But at least I knew what to expect. Now, not only had my ex-boyfriend been murdered, but my apartment burglarized, and I was about to take an insane trip leading God-knows-where.

"I don't have time to talk," I said to Miles.

"I brought you something in case it happens again." He fumbled in a baggy pocket of his cargo pants.

I didn't want to see whatever he was going to pull out of his pants.

"I'm really okay," I said. "You don't need to give me anything. I'm going out of town."

Miles stopped digging through his pockets. "Do you want me to look after your place while you're gone?"

"You don't need to do that. Look, my landlady already had the door fixed."

"You still need protection," Miles said.

"I'll be okay."

Taking care of myself isn't something I spend time worrying about. What I'm less confident of is my ability to pull off the more practical aspects of day-to-day life, like whether I could finish packing in time to make my flight. I left Miles in the doorway as I pulled a few more items from the closet.

"Can I help?" he asked a few moments later, his mouth only a few inches from my ear.

I was about to yell at Miles for his creepy behavior when a car in front of the house beeped its horn. *That* was the cab. I zipped up the backpack, grabbed my messenger bag, and pushed Miles out the door. If I'd forgotten anything, I could buy it 5,000 miles away.

# CHAPTER 11

The cabbie drove almost as fast as me, and soon I was shuffling through the airport security line. I loaded my messenger bag and small backpack onto the conveyor belt and waited.

And waited.

The screener behind the X-ray machine frowned. He motioned to a man with a mustache.

Mustache walked over to the X-ray machine and leaned over. He frowned as well. They backed up the conveyor belt. It was my backpack the screener held in his hands.

"Excuse me, ma'am," Mustache said to me. His biceps flexed under his dress shirt. "Is this your bag?"

He lifted the backpack in his large hands. I watched in horror as he removed a can of pepper spray.

Oh, God. Miles. He had wanted to give me something to protect myself.

"Ma'am," Mustache said, "please step this way."

I stepped into a roped-off area. At least I wasn't behind a closed door. Yet.

"Is there a problem?" a familiar voice said.

I turned and saw before me a figure I hardly recognized. Lane was dressed in a charcoal gray suit with a red dress shirt unbuttoned at the collar. The bright color set off his eyes, their hazel color appearing almost bronze. His hair was combed with a gel that held his tresses perfectly in place. Even his thick glasses took on a different look with the new ensemble. They were a trendy accessory now. Not a studious reading tool.

"Wow," I said.

I hadn't meant to say that.

Lane ignored me. It was probably for the best, since who knew what I would say next. He stepped forward and spoke with the security guard in hushed tones.

Mustache stepped out of the roped-off area and led Lane a few feet away. I could no longer hear their voices. Lane didn't look at me, but Mustache glanced over at me every few seconds.

He nodded slowly at Lane. Lane put out his hand for Mustache to shake. They shook hands in that curt, firm way that competitors do.

Lane picked up a small bag on the ground at his feet, then strode quickly toward me. With his free hand, he took my hand in his. I felt a sharp jolt of electricity. It must have been the carpet.

"Grab your stuff," he said.

I stared up at him.

"What?" he said. "I didn't want you to miss your flight."

"You followed me!"

"Aren't you going to thank me? That was pretty stupid to try to bring pepper spray on a flight. I thought Nadia said you knew judo or something anyway?"

"I didn't put that can in my bag," I snapped, dropping his hand.

"You didn't?" His eyes darted around.

"Long story," I said. "You don't need to worry about it."

"You sure?"

"What did you say to the security guard?"

"We should get out of here," he said. "Muscle man might change his mind."

I grabbed my bags and shoes and let Lane lead me away from the security area. I stopped once we were a few dozen yards into the concourse.

"How did you do that?" I asked, dropping my bags and putting on my shoes.

"You're lucky it was only pepper spray, not a Taser."

"But what did you say?"

"It doesn't matter," he said. "It worked."

"You're right. What matters is that you followed me."

"I followed your lead, but not you." He started walking again, looking around at the gate numbers. He pulled a ticket out of his dress shirt pocket without slowing, glanced at it, then put it back.

I caught up to him.

"I'm going to London," he said, "to write that article. All those paintings to back up this new hypothesis will be at the British Library in London. You wouldn't want my article to be full of shoddy scholarship, would you?"

He stopped in front of a gate. My gate. I flung my backpack onto the empty seat in front of me.

"No direct flights to Scotland?" Lane asked.

"Rupert was a lecturer in London. I'm stopping there before heading up to Scotland."

An announcement crackled on the speakers above, informing us that pre-boarding would begin momentarily.

"I'll be right back," Lane said.

He approached a flight staff member at the counter. He leaned over and folded his arms on the high counter, facing away from me. The young woman giggled and tucked a loose lock of hair behind her ear flirtatiously. She began typing on the computer. A few moments later, she handed two small pieces of paper to Lane.

"What was that?" I asked once he returned.

"I got us seats together."

"You—"

"Sorry they're in the back. Peak summer season and all."

He handed me a new boarding pass. I hadn't noticed my old one was missing out of the front pocket of my bag.

"What makes you think I want to sit with you?"

"Aren't you worried about your burglar? He didn't get what he's after."

"He can't. It's in a safe deposit box."

"He doesn't know that. If I were him, I wouldn't let you out of my sight."

My resolve of the night before was nowhere to be found today. I was all too aware of my tense neck muscles as I scanned the waiting area. I half-expected to see the stocky man who'd caught my eye at Zeitgeist the night before.

I didn't.

No one I even vaguely recognized was in sight.

Just Lane.

"How would the burglar even find me?"

"Nobody knows you're here?"

"Well of course people know I'm leaving. I can't very well take off without anybody knowing I'll be away." Very few people, in fact. Not that I was going to tell that to Lane.

"There you go."

The man had a way of leaving me speechless.

"That's our group they're calling," he said, standing up.

My stunned silence continued as we boarded the plane and got ourselves situated. I suspiciously regarded the man with sideburns and too much cologne who sat down in the aisle seat next to us.

"I didn't see anyone go up to the counter after me to switch their seat." Lane said. "He wouldn't be near us."

"Then why do you look so worried?"

"I'm not worried," Lane snapped. He tugged at the collar of his shirt, even though it was already loosened.

"At least I know you're a bad liar."

Giving up on his collar, Lane crossed his arms so firmly that his knuckles began to turn white.

"Ah," I said. "You're afraid of flying."

"I wouldn't use that strong of a word." Lane faced forward and didn't look at me as he spoke.

Since Lane didn't seem to want to talk about it, I picked up a magazine from the seat pocket in front of me. My heart sped up whenever a flight attendant passed our aisle to prepare for takeoff, so my nerves didn't seem to be doing much better than Lane's. At least he was no longer gripping his arms. He'd moved on to gripping the armrests.

"Isn't there something you can take?" I asked.

"Not if I want to be alert."

"You don't need to be alert for a nine hour flight."

Lane relaxed his arms and faced me. "Yes I do. You should be more concerned about yourself. Your ex is *dead*." He spoke so quietly I could barely hear him, but his voice was as serious as I'd ever heard it.

"I know that. I'm quite aware that I'm sitting on a plane with a stranger, part of an apocryphal treasure is hidden in my safe deposit box, and some unknown party is after it—and possibly me."

Lane gripped the armrests even tighter as the plane lifted off with a gentle bump. I looked out the window as the buildings below shrank. The ground turned into meaningless patterns before cloud cover swallowed up the airplane. I leaned back in the seat.

"No one has made an attempt on my life," I said. "No one is going to take a shot at me, which ricochets and blasts through one of these airplane windows and sends us dropping out of the sky, as we cling to our seats for dear life while other passengers get sucked out of the hole around us one by one—"

A loud click sounded.

I jumped in my seat. The seatbelt cut into my abdomen, holding me in place. Lane grabbed my hand so tightly it ached.

A whirring sound followed the click. It was only the plane's wheels retracting.

Lane let go of my hand. He ran his hands over his face. When he put them down I saw he was laughing. The noise from the plane drowned out much of the sound, but the expression on his face was a welcome one.

"Touché," he said. "I might be being overly cautious, but it's only because you're not taking this seriously enough."

"I *am* taking this seriously. But if I let the truth consume me, where would that leave me? I'd still be hiding under the covers of my bed. I can't let myself think about it. Oh good, it looks like the beverage service will be starting soon."

If all people were my size, economy class airline travel would be quite comfortable. Though I suppose if everyone were my size, they would make the seats smaller. I took a gin and tonic from the flight attendant, curled up on the seat, and promptly fell asleep.

When I awoke, the shade of the window next to me had been drawn and I could see the sun peeking out from beneath it. My neck was stiff, and my mouth was dry. The seat no longer felt as comfortable as when I had first sat down.

I stretched my arms above my head and wriggled my feet under the seat in front of me. Lane pulled the airline headphones off.

"You don't do anything without doing it wholeheartedly," he said. "You eat like you mean it. You drink like you mean it. You even sleep like you mean it."

"What time is it?"

"We're landing in a little over an hour."

I yawned. "Anyone try to kill me in my sleep?"

Lane didn't dignify the question with a response.

A flight attendant walked by, collecting empty breakfast trays.

"You didn't wake me up for breakfast?"

Lane reached down into the seat pocket and pulled out a miraculously resilient ham and cheese croissant and a tiny bottle of water. He handed them to me.

I tore into the breakfast sandwich. Lane put his headphones back on and resumed innocently watching a British sitcom on the screen on the back of the seat in front of him. I studied his profile. He couldn't possibly be involved in whatever was going on. Yet there was still something about Lane I couldn't quite put my finger on. I poked him in the arm. He lowered the headphones.

"Where are you going when we arrive?" I asked.

He shrugged. "I figured I'd find a hotel and then head to the British Library."

"I accept your offer of sticking together."

"My offer?"

"You said I had to be careful. Sticking together is the best way to do that. You're involved now, too."

There were two possibilities. Either Lane was right that an unknown party was after me and it was safer to stick together, or after being presented with such a tempting treasure Lane himself had...okay, I hadn't figured out exactly how he could possibly be involved. But if he was, I needed to keep an eye on him.

Either way, from the sleepy looks of all the passengers around me, I'd gotten more rest than any of them. I was starting out ahead.

# CHAPTER 12

We rode the Underground from Heathrow into the city. Much of the journey into London is above ground. We watched the outskirts of London speed by, passing by rows of sprawling stone houses with the wash hung out to dry.

I hadn't been back to London in over a year. Apart from the time I'd spent with Rupert, I passed most of my time in London looking at India Office Records in a reading room of the British Library. It was an intense year, and I finished my dissertation by the end of it. Rupert, on the other hand, was happy to prolong the student experience. His archaeology dissertation (the subject of which I was never entirely certain) was a never-ending work-in-progress that his heart was never committed to. Born wealthy and knowing parental money would keep coming as long as he was still in school, Rupert had chosen one of the longest courses of study available. While flitting around from one archaeological subject to another, he took his time, enjoying life. That was Rupert's strong suit. And we certainly did enjoy the finer things in life that year.

Spending my days studying the lives of people who had lived long before me left me with a desire to live my life to the fullest each night when I left the hallowed library halls. Not because the research was mundane and I needed some excitement, but quite the contrary. The pieces of history that survive are the dramatic ones. The kind that can make you wonder why your own dreary existence is worth living.

My research area is especially full of drama. Adventurous traders, proud rulers, courageous soldiers. No, my days weren't boring. But my nights with Rupert were even more exciting. Had he lived in a previous century, I have no doubt he would have voluntarily headed to India in search of his fortune like some of his ancestors.

The train headed into underground darkness as we neared central London. I pulled my thoughts back to the present.

Lane and I found adjoining rooms in a quiet Bayswater hotel. I quickly freshened up, then slipped my heels back on. I heaved my messenger bag across my chest before knocking on Lane's door.

"I'll share a cab with you to the library," I said when he opened the door. "There's something I want to look up there before I make another stop."

He yawned in response. His shoes were off and his dress shirt half unbuttoned. I pulled my eyes from the latter.

"Haven't you ever heard of a nap?" he asked. "It's not even noon here. The library will be open all day. And it's only a quick tube ride from here."

"A cab is much more efficient. Besides, you don't want me to go out there all by myself, do you?"

Lane raised an eyebrow. He was quite good at it.

"I didn't see anyone suspicious when we got off the plane," he said. "There's probably nothing to worry about."

"You don't believe that."

"No. But you don't believe you need a bodyguard, either. What do you want?"

"Your help."

His eyebrow shot up again.

"I thought if we got started now," I said, "we could meet for dinner. We could compare notes before I leave for Scotland tomorrow."

Fifteen minutes later we passed the sprawling King's Cross/St. Pancras station and arrived at the British Library. As we walked inside, I thought I noticed Lane give a fond look to an object directly inside the doors. The metal bench in the shape of a book with its pages flipped open is one of my favorite items in the library as well.

The main section of the library is open to the public. The reading rooms for specialized research are different. You need to apply for a reader's pass with your credentials. Lane didn't stop at the office to apply for a pass. Perhaps we'd crossed paths before without knowing it.

We dropped off our bags in lockers before entering the reading room. Bags are prohibited in all reading rooms, along with coats, umbrellas, food, drink, and even pens.

With all the hoops you need to jump through to gain access to the specialized reading room mini-libraries, you might think the rooms would be sparsely populated, quiet places. To the contrary, the room with the India Office Records seats a hundred and often fills to capacity, especially during the summer when visiting scholars are numerous.

I wasn't after a seat, though. I was after Jeremy, the librarian I had known while doing research at the library. He worked in the Asia, Pacific & Africa Collections. I spotted him right away. He was tough to miss.

"Jaya Jones," Jeremy said in his familiar, elegant voice. He rested his elbows on the high counter of the information desk. Though he'd only spoken two words, I was reminded of how well he could have fit into a film adaptation of a Jane Austen novel. Or maybe an audio recording. I didn't recall any black aristocrats in Jane Austen. He leaned forward over the desk and kissed the air next to my cheek.

"What brings you back to our fair city?" he asked. "Let me guess. You missed the challenge of walking in your fabulous heels on our cobblestone streets."

Jeremy is only a few years older than me. He looks even less like a librarian than I look like a professor. Like me, he appears younger than his true age. Unlike me, he's happy about it. His brightly colored ensemble of purple corduroys and a yellow sweater fit too tightly, but he pulled the look off with great success.

"A bit of a detour," I said. "You were always amazingly ingenious in what you could find. I thought I'd see if you could help me. I'm looking for some Indian rubies."

Jeremy watched closely as I lifted a small notebook from the library-approved plastic bag. I removed a photograph from the notebook's pages.

I pushed the photo of the ruby bracelet across the desk for him to see. He glanced at the front with only moderate interest. He lifted it up to more carefully inspect the back.

"Where's the reference?"

"That's why I need you, Jeremy."

I filled him in on how I thought the bracelet was from a set of Mughal jewelry from at least a few hundred years ago, and told him I'd check in later that day.

As I walked toward the exit, I felt a wave of apprehension wash over me. I looked around the high-ceilinged room. It was filled with people, some deep in concentration hunched over tables, some hurrying around. I spotted what I thought was the top of Lane's head in a corner of the room. I hesitated, then walked over to him. The reference binders look much the same, so I couldn't tell what he was looking up.

His face lit up when he saw me. I felt my own face break into a smile. Was I blushing? What was the matter with me?

"Got anything?" I asked.

"I think so. It shouldn't take too long to find something, now that we're here."

"See you tonight," I said, then headed out of the safe haven of the library to find out what Rupert had been up to.

# CHAPTER 13

If I didn't want to sell my roadster to pay my phone bill, I needed a new cell phone to use in the UK. Especially if I was going to call Sanjay as I'd promised. I found a mobile phone dealer on Tottenham Court Road who popped out the sim card from my phone and gave me a new card with a prepaid UK plan. Before heading off, I sent Sanjay a quick text message to let him know I'd arrived safely.

I made a quick stop in a Tesco Metro supermarket to grab a packaged egg-mayonnaise sandwich. It was not a frivolous stop. A girl has to keep up her energy to be productive. One of my favorite things about Britain has always been the food. Though mocked by some, I appreciate the straightforward nature of British cuisine. So much of it is easy on-the-go food. And on-the-go I went. I headed down the bustling street toward my next task: tracing Rupert's whereabouts.

It was a pleasant, sunny day. Throngs of tourists and Londoners walked along the broad sidewalk. The tourists ambled along, dressed in bright, summery colors. The locals, in their more subdued hues, easily maneuvered around them. Black cabs hurried along in the street. Pigeons flapped their wings to move out of the way. It was almost as if life was normal again.

Almost.

I couldn't quite place the reason, but something made me nervous as I walked. I was more worried than I'd admitted to Lane. I hurried into the tube station on the corner.

The Picadilly line went straight to South Kensington. It was quintessential Rupert to have lived in such a posh neighborhood while still a student. I emerged from the Underground at Gloucester Road and walked down the familiar blocks. Within a few minutes, I stood in front of Rupert's old flat. I didn't know if he had still been living there, but I had to start somewhere.

My unease grew stronger as I stood there. It was the same nervous feeling. I shook it off and knocked.

An attractive brunette opened the door. She told me she and her husband had moved in a year ago, but she wished me luck finding Rupert. She said she could tell Rupert and his roommates were sweet guys because when she first moved in, a neighborhood stray cat thought dinner ought to be on the stoop of the ground floor flat. "Sweet" was not an adjective I would use when describing Rupert and his friends. It was a good bet it was an opportunistic cat.

My next stop had a better chance of success. I'd heard that after Rupert finished his degree the previous December, he began lecturing at King's College in London. I sent him a "happy graduation" card at the time. His family connections had probably helped him get the job, but to be fair, Rupert was highly intelligent. He could do a lot when he set his mind to it. Which wasn't to say it was a frequent occurrence.

I found the department of archaeology in the modern King's Cross building on The Strand. Though it was summer and many of the students were gone, a smattering of voices could be heard in the hallways. At the main office, a very round and very freckled red-haired man stared at me from where he sat wedged into his seat.

"Can I help?"

"I hope so," I said. "Do you know Rupert Chadwick?"

His pudgy nose scrunched up, turning his narrow eyes into even smaller slits.

"He isn't here anymore." He spit out the words. I didn't get the impression he'd heard Rupert was dead.

"Quit before the end of term," he added.

I wasn't surprised Rupert had rubbed someone the wrong way. Still, that was not the answer I expected. What would have made Rupert quit so soon? A lecturer was the bottom of the ladder of university instructors, but King's College was an excellent school in the heart of his beloved London.

"Do you know where he went?"

"Not likely. He moved away."

"I was really hoping to track him down."

The man looked at me coldly.

"It's just...he owes me some money," I said.

His face relaxed. "Sounds like something the prat would do. Wish I could help."

"Maybe someone else here was friends with him."

He scratched the side of his large, red neck. "Not that I know of. What'd he want the money for? Always the posh ones who'll take you for it."

"Something stupid, I'm sure. Do you know why he quit?"

"Don't think I can help. That was a mystery around here, that one was."

"A mystery?"

"He didn't say a word to anyone."

I walked slowly down the hallway toward the main entrance. I was at a loss as to what to do next. I was sure Rupert would have stuck with a real job for at least a semester. I thought I would have been able to find someone who knew what he was doing. Now I had no choice but to arrive blind at the Scottish dig.

I stopped in the ladies room to freshen up. I splashed water on my face, then looked in the mirror. In spite of Lane's proclamation that I slept like I meant it, I was tired. I looked it. I needed some coffee.

I left the building, thinking I'd see if one of my favorite cafes was still in business. I walked a few yards before I realized I should have turned the other way to reach the Embankment tube stop. I turned around and passed by the main doors to the university again. As I walked by, I got the feeling someone was calling my name.

I looked back toward the expanse of the building. Maybe the man who disliked Rupert had thought of something helpful. Between his red hair and girth, he would be hard to miss. But I didn't see him. I walked back inside, but he wasn't there either. Odd.

Back out on the sidewalk, the feeling was there again. Someone was calling my name. The name Jaya wasn't uncommon in England, with its large South Asian population. It was conceivable that someone would have been calling out to their friend Jaya down the street.

I wasn't *hearing* anything, though. I was feeling it.

Someone was watching me.

# CHAPTER 14

I stopped abruptly, my heart thudding in my chest.

Whatever had been going on in San Francisco wasn't the same thing going on in London. My feeling of unease was completely different. This wasn't a vague sense of uneasiness. Someone was following me.

It was stupid of me to stop in the middle of the sidewalk. My pursuer would think I was onto him. Thankfully, a second later I had a rational thought. I was in front of Somerset House, a picturesque tourist attraction next to King's College. Somewhere in the depths of my bag, I had my camera. I fished it out and took a picture of the charming Palladian stone structure.

It really was a beautiful building. Hopefully enough so that my pursuer wouldn't find my actions suspicious.

I was about to put the camera back in my bag and walk on, when I had a better idea. I left the small camera in my hand. I made sure the lens was facing backwards, and not covered by the palm of my hand.

I walked quickly, still on my path to the Underground station. Instead of sticking to the main streets, I cut through the expansive courtyard of Somerset House. I clicked the shutter of the camera as I walked, capturing whoever was behind me.

There was one problem. Although I could look at the digital pictures on the camera as soon as it was safe to do so, I didn't know who I was looking for. Since it was summer, tourists filled the courtyard. They milled about the numerous fountains. They came and went from the multiple small museums housed there.

I needed to find somewhere more secluded, where I could isolate whoever was following me. Otherwise, for all I knew, my follower could be the handsome dark-haired man sitting by himself with an unopened paperback novel in his hands. No, wait. A voluptuous woman walked up to the man with outstretched arms. Okay, so he wasn't my spy. Perhaps it was the small woman who was slowly—too slowly, it seemed—reading an informational panel in front of one of the fountains. But then again, maybe she was just very interested in architecture.

I had to get out of there before my imagination started to rival Nadia's.

A side exit from the courtyard led to a smaller street that would lead to the waterfront of the Thames River. The waterfront street would lead to the Embankment tube stop. As I walked out of the courtyard, I continued to snap a photo every few seconds.

The sidewalk on the street was almost as crowded. This route wasn't going to be as helpful as I thought. I needed somewhere more remote. After a few more steps, I had an idea. Stone stairways were the most direct routes to the waterfront. The university and Somerset House were set on the high ground overlooking the river, on the same level as Waterloo Bridge. The Embankment and adjoining gardens were level with the river.

I weaved through the crowd, snapping more photos. I caught the briefest glimpse of a breathtaking view of the city before ducking into the maze of stairs leading down.

The stone stairway was quiet and deserted, as I had thought it would be. It was, in fact, exactly what I had expected. I hadn't counted on what that meant. The noise of the camera shutter clicking became louder in contrast to the quiet. Too loud. I took my hand off the shutter.

I was alone in the dusty concrete enclosure. I didn't see another soul as I rounded the curve onto the first landing.

I did, however, hear a sound.

Footsteps crunched on pebbles behind me. Someone was approaching.

Why was someone following me? What good could it possibly do them? They didn't actually think I had the bracelet with me, did they? Surely my life hadn't become like a paperback thriller where people dropped like flies because the bad guy thought they knew something compromising. Nothing had happened on the plane. Nothing would happen now. Right?

Alone on that solitary alley of stairs leading down to the dark river, I wasn't so sure.

I increased my pace, half-running to the street below. I snapped two shots with the camera as I flew down the rest of the stairs.

Rounding the last corner that let out onto the street, I ran straight into an anorexic woman sucking on a cigarette for dear life. On second thought, she was sturdier than she looked. I was the one who fell down.

My camera strap tangled around my wrist. The strap had kept the camera from bouncing away from me along with my bag. But it hadn't saved the camera from the brunt of the fall. I wouldn't be taking any more pictures of my pursuer.

I scrambled up and walked hurriedly off after apologizing to the woman, barely taking time to dust off my bruised knees. I didn't feel the sting. The smoke from the woman's cigarette had pushed all other thoughts from my mind except one.

Could *Lane* be following me?

The idea was preposterous, surely. But then, so was this whole escapade. I couldn't imagine what Lane could possibly gain by following me. If he was concerned about my well-being, he could innocently propose that we stick together. He didn't have to sneak around.

The more I thought about it as I hurried down the Embankment, there was no reasonable reason for Lane to follow me. The only thing that made less sense was his grand conspiracy theories. The theories he had been trying to shove down my throat.

I whirled around on my heel. No Lane. Nor was there anyone who looked familiar. There was one way to know for sure if it was him.

I stepped to the edge of the road and hailed a black cab. I felt the soreness of my knees as I stepped inside.

"The British Library," I said.

I didn't have time to stop at the lockers. I dropped my bag on the floor outside of the reading room and hoped for the best. I hurried up and down the stacks. My palms grew clammy on my second sweep of the room.

Lane wasn't in there.

# CHAPTER 15

I walked frantically along the edges of the reading room, making sure I hadn't missed Lane. Nobody paid the slightest bit of attention to me. An agitated academic searching in vain for documents wasn't an uncommon sight.

Lane could have needed a coffee break. It was possible. He'd been tired, after all. There could be any number of reasons why he wasn't there. It didn't mean he was the one following me. But in his absence, there was no way to be sure.

Giving myself a moment to collect my confused thoughts, I leaned against a pillar underneath the wall of paintings.

That's when I saw him.

Lane sat at a large table in a smaller room, separated by glass doors, off to the side of the main reading room. It was a room used for viewing oversized documents like maps.

I watched him through the glass for a few moments, letting my relief sink in. It looked as if he hadn't moved in hours, except for scribbling in the notebook that lay open in front of him. Several items in addition to the notebook lay flat on the table. His glasses slipped down his slender nose as he looked down at one of them, deep in thought.

Lane gave a nearly imperceptible startled jerk of his body as I opened the glass door to enter the small room. He looked up and readjusted his glasses.

"What's up?" he asked in a low voice.

"I'm being followed."

Lane's face darkened as he looked out into the main room.

"He's not there now," I said. "I hopped in a cab."

"Did you see who it was?"

"It was more of a feeling."

"But you're sure?" He kept glancing between me and the room beyond.

"Yes, I'm sure. This wasn't one of our theoretical conversations in San Francisco. There was someone watching me."

"Where did it start?"

"I've been thinking about that. It must have been when I left here."

"But how could—"

"You found it!" I exclaimed, pointing at the object in front of Lane on the table.

It was my bracelet. Only it wasn't.

I hadn't noticed it immediately because the ruby piece was only a portion of a lively, colorful painting of dozens of people in a festive royal court. Mughal courts would have looked like a lot of fun if I hadn't known that the women were most likely part of a harem.

One corner of the painting was highlighted more than the rest. Set slightly apart from the other subjects, a fair-skinned woman wore a thick armlet of gold and rubies clamped to her upper arm. The shape of gold and rubies was the same as the one Rupert had sent me.

The painting had the effect of making the ruby piece look unworldly. Leaning over the table to get a closer look, I could see why scholars thought it wasn't real. The gems seemed too large to be real.

The armlet dwarfed the other pieces of jewelry that adorned the girl and the people around her. It looked as if it could be a symbol, much like when rulers of high stature were depicted standing on a globe.

"It's one of them," Lane said.

"Who is she?" I pointed at the stunning woman. I wondered if she had been as beautiful in real life as she looked in the painting.

"I don't know," he said. "Not yet. That's the trouble with the destruction of original documents." He spoke in a quiet voice I hardly recognized. His eyes held an intensity that stunned me.

"Wars," he continued. "Infighting. Poor record keeping. Most of all, the simple ravages of time."

As he spoke the words, I shivered. He spoke with a prepossessed authority. If I were the type of person to succumb to romantic fancy, I would have been convinced he had been there himself.

"The artifacts we're left with," he continued, "are imperfectly understood at best."

"And we," I said, "put the pieces together."

My statement shook him out of his reverie. He had the faintest smile on his lips as he looked down at the corner of the painting. When he looked back up at me, his eyes were back to their usual veiled countenance.

I took a last look at the painting before stepping toward the door.

"Wait," he said. "Where are you going?"

"You said you hadn't figured it out yet," I said. "I'm leaving you in peace to finish working."

"But what about—"

"I lost him," I said.

"I don't think it's a good idea for us to go off on our own."

"That's a nice opinion," I said. "It doesn't happen to be mine."

Lane stood up. I was already at the door. He took a step forward toward me, but stopped and looked at his materials strewn about the desk. There was no way he could follow me out.

"See you tonight," I said with a wave.

"Jaya—"

"Be aware of anyone suspicious," I said as I walked through the door.

I glanced back to make sure Lane hadn't followed me out of the side room, then stopped to check in with Jeremy at the main reading room desk. He said he'd found enough possible references that I could spend the rest of the summer going through the archives, which he added was fine with him. The place could use a breath of fresh air. I told Jeremy I'd be in touch, then went in search of my bag, which I found where I had left it outside the reading room.

I checked to see if my camera would turn on. No luck. Instead, I found a thirty-minute photo shop. I handed over the memory card and asked for prints.

I drank a large coffee around the corner while I waited, then ordered another one after picking up the photos. Tucked in the back corner of a Pret A Manger cafe, I drank syrupy coffee and flipped through the pictures.

Most of the photos prominently featured sky or sidewalk. No one in a suspicious-looking broad hat or trench coat jumped out in any of the shots, though in one a man was in fact wearing a trench coat. In another, a pair of bright red sneakers in the crowd reminded me of something Rupert would have liked. He had a similar pair before. I had always found them a bit showy for men's shoes, but he was quite attached to them.

I sipped my coffee, feeling unsettled by this newfound sentimental bone in my body. I flipped through the photos one more time before giving up and heading back outside.

As I walked down the street, I realized I hadn't felt the sensation of being followed since I'd hopped in the cab. I took a deep breath of not-so-fresh air. Without any other ideas, I walked back to the hotel.

I had left a "do not disturb" sign on the door to my room. Everything appeared to be exactly as I'd left it. I had left my extra pair of shoes a few inches inside the door, leaving only enough room for me to slip out. Unless the tooth fairy had let herself in, nobody had entered the room.

I found my music player at the bottom of my bag and slipped on my headphones. I found a soothing tabla track and lay down on the bed for a nap. I set the alarm so I'd have enough time for a run and a shower before dinner.

At the appointed meeting time, I made my way down to the lobby with wet hair and a growling stomach. I found Lane already waiting for me. He was seated in a worn yet regal high-backed chair at the window. He was leaning back in a relaxed pose, an unlit cigarette in his hand. He faced the window, but he must have sensed my presence and turned his head.

"You could have waited for me outside so you could smoke," I said.

"I didn't think that would be a good idea," he said. "I'm being followed, too."

# CHAPTER 16

I instinctively backed away from the window.

"He's not here now," Lane said, watching my maneuver. "I lost him at another hotel before coming back here."

"Did you see who it was?"

"I think so," he said. "Normal-looking guy. Fair skin. Brown hair. Not especially tall. Nothing distinctive. He didn't try to approach me. He hung back. Can you sit down? You're making me nervous."

"Would you recognize him if you saw him again?"

"If I'm right about who it was," Lane said. "There's a chair right here, you know."

"I have too much energy to sit. What makes you think you can't be sure?"

"He didn't seem to know what he was doing," Lane said. "It made me wonder if it was just some weirdo. I don't think so, but—"

"See if he's in here," I said, handing him the stack of photos.

"Great picture," he said, holding up an out-of-focus picture of a crooked phone booth.

"I couldn't very well let him see I was taking pictures."

"Hmm."

"Do you see him?"

"How am I supposed to recognize anyone in these pictures?"

"It's a lot better than what you got: 'Average guy, average hair, average everything'."

"I lost him, didn't I?"

"So did I. It wasn't hard to do."

"Actually," Lane said, "I don't think you did. He only followed me after you came back to the library."

It took me a moment to recover my voice. "But I caught that cab."

"Twenty pounds says the first cabbie we ask has been given the order to follow another car at some point in his career."

"But—"

"How else do you think he was back at the library to follow me?"

I sunk into the plush chair next to Lane. It was stiffer than it looked. At least my bruised knees didn't feel as sore as I had feared they might.

"I'm beginning to wonder if I'll ever figure this out," I said, looking out the lobby window. "It doesn't make any sense."

"One piece at a time," Lane said, easing his lean body out of his chair. He offered me his hand. "I spotted a decent-looking pub down the street. I'll buy you dinner and fill you in on the rest of what I found at the library."

Slinking into back corner tables was becoming all too common. I didn't think twice about it when Lane led us to the farthest table in the back room of the Prince Alfred pub. Probably because the pungent smell of hearty bar food made my knees weak.

"I found her," Lane said, resting his elbows in satisfaction at the edge of the table.

"The woman in the painting?"

He nodded with that rare giddy look I was coming to recognize.

"It's Nur Jahan," he said.

The name was familiar.

Lane's eyes were locked on mine. I could see the excitement in them. Searching through all the dead ends, he'd found what he was after. I understood, and he knew that I did.

A waitress stepped out from behind the bar and set two glasses down on our table with a clunk. The spell was broken.

Who was I kidding? It had probably never been there in the first place.

"Nur Jahan?" I said, studying the bubbles in my gin and tonic.

"She was Jahangir's favorite wife."

"Oh, his *favorite* wife." I met his gaze. "Are you going to tell me another great Indian love story to supplement my underdeveloped appreciation for the love story of the Taj Mahal?"

"You have a lot of contemporary biases for a historian."

"I don't have to agree with what they did to understand it."

"He's in the history books as one of the most powerful rulers of all time," Lane said. "And it's widely accepted that he was addicted to drugs. To the point of incapacity. Nur Jahan did a lot of the ruling while Jahangir was in power. She was a great deal ahead of her time as a feminist. I'm surprised you don't know more about her."

"She wasn't the one who signed the agreements with the East India Company. An unnamed woman in the corner of a painting couldn't have come that far. Even if she did get to wear some jewels. But they both lived before things got really interesting. Ask me anything from the militarization of the Company at the Battle of Plassey in 1757 through the major turning point for British India at the Sepoy Uprising of 1857. I can answer the question blindfolded. I can also do pretty well with any information having to do with the British Raj leading up to Indian independence another century later, in 1947. Interesting about those dates, isn't it?"

Two heavy plates, heaping with hot food, clanked down onto our table. The scent of beer batter and vinegar was heavenly.

"Everything the Mughals possessed had to go somewhere after they lost power," Lane said. "Jahangir and Nur Jahan lived during the opulent height of the Mughal Empire. There are lots of more prominent paintings of Nur Jahan."

"Then why wasn't she identified in the painting you found today?"

"I'm getting to that," Lane said. He paused to start on his meal. He was enjoying the drama of his delivery, I could tell. He savored the mushy peas on his plate more than was necessary. I wasn't going to give him the satisfaction of seeing my impatience. I turned back to my own fish and chips.

"This particular painting wasn't well documented in general," Lane said. "Remember, it's not uncommon. Jahangir subsidized hundreds of artists during his reign. Some notes put together by a non-contemporary scholar suggested that the woman was Nur Mahal. I didn't put it together right away. Not until I found the date attributed to the painting. 1611."

"I don't get it. What's special about that year?"

"Nur Mahal didn't become Nur Jahan until 1616."

"Of course," I murmured. "He changed her name."

"You know how their names worked."

"None of these names were their birth names. Jahangir means Great Conqueror of the World. His real name was something like Selim, right? What about Nur Mahal?"

"I had to look it up to find the details," Lane said. "When they got married, Jahangir named her Nur Mahal, meaning Light of the Palace. As their love—and her power—grew, he renamed her Nur Jahan: Light of the World."

"Those dates also explain why she wasn't featured more prominently in that painting you found."

"What's especially interesting," Lane said, "is that once she was married, and featured more prominently in paintings where she's identified, I couldn't find a single instance where she was wearing your rubies."

"We already know they disappeared."

"I wonder," Lane said, "how your ex found it."

"Same as you, I suppose," I said. "An archaeologist could get access to the reading rooms."

Lane pushed his plate away and lowered his voice. "He didn't."

"How could you possibly know that?"

"The materials I requested," Lane said. "None of them had been checked out in over a year. Whatever your ex was up to, it wasn't scholarly Mughal research in the hallowed halls of the British Library."

# CHAPTER 17

"You realize we can't go back to the library," Lane said.

I couldn't meet his gaze. "I know. Whoever is following us now knows to look for us there. I'm sorry you'll be in danger if you try to finish your article."

"Jaya—"

"You'll probably be able to go back soon. This was always only my first stop. I'm getting out of here tomorrow. It's me they want, right?"

"You can't—"

"Can't what?"

"You're going to the Scottish dig *by yourself?*"

"I know it's hard to believe," I said, "but archaeologists attend digs unchaperoned all the time. They're no braver than historians. If they can do it, I can too."

"You can drop the sarcasm," Lane said. "Murders don't happen at the average dig."

"Then what do you propose?"

"I can't go back to the library any more than you can," Lane said. "I could go with you to Scotland."

"You want to come with me?"

"Based on what's going on, it makes the most sense. We should stick together."

"In that case," I said, "I have a plan. You're my rich new boy-friend, who dabbles in archaeology. I'm bringing you to the dig to rub Rupert's nose in it."

"You are something," he said, his lip curling in amusement. "You already thought this through. You want me to be your cover for showing up at the dig."

"You're the one who said you wanted to tag along."

"It's a good idea," Lane said, holding up his hands in a placating gesture. "What was your story going to be on your own? Surely you weren't going to walk in and say Rupert sent you a note saying one of them was going to murder him."

"You're the one who said you thought he sent me the bracelet to get back together with me. Who's to say I wouldn't follow him across the world to get back together?"

"Would his friend at the dig believe you'd do that?"

"Our plan is more believable."

We walked back to the hotel in silence, glancing around nervously whenever the bushes rustled. As soon as we entered the hotel, I was suddenly so tired that I could have fallen asleep in one of the chairs in the lobby.

"My key doesn't fit," I grumbled through a yawn as I tried to open the door to my room.

"That's because this is my room," Lane said, pulling my hand back from the door handle.

His hand was gentle, but I felt his strength. He drew the key from my fingers. He led me over to my door and unlocked it for me. He pushed the door open and quickly scanned the room.

We stood close to each other. I could feel Lane's breath on the top of my head. He hesitated in the doorway.

"Get some sleep, Jones," he said.

I felt cool metal as he pressed the key back into my palm.

"We want to catch the early train," I said, yawning again.

"Train? Shouldn't we catch a flight? I know I'm not the biggest fan of flying, but I can handle it."

"They'll be out at the dig all day. We've got time."

"Come get me in the morning when you're ready to leave."

I didn't remember falling into bed, but I awoke to bright sunlight streaming across the bed, hitting my face.

I'd overslept.

I meant for us to catch the earliest departing train to Scotland from King's Cross Station. That way we'd have time to examine our new surroundings. Even with our late departure, with the seven-hour train ride we'd still arrive in the late afternoon.

English train stations, full of hearty British food and interesting people from around the world, are some of my favorite places on earth.

The trains themselves fill me with much the same feeling, with the added benefit of scenic landscapes passing before my eyes. A romantic might think of *Murder on the Orient Express* or some other classic book involving intrigue on a foreign train. I, however, am not a romantic. It's the meditative respite I appreciate.

Lane and I boarded the Scotland-bound train and found seats in a coach car. We dumped our luggage in the compartment at the end of the car and settled into our seats. We barely made it before the train pulled out of the station.

I hadn't had time to buy food at the station. Since the train had both a dining car and a roving snack cart, I wasn't worried about keeping properly nourished.

The engine hummed and we started moving. As we chugged along smoothly, I looked out the window. Lane was reading a book, but when I turned from the window he looked up at me.

"You like it here, don't you?" he said.

It should have made me nervous that he was always able to read my mind. For some reason, it didn't.

"It's the perfect balance," I said. "When I'm overseas in an English-speaking country, it's similar yet different enough at the same time. It's liberating."

"I know," he said. I had the feeling he wasn't making small talk. That he did know what I meant.

"I'm not supposed to fit in here," I said. "I'm a foreigner in India, where I was born, and to some extent I'm even a foreigner at home. But here, it feels much more natural being asked where I'm from since I'm not in one of the two countries I'm actually from. There aren't the same expectations about who I'm supposed to be."

"It gets tiring being an outsider in places where you're not supposed to feel that way."

I looked at him—really looked at him. Not his physical features, but at what the image he presented seemed to be hiding.

"Where are you from?" I asked.

A flash of emotion shone in his eyes for a moment. Indecision?

"Minnesota."

"You don't look like you're from Minnesota."

"I'm from Minnesota like you're from India."

He returned to reading his book. He stayed on the same page for an awfully long time, shifting in his seat.

"What is it?" I asked.

"Nothing."

"Something."

"What's your favorite color?" he asked.

"That's not what you wanted to say."

"We have to get to know each other," Lane said. "I'm supposed to be your significant other. We need to know the basics about each other."

"Red," I said.

"Figures."

"What's that supposed to mean?"

"Nothing. I'm a good guesser."

"What's yours?"

"The same."

"Favorite author?" I asked.

"Dostoyevsky."

"Really?"

"And yours?"

"Borges."

Lane's left eyebrow arched. I was again struck by the gracefulness of the simplest of his body's movements.

"Which grocery store do you go to?" he asked.

"That's a good one," I said. "This was a good idea. I don't go to the grocery store."

"How is that possible?"

"I listen to my body," I said. "I never know in advance what I'm going to want to eat, so I wait until I'm hungry and then follow my gut. I've always lived in urban places, so it's easy. My gut has a lot of options."

"I cook," Lane said. "In our pretend life together, I cook dinner for you all the time. And you like it, because we're not fulfilling our proper gender roles. What? That's funny, huh?"

He laughed along with me. His teeth were pristine. Interesting.

"How long have you smoked?" I asked.

He shrugged. "It's one of those things you pick up in your youth."

"How old are you, anyway?"

He shrugged again. "Let's say I'm thirty-five."

"How old are you really?"

"Thirty-five."

"Oh, you're a riot."

"My turn," Lane said. "How do we say we met?"

"Good question." I thought about it for a moment. "I was doing research for an article. I needed the help of an art historian. The less we have to make up, the better."

"Nice," he said. "Sticking to real-life facts as much as possible. So I'm myself."

"With a few extra million dollars lying about," I added. "You certainly look the part in that tailored suit."

"Let me get this straight in my mind," Lane said. "I'm financing this romantic summer vacation, a whirlwind European tour, during which you drag me to Scotland. Your ex told you he was on this small, underfunded dig. He tells you he wants to see you, not knowing I'm in your life. You know that in addition to my interest in art history, which is something I do to pass the time, being independently wealthy and all, that I have a fondness for archaeology. So, you think you can do two things at once. One, you'll give me a nice present by finding a dig that would be willing to let me help. Two, you get to rub your ex's nose in my presence. We head up here before learning about his accident, which we accept as accidental."

"You're good," I said. "Did you think that up on the spot?"

"Last night. But there are still some holes."

Rain began to patter on the windows of the train. I hadn't noticed that the blue sky had turned to gray.

"I know," I said, looking out at the rain. We'd come far enough that urban London had given way to greenery. "Our story doesn't matter if someone there already knows we know more than that. We're in the impossible situation where we need to find out what they know. But if someone there does know something useful, then it means they probably know our story is a lie."

"They might not know. Whoever is following us hasn't remained at the dig. All we can do is try. Tell me about the dig."

I went over the few facts I knew. Professor Malcolm Alpin's underfunded Pictish dig in the middle of nowhere, the staff that included Rupert's best friend Knox, and the Fog & Thistle Inn that Rupert had listed as his address.

"Damn," I concluded.

"Damn?"

"The guy following us," I said. "He doesn't fit."

"There's nothing else we can figure out before we get there," Lane said. "How long have you played the tablas? That's what I saw in your apartment, wasn't it?"

I opened my eyes. The rain was letting up.

"Technically," I said, "it's the tabla, singular, for the pair of drums."

"So how long?"

"As long as I can remember. It's the only other language I truly speak."

He nodded, his eyes locked on mine.

"I studied classical tabla," I said, "but when I listen to it, modern fusion is my favorite. The Asian Underground. Bhangra. I feel like...."

"Like you understand them."

"No," I said. "That's not quite it. It's like they understand me. It's not the same thing. The music isn't only straddling cultures or generations. At its center, something new had to grow out of the mix."

Lane held my gaze for a second past when I stopped speaking. Some emotion flickered in his eyes, and he turned away.

I watched him for another moment before the mystery of him, on top of the mystery we were solving, became too oppressive for me to take.

"I'm hungry," I said. "I'm going to the dining car."

"I'm sure the food cart will get here soon."

"Maybe, but who wants to chance it?"


The dining car was several cars down from where we were seated. The endless length of British trains never ceases to amaze me. I walked down the gently rocking corridors through at least five cars. I was passing through the sleeper car when it happened.

Two strong arms reached out of an open door and pulled me inside. The door shut behind me.

The arms twisted my body around until I was facing my attacker. As his arm reached across me to lock the door of the small compartment, I stood staring up into the eyes of Rupert Chadwick.

# CHAPTER 18

The breath was momentarily knocked out of me. The arms that dragged me into the compartment were unquestionably not those of a ghost.

A second wave of surprise hit me as I noticed something else. Rupert's shoes. The faded red sneakers were the shoes of the partially hidden man in my blurry photographs.

In the precious fraction of a second before I was able to gather my thoughts and my breath, Rupert grabbed his chance. He leaned down and kissed me on the mouth.

He didn't have to lean far. Rupert was only five foot five. I had always suspected my height was one of the things that attracted him to me. As for what attracted me to him? Well, even at the worst of times, no one could claim Rupert was boring.

He pulled me toward him, kissing me more deeply. He didn't hold me for long, but his grip was intense. Especially for that of a man who was supposed to be dead.

His lips finally released mine. "All right?" he said, grinning.

That refined accent of his was full of vigor. The sound filled the space of the small compartment. The steady background noise of the train faded away.

"How dare you let me think you were dead!"

I felt foolish that I hadn't thought of something more clever to say. But when presented with a situation such as this, really, what else is there that can be said?

"Why, darling," he said, beaming, "I didn't know you still cared."

A big part of me wanted to bring down my heel on his foot. Hard. But at the same time, seeing him alive, relief and compassion won out. Rupert's face was uncharacteristically gaunt. Deep, dark circles stood out under his blue-gray eyes. A sizable bruise covered his jaw. A bandage poked out of his left shirt sleeve near his wrist. Even though he wasn't dead, whatever was going on had ended up with him getting himself hurt. But in spite of his ailments, his eyes were as lively as ever. They sparkled as he continued to grin at me.

That was too much.

I raised my arm to slap his face. He must have anticipated the move, for he was able to block it and grab my arm instead.

If that's what he wanted, that's what he would get. I raised my other arm and slapped his bruised cheek. Not hard. But it was the principle of the thing. He swore something indecipherable, releasing me and taking a step back.

It's amazing how easy it is to forgive someone's faults when you think they're dead. My memories had absolved Rupert of his cocky arrogance. And he was arrogant. First, assuming that I would help him with his scheme. Then, letting me believe he was dead.

"Always so predictable," he said, rubbing his jaw while he grinned at me. "I knew you'd head for the dining car sooner rather than later. All I had to do was wait."

"You're a terrible spy," I said. It was difficult to speak with a level voice. "I can't believe you've been following me. You didn't even let me know that you weren't...that you...all the effort, and you couldn't even...I mean...." I gave up trying to be calm. "You even broke into my apartment!"

"What? I never broke into your flat, Jaya." He wasn't smiling any longer.

"You—"

"Hold on, love," he said. He sank down into one of the two small seats in the compartment. For a moment he looked seasick.

With his casual attitude and his kiss, I assumed his injuries weren't serious. But Rupert didn't suffer from motion sickness. He wasn't doing well.

"I might not have gone about this in the best possible way," he said. "But when I first saw you with that tosser at the library, going after the treasure for the two of you....I didn't know what to do."

He looked up at me imploringly. His voice sounded heartfelt. But with Rupert, you could never really tell.

"We were trying to figure out who killed you, you jerk," I said. "I don't care about a stupid treasure. We don't even know what we're looking for. Why did you bother to mail me the bracelet if you were going to steal it back?"

"Wait," Rupert said slowly. "Why did you think someone killed me?"

"Anna sent me a link to the article in the paper about your death. Remember her? The date of your supposed death was reported as the same date as the postmark on the package you sent."

Rupert swore under his breath.

"And you put together—"

"Why have you been sneaking around?" I asked. "Why didn't you—"

"You were with that strange fellow," Rupert said, a sour expression transforming his face. "I didn't know what was going on. I'd been searching the library for days, and then all of a sudden you show up making kissy face with some other bloke. I bloody well didn't expect that you'd show up across the pond, did I?"

"*You* did."

"What are you talking about, love? This business about your flat? You're talking about your flat in America? That wasn't me. How could I have done that?"

He stared at me, confusion evident in his eyes. I again noticed how drawn his face was.

"You don't believe me?" he said. "No bleeding way I could get out of the country on my passport. I'm supposed to be dead."

"But then how—"

"Some lucky nutter's got the ruby, then?"

"No," I said, feeling suddenly claustrophobic in my surroundings. "It's safe."

Relief showed on Rupert's face. I, however, was less than reassured. I should have been happy it was Rupert who had been following me in London. But I wasn't. That meant someone else had broken into my apartment in San Francisco. Someone who Rupert knew nothing about.

If he could be believed.

"Rupert," I said, "tell me what's going on. Why did you write that you needed my help?"

"Right, then...." he trailed off.

"You conceited bastard! You let me think you were dead."

I tried to pace around the small quarters. I had to do something to quash the urge to hit Rupert again.

"Hold on, then," Rupert said. "I tried to get in touch with you. You didn't get any of my messages? Is that why you're angry?"

"Messages? Really, Rupert."

"I emailed you first."

"Where?"

"At your *email* account," he said tersely.

"The university one you knew from when I was finishing my degree? I don't use that anymore."

"Bloody hell, how am I supposed to know that? I rang up and left you a message, too. Your old mobile phone number I knew didn't work, so I called that other number you had. I left a message on the machine. You can't say I didn't try."

That explained the phone call from my brother. I needed to remember to yell at Mahilan later for all the trouble his Hindi-only policy was causing.

Rupert took my silence for annoyance directed at him.

"It's not easy to track people down when running for your life," he said, tugging at the sleeve that covered his bandage. "You never gave me your new number. I only had your address since you sent me that graduation card—"

"You kept it?"

Rupert's cheeks flushed.

"It doesn't matter now," he said. "The point is, I'm trying to protect you."

I tried to scoff. I'm pretty sure it came out more like a snort.

"Someone did try to kill me," he said, the blue in his eyes shining brightly with urgency. He held up his bandaged arm for me to see.

"I thought I needed your help," he said. "But then it didn't seem worth it once things got more dangerous. I never in a million bleeding years thought you'd show up after you'd gotten my messages asking you to do nothing except hang onto the artifact for me."

"What the hell is going on, Rupert?"

"Listen, love," he said, pulling me down onto the seat next to him. He kept my hand in his. I didn't try to remove it.

"I sent you that ruby before I knew how dangerous this whole business was. I thought I was being cautious when I sent the artifact to you. But now...now it's best you go home and stay out of it."

"I'm already involved."

"I'll still give you a cut," Rupert said, caressing my hand. "Not that wanker, but you—"

"That's not what I mean." I pulled my hand away. "Someone besides you knows about it. Weren't you listening to me? He broke into my apartment. He also hurt the person who interrupted him."

"That's not possible," Rupert said, rubbing his jaw slowly. "Your burglary can't be related. Only a few people know about it. They're all still at the...ah...."

"I already know about the dig."

"You do?"

"I also know you quit your job lecturing, and that you and Knox are in over your heads."

Our faces were inches apart in the small space. Rupert's face looked even more haggard up close. I spotted a few strands of gray in his hair.

"I can help," I said. "You did ask for my help, remember?" He smiled. His eyes moved over my face. "There is one way you can help," he said. He moved in to kiss me again. I stopped him by pressing my fingertips to his lips.

"Tell me," I said.

He laughed gently, shaking his head from side to side.

"Oh, Jaya," he said. "I knew I had to see you again."

"Dammit, Rupert. I came all this way to find out what got you killed. You better start telling me what's going on."

"I really don't know." He wasn't laughing any longer.

"Fine," I said. "Then I'll formulate my own hypothesis. You and Knox stole a valuable piece of ancient jewelry. You stupidly bragged about it, so then you needed to go into hiding, hoping things would blow over. That's why you quit your position. You found a remote dig where you could lay low for the summer. Only you didn't realize Knox's photograph would be posted on the dig's website. Whoever you stole the piece from was able to find you easily after seeing the picture. They tried to kill you, so you played dead so they wouldn't try it again—I haven't worked out how you managed that yet. But whatever the answer is, the best thing for me to do is to drop off the bracelet with Interpol, and take you to a doctor."

"Christ, don't do that," Rupert said, his face pale. "That's not what happened. It's not stolen, I swear."

"Why should I believe you if you don't tell me where it's *not stolen* from?"

"Have I ever let you down before? Wait, don't answer that. You've at least got to believe me that we're both safer if they think I'm dead."

"Who are *they*?"

"I'm not sure. Honestly!"

The exclamation took the wind out of him. He put his head in his hands and rubbed his temples. He didn't look well.

"Knox and I found out something...how should I put this? Something interesting," he said, looking back up at me with his elbows resting on his knees. "Before we had a chance to find it—"

"Stop," I said. "You had the bracelet already. You're after more. I get that. But you don't know where the treasure is?"

"Of course we don't know where it is." Rupert blinked at me. "Why else would we bother asking for help?"

# CHAPTER 19

My head spun as the train rocked back and forth.

"Go on with the story," I snapped.

"Right. Before we learned where the treasure was, someone cut the brakes of my car—that brilliant old Jeep, remember?—and I barely got out before it went over the edge of the road onto the rocks below." He rolled up the sleeve of his shirt so I could see the full extent of the injury.

"Have you got any idea how steep it is up around Aberdeen?" he asked. "The students go rock climbing on those cliffs."

I nodded distractedly as I looked at the ragged bandage. Unless he was faking it, his injuries were serious.

"It was right at the edge of the ocean," he said. "I figured I could make like I had been swept out to sea with the tide. You were right, I thought it would be best if everyone thought I was dead. I was already covered in blood from getting scraped up when I jumped out of the car. I climbed down the rocks and let myself bleed some more on the rocks next to the Jeep. For good measure and all that."

"You're pretending to be dead so you can find your attempted killer?"

"Well, of course that would be nice, too. Don't look at me like that! I thought I could have the whole treasure bit sorted out in a few days, once I had total freedom without whoever is out to get me still after me. Then I thought I could show up and pretend I'd had amnesia from the accident. My head did get a right bump." He let go of my hand and rubbed his jaw again.

"It's been more than a few days," I said. Sometimes I wondered if Rupert was for real.

"I wasn't as fit as I would have liked, was I? I only got myself sorted a couple of days ago. I came down to London to look something up. Been searching the bloody library for days. Luckily nobody pays attention to you if you keep your head down in a library. That's when I saw you and that bloke."

"But you hadn't requested any materials on the Mughals."

Rupert's eyes narrowed. My breath caught.

"You were looking at something else," I said. "Tell me."

I took his hand back in mine, which he readily surrendered, then squeezed his forearm. He yelped and pulled away. A new spot of blood showed on the bandage. He wasn't faking his injuries.

"You're brutal," he said, rubbing his arm.

"I had to be sure you weren't faking it."

Rupert wisely kept his mouth shut.

I opened my bag and removed a packet of bandages. Yes, when searching for a murderer in a foreign country I find it wise to carry first aid.

"I've already got some, if you haven't noticed," he said.

"You don't appear to be using them very well." I winced when I saw the gash on his arm. "Did you wrap this yourself?"

I pulled off the last of the sloppily wrapped bandage with only a minor protest from Rupert.

"You should have seen the car." He tried to laugh.

"Did anyone try to kill Knox?" I asked.

Rupert didn't answer immediately. He watched me open a packet of strong-smelling antiseptic, avoiding looking at me.

"If they didn't," I continued, "that would suggest—"

"I know," he said. "That would suggest he was in on it." He squirmed as I wiped the antiseptic across his arm.

"Have you told him you're alive?"

"I can't believe my best mate would try to kill me."

"But you haven't told him."

"No." He rested his hand on my knee. "You're the only one I can trust, love."

"How sweet," I said through my teeth, "since you've so conveniently forgotten that you asked for my help."

"Before I knew what was going on!"

"It still doesn't sound like you know what's going on." I finished with his new-and-improved bandage and sat back.

"Not exactly."

"Where are you staying?"

"That would be telling."

I pushed his hand off my leg and stood up.

"Why did you follow me and pull me in here?" I asked.

"I wanted to know what you were doing. I don't want you to get hurt."

"I wish people would stop thinking I can't take care of myself."

"Other people are saying that?" He wiggled his arm around, getting a feel for the new bandage. "Who's the bloke?"

"An art history graduate student at Berkeley. He was helping me identify the artifact, since you failed to do so."

"Are you an item?"

"My love life is none of your business. Not anymore."

"Hmm."

"Why did you follow him rather than me yesterday afternoon?" I tried pacing again, but failed as my arms kept bumping into furniture in the small compartment. "You could have talked to me."

"I was going to," he said. "After I got a sense of what you were doing, I was working my way up to it. But then you hailed a cab and I lost you."

"You didn't follow me in another taxi?"

"As if a cab would do such a daft thing for a fare. No. I went back to the library, where I had first seen you. I didn't find you, but I found him. What's his name?"

"Lane."

"Do you really have to look at me like that? I thought you were grateful I was alive."

"How did you find us today?"

"I was hoping Lane would lead me back to you last night, but I lost him. Based on what you were doing, I thought you'd go next to the address on the package I sent you. I remembered how much you love trains, so I knew you'd take the train. I waited at the station since six this morning. You used to be a morning person."

He yawned and closed his eyes. He wasn't just tired. He needed a doctor. Ashen skin stretched over his gaunt face. I wondered if he'd gotten an infection from his injuries. Though I'd done my best with my small first-aid kit, the cut on his arm didn't look good.

"Aren't there anonymous free clinics in this country?" I asked. "Isn't that what the NHS does?"

He opened his eyes and smiled. I saw a hint of the unidentifiable charm I had once known.

"I'll be all right," he said. "I'd be better if I could convince you to go home. No? I didn't think so. At least give me whatever mobile number you're using now, so we can keep in touch."

"We're not splitting up."

In the close quarters all he had to do to reach me was lift up his good arm. He pulled me down onto his lap.

"You know that's not what I meant," I said, extricating myself from his grip.

"My idea was more fun, though."

"You hardly look up to it."

"That would be my cue to change the subject if I know what's good for me. Right. I'm not going to talk you out of going to the dig. I know you well enough for that. I can't go with you, you understand. You'll be my eyes and ears, as they say. You can keep an eye on them. You can figure out who tried to do me in."

"While you do *what* exactly?"

"Find the treasure, of course."

# CHAPTER 20

In spite of repeated threats that I would murder him myself, I couldn't get any more details about the treasure from Rupert. He insisted everything was now under control. Except for the small detail of an unknown murderous villain on the loose.

He didn't want to "burden" me with whatever plot he and Knox had hatched, including the small detail of why he thought I could help him in the first place. To put my mind at ease, he assured me it wasn't illegal and would not offend my integrity. In spite of this fact, he turned a shade paler each time I mentioned the idea of turning to the police for help.

He insisted it had to have been someone at the dig or at the Fog & Thistle Inn who had attempted to kill him. Nobody else could possibly have known what they were up to. The dig and their housing were close quarters, so it was entirely possible that someone learned he and Knox had the ruby bracelet.

"It might be as easy as seeing who left the dig," I said.

"What, your burglary again? You live in a city, love. Crime happens. Luckily not while your pretty little head was at home in this case."

"It wasn't a coincidence."

"Nothing else makes sense," he insisted.

But in spite of his protestations, I saw that it unnerved him.

"Look," he said, rubbing his sore jaw, "just promise me you won't trust anyone."

As he filled me in on more details about the dig, I saw how serious he was about making sure I knew what I was getting into. Sometimes Rupert did surprise me.

Malcolm Alpin, the professor heading up the dig, took his work seriously. Knox Bailey and Derwin McVicar were Malcolm's crew for the summer. Since Knox withdrew from his archaeology PhD program before being formally kicked out for plagiarism, he was able to stay involved in the field to some extent. I didn't know Derwin, an archaeology graduate student studying under Malcolm Alpin at St. Andrews.

Rupert stressed that it was best not to offend Malcolm, as he pointed out I had been known to do to a scholar or twenty. If Malcolm didn't like me, he would have no problem banning me from his site, even though he desperately needed additional help.

The dig's crew members were housed at the Fog & Thistle Inn. The landlord of the inn ran the place with his wife. Two local characters spent a lot of time in the small pub below the rooms, but otherwise it was a low-key establishment.

Rupert couldn't think of any reason that any of them would have made an attempt on his life. At the same time, he continued to insist that it had to be one of them. I was relieved to learn that nobody knew he had sent me the ruby artifact.

His cell phone had been washed away with several other items in his Jeep. He hadn't wasted his limited post-mortem funds on a new phone. He was dead, he said, so who was going to call him? I gave him my new number so he could reach me.

I was trying to decide on a strategy for coercing Rupert into telling me more about the treasure he and Knox were after, when he cocked his head to one side. A smirk spread across his face.

"It's been lovely," he said, standing up.

"You're not sending me away until I'm satisfied," I said.

"But I thought you said you didn't want to—"

Why did I only know infuriating men?

"You're going to tell me—"

"This is my stop," Rupert said. He stepped around me and grabbed the door handle.

The screech of breaks sounded as the train slowed.

"You can't mean to get off here," I said. "We're in the middle of nowhere."

"Precisely."

The train came to a halt.

Rupert stepped forward unexpectedly and gave me a quick yet intense kiss on the mouth. He let go of me just as quickly. In my brief confusion, he slipped past me. The door slammed into me, and Rupert ran out of the compartment.

I followed quickly, but stopped on the train's steps. Rupert was already halfway down the platform. He must have been using all of his reserves of energy.

Both Lane and my bag were on the opposite side of the train. I'd never catch Rupert before the train departed. As the train engine revved up, I watched his red sneakers disappear around the corner of the small town train station. The train started up again. Dumbstruck, I stood watching the platform fade into the distance.


I returned to my seat with a cup of overpriced tea in my hands. I'd already polished off a muffin on my walk through the train cars. I didn't need a lack of calories to make me any shakier than I already was from my encounter with Rupert.

"Long line in the food car?" Lane asked.

I took a deep breath.

"I saw Rupert."

Lane looked me up and down. His eyes were wide with concern, showing the reflection from the train window of the deep azure sky outside.

"Jones," he said. The soft waves of his hair swayed back and forth as he shook his head gently. "I'm sorry. I know it must be difficult for you to accept that he's—"

"He's not dead."

"I know his memory lives on."

"You're not listening to me! He faked his death."

"He's here?" Lane stood up. "On the train?"

I pushed him back into the seat.

"He's gone."

After a few deep breaths, I told Lane what I had learned from Rupert. He processed the information quickly. As I spoke, I realized how little I actually knew. I'm apparently not at my best after learning that a dead ex-lover is alive but not well.

"We've got to find that treasure," Lane said once I was finished telling him all I knew.

"I get the point that you're ambitious. But don't you think it's more important that there's someone out there willing to murder people over this?"

Lane held up his hand to quiet me. I looked around to see what I was missing. Two people were sleeping. A Scotsman was giving travel advice to an American couple a few rows in front of us. An English couple was arguing. None of them were paying any attention to us. Except one. An elderly woman with bright silver hair sat by herself across the aisle from us. A ball of fluffy green yarn lay in her lap. Her hands worked in swift, practiced strokes as she pulled the yarn with her knitting needles. She must have had a lifetime of practice. She didn't need to look at her hands as she worked. I looked at her, and she smiled unabashedly back.

I turned back to Lane. "Why did you shush me? There's nothing to worry about."

"You shouldn't underestimate people," he said. I would have thought he was joking except that he said it in a voice so close to a whisper that I had to wonder.

"Miss Marple?" I said, following his lead with a quiet voice.

"I doubt it. But you need to be more careful. We don't know what's going on. That's why our main priority needs to be finding the treasure."

"How can you—" I reminded myself to lower my voice. "That is not the most important thing."

"But it *is* what we have the most control over. We're not the police. We're historians. We know how to find missing pieces of history. Not attempted murderers."

I pressed my head against the back of the seat, and willed my shoulders to relax.

"We need more information from your ex," Lane said. "I'm sure the shock from seeing him alive was why you weren't able to learn much from him."

"You have no idea."

"We need to try again," Lane said. "How do we reach him?"

"We can't," I said. "His phone was swept out to sea. He only has my number to reach us."

"How convenient."

"He doesn't know any more about who tried to kill him. I'm sure of that. He didn't even tell his best friend he's alive."

"But the treasure—"

"What *is it* with you?"

"He's wasn't killed, Jaya. I don't want to see you or anyone else get too far and end up dead. If we focus on the treasure, we'll be doing what we know best. If we can get the information we need—from your ex, or his partners at the dig—then we can get out of there quickly. Without giving anyone a reason to do to us what they did to your ex."

"This isn't about doing what's easy." I grabbed my bag and stood up.

"Where are you going?"

"Our stop is Aberdeen," I said. "I'll meet you on the platform."

"You tell him, dearie," the silver-haired woman said as I stomped briskly away.

# CHAPTER 21

The sky outside became fierce as the train thundered into Scotland. I sat alone in an empty back row of a train compartment as far away as I could get from Lane Peters.

Dark clouds tumbled by. Hail splattered across the window. The train cut inland briefly, revealing a bright blue sky for a few precious moments. Before long, the sky was again swallowed up by clouds.

What was it about the idea of a long-lost treasure that could turn the brain of a normally rational man into single-minded idiocy? On Rupert's part, I knew he wasn't the most rational of men to begin with. But I wasn't ready to forgive him for his childish stunt of following me around London. Rupert's actions had shaken me more than I cared to admit. Now that I knew it had been Rupert following me, I had fury to deal with on top of my fears.

I had thought Lane was different. I was wrong.

I turned up the volume on my headphones to a level that I'd probably regret if I lived to be eighty. I'd worry about that later. I skipped through tracks, first trying some of my classical tabla favorites, then the more upbeat Asian Underground beats, danceable bhangra, and last, some of my dad's '60s folk music that had stuck with me. None succeeded in distracting me.

I tried watching the scenery out the window. The train swept along the eastern seaboard. To the west, the landscape was dotted with sheep grazing on grassy pastures lush from the frequent rains.

We passed lone houses, stone churches with granite gravestones, and crumbling ruins of old abbeys. To the east, jagged cliffs stretched along the edge of the sea, with the occasional fishing village and harbor.

We headed north into the Aberdeenshire and Grampian Highlands, where the Scottish Highlands begin. The plan was to disembark in the city of Aberdeen and rent a car to drive to the Fog & Thistle Inn. Providing I managed to stay sane that long. It didn't seem likely at the moment.

I flipped through the guidebook I'd picked up in London. Unable to focus, I was about to toss it back into my bag. The title on the page caught my eye, snapping me out of my funk. An old estate in the Grampian region was now open to the public. The title read: Relive the Romance and Splendor of the British Raj.

I turned to the map showing the estate's location, forgetting all about Rupert and Lane. The newly opened Gregor Estate was only a few miles away from Rupert's Pictish dig. Could that be why he and Knox were at the nearby dig?

The British Raj wasn't technically the same thing as the East India Company, but it was damn close. After the 1857 uprising that killed scores of both British and Indian soldiers and civilians, the Company was absorbed into a system of colonial rule directly from the British Crown, known as the British Raj. It was hardly a "romantic" time as the guidebook claimed, but it did involve vast amounts of wealth. The kind of wealth that could secretly buy lost ruby treasures like the one Rupert sent me.

When I stepped off the train in Aberdeen, Lane was already standing on the platform. He was leaning against a signpost at the far end, halfway through a cigarette, his bag at his feet. He looked as if he could have been standing there for hours.

My stomach clenched. His relaxed pose reminded me of another time when I'd seen him looking contentedly as if he hadn't moved in ages. The reading room. If he could look that at ease on cue....

But I knew it hadn't been Lane following me. I needed to relax. I took a deep breath of the clean coastal air. Though there wasn't a cloud in sight, the air smelled of fresh rain and the ground was slightly damp. I walked up to Lane.

"You were right," he said. "I realize how what I said must have sounded to you. All I meant was that working with our strengths is what makes the most sense. If we solve the mystery of the treasure, it should also lead to the attempted murderer. Truce?"

He held out his hand for me to shake.

"Apology accepted," I said. "Let's go get a car. We've got somewhere to go before the dig."

"What did I miss?"

"Patience is a virtue."


I led the way to the car rental service at the end of the station.

"How about this one?" he asked.

A sleek, forest green Jaguar sat in the lot, looking down its hood ornament at the sedate sedans next to it.

"You're joking."

"Hardly. We're supposed to be on a leisurely vacation in Europe with the means to do so. We need to play the part."

"Why not," I said. I do love a sporty car. "In for a penny...."

"I'll cover it," Lane said. "Provided you actually tell me where we're going."

"On your research assistant salary? It's okay, I can get it."

"I worked for a while before I went to grad school. Did you think I'd been a graduate student for over ten years? Let me get it."

"If you insist. But I'm driving." I tossed him the guidebook. "Check out the page I marked."

* * *

The highway down to Stonehaven was a straight shot from Aberdeen. The stick shift on the left took a little getting used to, but driving on the left side of the road itself is easy. Lane, however, began to look nervous when I barely slowed as I took a tight curve along the coast. He breathed out a sigh of relief as I eased the car up the gravel drive to the massive Gregor Estate.

"It's a stretch, you know," Lane said.

"Hurry up." I hopped out of the car. "The book says they're only open for the next hour."

Lane followed me up to the ticket booth.

"Is there a collection of jewelry here?" I asked the lean man sitting behind a tall counter.

"He dragged you along with him to see the military history, did he, love?" He winked at Lane. "Sorry to disappoint. The family hasn't got any jewelry on display. No need to look so sad, love. There are some beautiful tapestries. The ladies seem to like those."

I smiled weakly as Lane thanked him. We paid our admission and joined a handful of elderly tourists in the main hall.

"Don't beat yourself up," Lane said. "You didn't really think the ruby set would be here, did you? Escaping the notice of the world aside from your ex?"

"I know you're right," I grumbled. "But the existence of this place so close to the dig...it can't be a coincidence. There's a connection. We need to find it."

I walked up to the huge portrait that dominated the room.

"Connor Gregor," I read, "1899."

A plaque explained that Connor had held a high-level administrative position in the British Raj. Connor seemed to have done pretty well for himself. His portrait hung above a hearth taller than me. On the opposite wall, an equally large landscape painting of the ocean crashing against the local cliffs dominated its own corner. Smaller paintings and photographs of other members of the Gregor family lined one side wall, and those impressive tapestries the ticket-taker had mentioned hung against the other.

I walked along the row of portraits. The Gregors were a rather unremarkable, fair-haired lot. *Mary, 1865,* her wispy blonde hair framing a narrow face with wrinkled lips pressed firmly together. *Morag, 1895,* with a visibly serious scowl in spite of eyebrows so fair you could barely see them. *Iain, 1927,* a thin mustache adding dignity to an already solemn face. And on they went, a serious family, indeed. The earliest portrait, *Willoughby Gregor, 1858,* had the same sedate pose except for his mischievous eyes.

The woman next to Willoughby stood out even more. And not only because she had sat for the portrait while much younger than the others. Her black hair stood out against her pale skin. Her large brown eyes were almost haunting. *Elspeth Gregor, 1859.* She didn't resemble the rest of the family. She almost looked like....

"There's a room full of guns," Lane said, coming up beside me and interrupting my thoughts. "But not a single piece of jewelry."

I looked back at the imposing portrait of Connor Gregor. His blue eyes stared across the room at me.

"What are you up to, Rupert?" I whispered to myself.

# CHAPTER 22

We arrived at the Fog & Thistle Inn close to five o'clock. A modest wooden sign announced a pub and rooms for rent. The Tudor building looked like a home. The heavy door creaked as we opened it. It led into a small pub with a bar and half a dozen tables. An unlit fireplace filled most of one wall. A small stone gargoyle perched at its edge.

The room was eerily empty. A few seconds after we entered, a man appeared behind the bar. He stepped into the light from the shadows of a room behind the bar, revealing black eyes and ginger hair. The juxtaposition was jarring at first, but as he welcomed us with a full Scottish brogue, his cheery demeanor was unmistakable.

"Douglas Black," he said. "Can I offer ye a pint to fill yer belly, or a bed to rest yer head?"

Lane explained that we were there to see the archaeologists, and Mr. Black was happy to give us his one remaining room. As we filled out the standard form with passport numbers, Mr. Black—the name that seemed more fitting for him than Douglas—explained that he and his wife were retired other than running the small establishment. They lived in the section of the house on the ground floor behind the pub. The rooms of the inn were on the next floor up. His wife cooked a set meal each night for the guests.

"They should be headin' back within the hour," Mr. Black said. "Their stones is down the way."

"Is the site of the dig easy to find?" Lane asked.

"Tis at that. But ye might as well wait, or ye'll pass 'em as they come."

"It's not far?"

"The professor invited me to visit the site," he said proudly. "Only a quarter of an hour's walk to get there. They're all stayin' with me and the missus. Except for Mr. Chadwick. He met with an accident last week. Went over the cliffs. Reckless driving." He shook his head sadly.

"I'm so sorry," I said. "And nobody else has left?"

"Left?"

"I thought perhaps someone might have been so distraught—"

"Nothin' like that. These are professionals."

"What about visitors?" Lane asked.

Mr. Black thought it over for a moment before shaking his head. His face clouded over as he turned his attention back to me.

"No," Mr. Black said, looking me straight in the eye. "But you be careful, young miss. It's not only cars that lose control. The winds 'round here will pick you right up and toss you out into the sea before you know what's got you. Especially someone as wee as yourself."

His eyes remained locked on mine in the moments of silence that followed.

"Well then!" He slapped his palms together. "Fancy a pint before ye head up to yer room?"

"I think I'll go freshen up first," I said, grabbing Lane's elbow before he could answer.

Mr. Black handed me the keys and pointed us up the stairs.

At the top of the steep wooden stairs we emerged into a narrow hallway with a slanted ceiling.

"How can they all still be here?" I said, shuffling dejectedly down the hall. "I was so sure it was one of them in San Francisco."

"It's too bad he didn't see anyone visiting the crew. But look—" He pulled his cell phone out of his pocket. "Even though we're in the middle of nowhere, full reception. It wouldn't be hard to secretly give an accomplice a call."

We found our room at the end of the hall.

"Cozy," I said, stepping inside. It wasn't much bigger than the sleeping car into which Rupert had pulled me.

The slanted ceiling cut across the room. A single bed had been pushed under the lowest part of the slope. A child-size bureau stood next to the end of the bed, and a chair was tucked underneath the small window opposite the door.

"I'll take the floor," Lane said, dropping his bag on the hardwood floor.

"Chivalry?" I asked, setting down my pack on the small surface of the bureau. It was a good thing we'd both packed lightly. "We should flip a coin or something."

"I'm not being chivalrous," he said. "I'm being tall. Look at the size of the bed. There's no way I'd fit in that."

I looked closely at the bed. Because it filled up such a large portion of the room, it gave a false impression of being at least a standard twin bed. I sat on the edge of the bed, sinking down several inches. I looked up at Lane. His head nearly touched the ceiling.

"At least take the quilt," I said.

"Will do."

"I'm bad at sitting still," I said, bouncing back up.

"I noticed."

"I'm going to go downstairs to the pub. Are you coming?"

"But I thought you said—"

"I needed a minute to compose myself."

Lane's eyes were an unreadable dark gray behind his glasses as he stood blocking the beam of light from the small window.

"I didn't like what he said to you about those cliffs either," he said. His voice held the trace of some strong emotion, but it was so faint that I might have imagined it.

"I'm sure he didn't mean to spook us. He doesn't know we're worried about someone who would actually send us off that cliff."

"But maybe he's worried about something, too."

"I wonder what he—"

A low rumble sounded a fraction of a second before the sound exploded. The small window shook violently, trying to escape from the frame. The thick glass pane rattled so loudly I was surprised it didn't break.

Lane whirled around. The explosive thudding sound came again.

"Wind," Lane said, exhaling loudly. "That dangerous Scottish wind."

I sighed. "I'm going down. I want to be there when the crew gets back from the dig."

"I'll see what I can do to secure the window. I'll meet you down there."

I made my way down the steep stairs, regaining my composure as my feet slowly touched down on each step. Though the stairs looked old and creaky, they were in fact solid and noiseless.

The pub was still deserted, save for two figures huddled together at the bar. A face turned toward me and met my gaze. The face froze. A visible shudder ran across it. The old man recoiled as if he had seen a ghost. He let out a rattling gasp.

"The dark fayrie," he whispered in a hoarse voice. "She's returned."

# CHAPTER 23

The eyes that stared across the room at me were the deepest of gray, and half-hidden in the shadows of bushy white eyebrows. Thin, weathered skin stretched over the cheekbones below, bracketing a narrow, crooked nose streaked with broken blood vessels. The sallow skin stretched down into wrinkles surrounding thin lips, which remained slightly parted after his outburst.

"The dark fayrie," he repeated, elbowing his friend. "The *bean nighe.*"

A *fairy*? I wasn't going to hazard a guess at the second thing he said.

"Nae, nae," the other man said. "Is a wee lass, is all."

"What do ye ken," the first man snapped back at his friend, but only taking his eyes off of me for the briefest moment.

"Yer scarin' the poor lass, Fergus," the second man said, turning toward me on his barstool. He smiled through the scruffy light beard that framed his face. "Miss, Fergus dunnae mean nae harm."

This man's features were less ragged than those of his friend, though his visage had been weathered by the years as well. His eyes were almost as black as Douglas Black's, though I caught a hint of sapphire in them. His unkempt sandy brown hair ran wild on his head, but his eyebrows didn't overshadow his large, friendly eyes. The two men wore workmen's clothes.

Uneven light and shadows emanated from the recently lit fire. I walked up to the bar in the dancing light.

"She's no *bean nighe*," the friendly one said to Fergus. "Buy ye a drink for yer trouble, miss?"

"Aye, aye," Fergus jumped in, the movement of bushy white eyebrows reflecting his enthusiasm. "Anythin' ye like."

"Ach," the second man said, chuckling to himself. "For luck, eh, Fergus?"

Fergus shot him a dirty look. "Angus," he said. "Go find Dougie to pour the fayr—the lass a nip."

"Thanks," I said, joining them at the bar. Fergus and Angus? They must have been the locals Rupert had mentioned.

Fergus tried to shrink back even further, but the bar prevented the movement. Angus stood up and pulled out a barstool for me. I sat down, and he turned away.

"Dougie!" he shouted toward the kitchen. His voice was louder than I expected based on his soft tone moments earlier.

"Did you say you thought I was a fairy?" I asked.

"Yer good folk," he said, giving me a gracious smile.

Douglas Black appeared at the bar. "All right?" he said. "Ready for a second round already? Oh, Miss Jones! What'll ye be havin'?"

"Best Scotch ye have fer her, Dougie," Fergus said.

Douglas Black's face showed his confusion. I took it as a good sign he wasn't used to seeing Fergus and Angus sweet-talk the ladies.

"Fergus thinks I'm a fairy," I explained.

Mr. Black broke into a hearty whoop of laughter. Fergus' eyebrows shot up in terror. Mr. Black laughed even harder. He wiped his eyes, then reached below the bar. He pulled out a wooden box.

Fergus and Angus looked at each other and nodded in appreciation. Mr. Black removed a bottle of amber liquid with rose-colored flecks floating near the bottom. The bottle was almost as wide as it was tall. The label was handmade, with a name written in a script I couldn't make out. Mr. Black poured a generous shot.

"Fergus is afraid you'll cast a spell on 'im if yer offended, Miss Jones," he said, handing me the glass.

Fergus frowned at Mr. Black.

"Yer deep in fayrie land," Mr. Black continued. "Banshees 'n bogarts 'n kelpies. Real fayries. Not make-believe Tinker Bell. Fayries is wee, but not tha' wee."

"So it's not just the land of the Picts?" I asked.

"Lots o' history in these parts," he said. "But I dunnae think yer a wee one. Go on, have a taste. I willnae be offended if yer wantin' somethin' else."

I raised the glass to my lips. The liquid smelled of earthen peat. It was a comforting scent, like a fire in the hearth. I took a hearty sip, and savored the warm earthy flavor on my tongue.

Fergus' eyes bulged as I swallowed with a smile on my face. Whatever I was drinking was no bathtub concoction. I took another sip, wondering how I'd missed out on the pleasures of whisky.

"Dunnae mind the boys," Mr. Black said with a grin. "They're harmless. Here most nights for supper and a nip. I need to be headin' back to the missus, but holler if ye need anythin'."

"I told ye," Fergus said, elbowing Angus in the ribs. "Only a fayrie lass could drink as tha'."

Angus stroked his fuzzy beard.

"What kind of evil fairy do you take me for?" I asked.

"Not *evil*," Fergus said hastily. "Miss...Jones, is it?"

"Please call me Jaya."

"Yer an archaeologist, Miss Jones, eh?" Fergus asked. "We've seen many a thing 'round these parts. Not wicked things, mind ye. Powerful things."

Fergus paused to take a gulp of the dark beer he was drinking. I got a better look at his nose as he tilted his head back. It wasn't crooked, after all. A thick scar ran down his nose at an angle.

"Ye dunnae ken yer roots, Miss Jones?" Fergus asked setting down his glass. "About the fayries?"

"I don't what?" I asked.

"Is an American lass, Fergus," Angus said. "They dunnae ken history."

"Aye, is it so?" Fergus asked.

"Oh, you mean I don't *know* fairy history," I said. "It's true. I'm afraid my fairy lore is a bit lacking."

"*Lore*," Fergus scoffed. "Ye hear the bird, Angus?"

"Aye," Angus said, sipping his beer.

"Wh'eel, lass," Fergus said, "ye've got a bit o' catchin' up to do."

Angus whispered something to Fergus that I couldn't hear.

"Ach," Fergus said, shooing Angus away. "Yer nae my *bean nighe*," he said to me, enunciating slowly.

"Fergus," Angus said.

"I'm gettin' there, Angus! The *bean nighe* is the washer at the ford. The banshee'll be back soon enough to claim my life, the way she claimed the life o' my wife. *Se do leine, se do leine ga mi nigheadh....*"

"When it's yer time tae die," Angus added softly, "ye'll see the fairy hag at the stream, washin' yer bloody shirt. She doesnae show herself before midnight."

"Half eleven," Fergus snapped. "Fer my wife, as I ken."

I wondered at the logistics of that legend. Why would anyone be walking by a stream at midnight?

"I look like this death fairy?" I asked.

"Ach!" Fergus exclaimed. "I did nae mean—"

"She is tha', Fergus," Angus said with a calm shrug. "Is nae wrong to speak the truth."

"Her hair is dark," he said in a whisper. He lifted a trembling hand and pointed directly at me. "And her skin is fair with the tint o' the sea."

"Dunnae frighten the poor lass, Fergus," Angus said. "I dunnae think there's such thing as an American fayrie."

"She's nae American," Fergus said.

"Are ye listenin' to her speak, Fergus?"

"California," I said. "My accent. It's mostly from California. I'm not your *bean nighe*."

"She's the fayrie spirit of a wee lass who's died in childbirth," Angus said. He spoke in his usual measured voice that contrasted with his friend's. He spoke the words so peacefully, so softly, that it was almost as if he were part of the legend himself. "She's to wash the shirts o' the doomed, ye see."

I shivered in spite of the Scotch warming my body.

"Ye'll see the lass," Angus said, "at a burn not far from yer home."

"And ye'll ken," Fergus said. "Ye'll ken."

The two men nodded to each other.

"Did she appear to the man who died last week?" I asked.

They froze.

As sure as I wasn't a *bean nighe*, I was certain they knew something.

"A foreigner," Fergus said, shaking his head. "The man who died last week was a foreigner. It doesn't take them the same way."

"He was English," I said. "Not a—"

"Not Scottish, is whot I'm sayin'."

"No warning signs for him, then?" I asked.

Again Fergus and Angus glanced uneasily at each other. The effects of the Scotch dissipated as blood pumped through my veins.

"What kind of warning did he get?"

Angus glanced at Fergus before speaking.

"They dunnae ken what they're lookin' fer," he said.

"What do you mean?"

A glimmer of light reflected off my glass. I looked over my shoulder and saw through the window that the sun was sinking low in the sky. Still, not a soul appeared. Where was Lane?

"All sorts o' tales," Angus said. "The stones o' the Picts. The hollow hill o' the fayries. The tools of the Tuatha De Danann. They willnae find what they seek. Some things are nae meant to be found."

"They're diggin' up our cliffs," Fergus said, banging his nearly empty pint glass on the bar. "No good can come from tha'."

Were Fergus and Angus so upset about the desecration of their cliffs that they would kill to stop it?

But Rupert was only one of many members of the crew. And hardly the most important one.

"Did something bad happen to him because of their work?" I asked.

"Is nae my place to question the wrath o' God," Fergus said.

"Archaeologists have reasons for digging where they do," I said. "It preserves our history—your history."

"Ye be careful, Miss Jones," Fergus said. "Ye dunnae want to fall into a fayrie ring out along our cliffs."

"What do you—"

"Is best left alone!" Fergus growled.

He gasped and clasped his hand over his mouth as soon as he uttered the exclamation. "Ach, no!"

He slid off his barstool, muttering something about four-leaf clovers to protect him from the curse of displeased fairies. He disappeared out the door of the pub.

"Dunnae take offense of ol' Fergus," Angus said. He smiled, revealing teeth much whiter and more intact than his friend's. "Dunnae worry about all the talk o' fayries. Fergus thinks he was pulled into a fayrie ring. He's nae been right since 'is wife passed on. He fell into the bottle for years afterward. He lost those years to the drink. Not to the fayries."

"But he's your friend," I said.

"Ye understand, Miss Jones."

"You two come here every night?"

"The walk does us good. Now that Sally's not here to cook for 'im, an old bachelor can convince 'im to come 'round for Dougie's wife's pies. Right good cook, she is."

"Does anyone else come by?" I asked, looking around the deserted room.

"B'sides the archaeologist lot?" He nodded. "On the weekend evenin's it can be difficult to find a seat. An' Dougie's wife does a right good Sunday roast. B'sides that, Dougie's wife's lady friends, and the hill walkers might do."

"Fergus warns the hikers about the fairy rings?"

"He might do." Angus rubbed his beard. "Hill walking isnae fer the faint o' heart."

He explained that fairies were known to mislead travelers in these parts. I took that to mean that the trails were confusing. The four-leaf clover Fergus had been mumbling about was one of the protections against malevolent fairies. Another was turning your clothes inside out. Was that supposed to confuse a fairy, I wondered? Putting a knife under your pillow would also protect you.

"I like that last one," I said.

"A practical one, are ye?" he said with a wink.

I tried to turn the conversation back to the archaeologists, but Angus ignored my hints. He instead told me about Lammastide, the holiday in the summer when fairies would walk in the open from hill to hill. The date was fast approaching.

"Thorn trees on a hill will show ye where ye'll find a fairy home," he said. "Dangerous places, those can be. Dangerous places indeed. There's one on the way to their Pictish stones."

He turned away from me, glancing at the door of the pub. "Dougie!" he called out. "Another round here."

Douglas Black emerged seconds later. Angus ordered two more pints of bitter for himself and Fergus. I asked for another Scotch, but something new this time.

As Mr. Black poured our drinks, the door opened behind me. I felt a burst of cool air and heard the sound of a train in the distance.

Lane walked through the door, with Fergus next to him. I had been listening intently to Angus' stories, but I thought I would have noticed Lane slipping downstairs and outside.

Lane's hand was on Fergus' shoulder. The latter nodded vigorously, his head of thick white hair bobbing as he did so.

"What'll ye have?" Mr. Black asked Lane.

"Looks like the crew are on their way as well," Lane said.

At this news, Fergus and Angus took their drinks and shuffled to a corner table next to the fire. Lane took a seat next to me at the bar.

"Fergus certainly thinks highly of you," he said.

"What were you doing out there?"

"Play along," Lane said under his breath.

"With what?"

"We're about to make you indispensable to the crew."

The large door creaked open. It was time to meet an attempted murderer.

# CHAPTER 24

When that door to the pub swung open, I knew who I was looking at. Tan work boots, worn khaki trousers, shirt sleeves rolled to the elbow. And the finishing touch: a fedora. The man who stepped through the doorway was wearing enough dust and sweat to be a hands-on archaeologist, but not enough to make him unapproachable. He must have been at least fifty years old, but his broad chest indicated he wasn't one to delegate physical labor.

He took off the hat as he entered the pub, revealing flaxen hair sprinkled with white. I knew I should have been frightened, or at least on guard, with what he might have done. Instead, I was impressed.

"Drinks all around, Douglas," Professor Malcolm Alpin said with an English, rather than Scottish, accent. "We've made a discovery today."

"Right, gov," Mr. Black said, and got to work pouring drinks.

Knox was right behind the dig's leader. He was slightly rounder around the middle than I remembered. Otherwise he seemed to be the same affable Knox. He and Rupert could have passed for brothers except for the fact that their accents didn't match. Both shorter than average with brown hair and blue-gray eyes, their striking difference was that Knox had working-class roots.

He stopped right inside the door when he saw me. "*Jaya?*"

Behind Knox was someone I wasn't expecting. His girlfriend, Fiona. An archaeology graduate student, she must have been there for the dig as well. And Rupert hadn't told me. My jaw tightened. He knew Fiona and I didn't get along, and he hadn't wanted to deal with my reaction. She blamed me for encouraging Knox and Rupert's scholarly shortcuts, and was convinced I was the one who suggested Knox plagiarize a section of his dissertation. I hadn't known what Knox intended to do. But even if I had, I could never have stopped either Knox or Rupert from doing anything.

Fiona came to an abrupt stop beside Knox. I heard her sharp intake of breath as she saw me. In tan slacks and a matching fitted sweater, she looked as if she had stepped out of an upscale clothing catalog rather than out of a hole in the ground.

Fiona's hair is as black as mine. That's where our similarities end. She keeps her hair long and flowing, compared to my practical bob. The look fits with her ethereal eyes, which are a translucent shade of the palest blue imaginable. Curves follow her tall frame from head to foot. If ever someone looked like an attempted murderess....

I'm just saying.

"What are you doing here?" Fiona asked. It was not a friendly question.

"Jaya!" Knox said again, his shock having worn off. This time his greeting was accompanied by a bear hug. "What are you doing here?" His voice was curious rather than hostile.

"Hi, Knox," I said into his shirt. "Rupert didn't tell me why, but he invited me."

"Did you hear?" Knox asked, pulling back from the hug but leaving his hands on my shoulders. His forehead creased in a pained expression.

"Douglas Black told us," I said. "We must have already been on our way. It's such a shock."

The unfamiliar man at the rear of the group cleared his throat. He stepped around Knox, shooting him a dirty look. He carried two bags, one slung over each shoulder. His body sagged under their weight.

"Looks like we need some introductions," the professor said. He extended his hand to me. "I'm Malcolm Alpin. Please call me Malcolm."

"Jaya Jones," I said, returning his firm handshake. "This is my boyfriend, Lane Peters."

"I see you know Knox and Fiona. And this is Derwin McVicar." The younger man's shoulders weren't actually sagging. Derwin was the tallest man in the room; he had been slouching to avoid hitting his head on the door.

In spite of his height, Derwin couldn't be described as a large man. Beneath the thin fabric of the sleeves of his work shirt, knobby elbows and skeletal forearms were apparent. He gave a curt nod to me and then to Lane.

"I haven't had the pleasure," Fiona said to Lane, extending her hand toward him.

Knox scratched the back of his head as Fiona gave Lane a long handshake accompanied by a broad smile.

"I'm sorry about your friend," Malcolm said. "You must think us frightfully rude to be celebrating so soon after his recent accident."

"Not at all," I said. "You hardly knew him."

"He was a good man," Malcolm said. "A great help to us. We could not have made the discovery today without him."

From the way Knox, Fiona, and Derwin stared at Malcolm, he was speaking well of the supposedly dead.

"I'm going to freshen up," Fiona said, slipping away with a glance back at Lane.

"Are we going to go over our notes?" Derwin asked.

"We'll catch up on them tomorrow," Malcolm said, his eyes following Fiona. "Tonight is a much needed celebration."

Knox took one of the pints Mr. Black had set on the bar.

"You said Rupert asked you to come," Malcolm said, turning back to me. "Are you archaeologists interested in the Picts?"

"As I said, I'm not sure why Rupert asked me—"

"Jaya is being modest," Lane cut in. "She's become a great photographer, and we thought he probably wanted her to document this important dig. I did my undergraduate degree in archaeology, and it's something I take seriously. I thought I might be able to help out as well."

I tried not to glare at Lane. It was difficult.

"Brilliant," Malcolm said, slapping Derwin's back. "Not five minutes ago I was saying how helpful that would be to have a photographer."

"Mmm." Derwin nodded, his thin lips pressed together in an attempt at a smile.

"If you'll excuse me," he said, "I should put these bags away if we're not going to follow procedure and write up our notes."

"We haven't got a proper photographer," Malcolm said as Derwin slogged up the stairs with the heavy bags. "After what we've uncovered today, it would be brilliant to have one."

"We're happy to stay and help," I said. "But I didn't bring—"

Lane kicked my shin.

"Sorry, honey," he said. "I slipped." He turned back to Malcolm. "What have you found?"

"An inscribed Pictish stone that has been hidden for centuries," Malcolm said as he led Lane to the large table. I rubbed my newly bruised shin.

I made my way to the bar and grabbed the Scotch whisky Mr. Black had poured me. This one lacked the flavorful rose-colored flecks, but had its own aromatic punch.

Knox sat down on a stool at the edge of the bar. I took my drink and sat down next to him.

His stomach bulged over the top of his jeans more than looked comfortable.

"You look good," he said. A sad smile lingered on his face. "It's good to see you again. Wish it was under other circumstances."

"I think I'm in denial."

"Rupert didn't tell me he'd rung you up."

"I don't know why he got in touch. He said it was a surprise." I should have rehearsed. It was one thing to make up a fictional story while it was a hypothetical exercise. Lying to an old friend was quite another.

"I thought it was an immature attempt to get me back," I said, "which is why I took him up on it." I pointed over at Lane. "My new boyfriend. Taller, richer. I wanted to rub it in Rupert's nose. I figured Rupert's invitation would give me a chance to surprise him with my successful life. I feel so bad, now that he's...."

Knox sighed and nodded. He rested his dusty elbows on the bar and took a drink of his beer.

"The sad bastard," Knox said. "Such a daft thing to have happened."

"I guess it shouldn't matter to me anymore," I said, "but it does. Even though I hadn't seen him in ages."

The words were true. When I looked past my anger, which admittedly required digging deep, something was there. I wished I knew what. But I didn't travel halfway across the world to sort out my confused feelings for an old boyfriend. I was here to find out who had tried to kill him and was now after me and the ruby treasure.

"What happened?" I asked.

"No idea. I never thought of him as a reckless driver, but I guess you never really know what's going on with someone."

"I didn't even know Rupert was studying the Picts," I said, watching for Knox's reaction.

Knox squinted at me. "It's a gig," he said. "Basic pay for the summer. Not too bad."

In spite of being caught plagiarizing, Knox wasn't stupid. He had grand ideas that inspired Rupert and won Fiona as a girlfriend, and he'd gained admission to a good university. I suspected he had simply given up at some point after meeting the even more talented Fiona and Rupert. He couldn't keep up with them. By the time I met Knox, he had already stopped trying.

"Fiona has a grant for the dig," Knox said. "She arranged for us to come up."

He took another long drink of his beer. I inhaled the scent wafting out from behind the bar. I was too hungry to concentrate. I hoped Mrs. Black was making something tasty and filling. Now that I knew Rupert was alive and I wanted to kill him myself, it wasn't nearly as easy to focus.

"You and Fiona," I said, "you're back together?"

"What? Well, you know how it is."

"Not really."

Knox chugged some more beer. "We're young, have to go see the world 'n all."

He licked a drop of beer off the rim of his glass. Knox was a puppy dog. Cuddly and with an eye for adventure, but never able to get anywhere without someone there to take care of him.

Douglas Black set down another pint in front of Knox, from which Knox immediately took a long swig. It wasn't hard to see how he'd gotten into his present shape.

An eruption of laughter echoed from the table behind us. Derwin and Fiona had returned and joined Malcolm and Lane. The fire crackled in the background. Fergus and Angus had their heads together over their table. No one seemed to be paying any attention to me or Knox.

"I didn't know you were still doing archaeological work," I said.

"Rupert didn't tell you?"

"We didn't keep in touch."

"No? I thought you two were still tight, from how he talked about you."

"But he didn't tell you why he invited me here?"

"Why would he tell me? I was only supposed to be his best mate." Knox shrugged, his head sagging. "I'm doing as much as I can. I worked at an auction house in London for a while. Appraising is more lucrative than lecturing, you know. It wasn't such a bad lot that I couldn't lecture like Rupert. You're teaching at a university in Los Angeles?"

"San Francisco."

"San Francisco. Never been to California myself, you know. Fi and I might go on holiday there when we can. You like it there?"

"Never a dull moment." I thought about nosy Nadia, my nearly-harmless stalker Miles, and Sanjay, who I really needed to call again before he contacted British authorities.

"We had some right fun that year you were here," Knox said, bringing his hands to watery eyes. "Bloody sad bastard."

I must have had a sentimental bone somewhere in my body, because I found myself about to confide in Knox. Not a good idea.

"What's this big discovery here?" I asked.

He gave a start, but then recovered.

"Oh, today, you mean," he said.

He wasn't holding up his end of the secret very well. I needed to talk with him away from the others.

"We found one of the stones Professor Alpin was on about," he said. "Another stone was found nearby. The professor guessed there'd be a cluster."

"New Pictish standing stones," I said. "That's a big deal, isn't it?"

Knox leaned toward me. His eyes were red.

"The old prof would be thrilled to fill you in," he said, rubbing his eyes. "I'm sure he'll tell you whatever I told you was wrong, anyway."

"I don't really care about the stones, you know. I was just asking to be—"

"I know, I know," Knox said warily. "Since when are you one for pleasantries, Jaya? This has been a bloody awful week. I don't want to think about Rupert or anything else anymore. Can't you leave me to drink my pint in peace?"

# CHAPTER 25

Knox sat with his head bowed over his drink at the bar as I joined the others.

Douglas Black emerged from behind the bar carrying hot plates of food. He served Fergus and Angus first, showing the proper respect for the old regulars, then came back with plates for the rest of us. When a steaming plate of meat pie with a side of carrots and buttery baked potatoes was set down in front of me, I found I was even hungrier than I thought.

Malcolm called over to Knox, "There's room here at the other end of the table."

"Ta," Knox replied. "I'm all right."

"Cheers, everyone," Malcolm said, raising his glass.

I poured more than a generous serving of both brown sauce and vinegar onto my potato. Malcolm was too polite to comment. Fiona wrinkled her nose.

"I was explaining," Malcolm said between bites of food, "that we're short-staffed this summer. I wasn't able to acquire as much of a grant as this work deserves. My theories aren't what you'd call mainstream. Locating this site through the discovery of a first stone wasn't enough. I have some detractors in high places."

"He thinks the Picts weren't Celts," Lane said, as if this was supposed to mean something to me.

"But the debate is far from settled!" Malcolm's eyes grew wide as he spoke.

Derwin nodded along with him, his Adam's apple bulging alarmingly. No wonder the locals were creeped out by this group.

"You two are acquainted with the mysterious Picts?" Malcolm asked.

"The professor is being sarcastic," Derwin said. "The Picts—or 'picti,' the painted people, as the Romans described them—aren't mysterious at all. Not in the most commonly used form of the word. Not like the *Druids*."

He laughed at his own joke. At least I think it was a joke.

"The mystery," he said, ignoring his food, "is because we haven't yet come to understand their system of communication."

"Much of the history of the region hasn't yet been pieced together," Malcolm said. "In the ninth century, Kenneth MacAlpine united the Picts and the Scots to form Scotland, but before that the details of the Picts have been harder to piece together based on lack of written records. All we have is the stones. But so far, they've defied deciphering."

"Conventional wisdom," said Derwin, "has the Picts as Celtic peoples, but there isn't any conclusive evidence to support that claim. It's purely backwards reasoning: 'The Picts put Celtic crosses on their stones once they were converted to Christianity in the fifth century, ergo they were originally Celts'."

I smiled at Derwin. Maybe he was my kind of scholar after all.

"Malcolm already has some evidence to support his theory," Fiona said, startling Derwin. Her translucent eyes were ghostly in the firelight, commanding the attention of the group.

"The Picts had a matrilineal society," she said. "The familial line was passed down from the mother instead of the father. But there's still not nearly enough known to be able to say much."

Malcolm looked at her fondly. "That's why discovering more stones is so important," he said. "Fiona joined my team even after I was slandered by my enemies."

"The professor," Derwin said, "has discovered this site of heretofore undiscovered symbol stones. He's working on a paper on the subject at St. Andrews, which I will be coauthoring after our discoveries this summer."

The fire flickered as a gust of wind circled the inn and crept into the fireplace. Conversation broke off as we all turned to watch the amber flames dance up into the stone chimney. Everyone except for Fiona. Her gaze was fixed on Lane.

Derwin stood up and stretched his long legs. He walked over to the fire, leaving his nearly untouched dinner behind. He stooped to warm his hands in front of the flames.

"It's a class-one symbol stone," he said. "It might even contain some new pictographic classifications—"

"Not likely," said Fiona.

"These class-one symbol stones," Derwin continued as if Fiona hadn't spoken, "are most important to identifying the origins of the Picts. They're the earliest carvings, and they don't yet have any Celtic additions to them to confuse things."

"I'm lucky Derwin turned to Scottish archaeology after studying geology as an undergraduate," Malcolm said. "He's been doing some fascinating research for his doctorate on P-Celtic versus Q-Celtic languages."

My eyes glazed over. I doubted it was from the strong Scotch whisky. I watched Knox's chubby fingers raise the pint glass to his lips yet again, drowning his sorrows at the bar. It was difficult to imagine him trying to kill his friend.

Unless it wasn't sorrow that was eating him up. Could it be guilt?

The quiet Angus looked out over his glass and caught my eye. The talkative group didn't seem to miss my company as I left to sit with the regulars. Angus pulled up a chair for me while Fergus scowled at the crew.

"What is it you don't approve of?" I asked.

"Who'd give a toss about the Picts," Fergus said, "when there's real history to be found."

"Fairy history?" I asked.

"The Tuatha De Danann," he whispered.

Angus nodded silently.

"From the clouds they came," Fergus said, "driven underground by the mortals to the sidh." He pronounced the word 'shee.'

"Fayrie mounds," Angus translated. "Hills where fayries dwell."

"The lass must know what a sidh is, Angus," Fergus said, shaking his head in exasperation.

For the time it took them to finish their drinks, they recounted several more fairy stories for me. Then Fergus removed a pack of cigarettes from his pocket, and Angus extracted a pipe. It was time for their walk home, they said.

Lane was no longer in the room. Neither was Fiona. I figured Lane might have been outside smoking, but I didn't remember Fiona to have been a smoker.

Knox had joined the rest of the crew. He, Malcolm, and Derwin sat around the table with their heads together, debating about how to remove the stone from the earth.

Malcolm got up from the table, pausing by the hearth. He rested his arm against the mantle, near the stone gargoyle.

"Brilliant day," he said. He tilted his head to me before heading up the stairs.

"Night, Jaya," Knox mumbled, and followed Malcolm.

"It's quite late," Derwin said after Malcolm and Knox were out of sight. "I'm surprised the professor indulged in this late-night merriment."

Derwin's vocabulary was from another era. Not to mention his name. I felt a twinge of pity. I imagined he was someone who would have felt more at home had he been born at another time. In the dim light of the fire, his pinched features were full of sorrow. Perhaps he wished he had lived before the grand halls of the nearby Dunnottar Castle had turned to rubble.

"From what you've told us about the discovery," I said, "it sounds like you deserve to celebrate."

"But the professor takes his digs very seriously," Derwin said quietly, staring into the fire. Was that fear on his face?

An uneasy feeling entered my mind. Before the thought could fully form, Fiona walked through the door of the pub. She walked up the stairs without pausing to acknowledge me or Derwin.

I was about to ask Derwin if he was all right, when Douglas Black emerged from behind the bar to clean up. He whistled as he began to stack up the chairs.

"Coming up?" I asked Derwin.

He shook his head, still looking at the fire.

"When the fire goes out," he said.

At the top of the stairs, I opened the door to my room as quietly as I could. I needn't have bothered. It was empty.

Lane had fixed the rattling window. A towel was snugly fitted along the bottom, and I didn't hear any rattling. I didn't hear anything at all.

I put my ear to the door. Something creaked softly. I couldn't tell if it was a door, let alone which one.

I sat down on the bed and pulled out my phone. Sanjay had left me two voicemail messages and three texts.

"Bad timing," Sanjay said as soon as he picked up the phone. "I was expecting you to call ages ago. I'm practicing the snake charmer basket now. You know that one requires a lot of concentration."

"You want me to call you later?" I asked.

"Of course not. Just give me two seconds."

I heard a hissing that I hoped wasn't coming from a real snake.

"Okay," Sanjay said. "I'm all yours."

"We're safely in Scotland."

"*We*? Who's *we*?"

I really needed to start writing down what I was going to say to everyone so I could keep things straight. How would I explain Lane to Sanjay?

"I mean we the crew of the dig," I said. "What else would I mean?"

"Why didn't you tell me Nadia didn't know what was going on?"

"You told *Nadia* about the ruby? Why were you even at the house?"

"I wasn't," Sanjay said. "She called me."

"But she hates you."

"She hates me? You told me she hated magicians in general because we deceive people."

"That's what I meant." I hoped I sounded convincing. "Why did she call you?"

"She was worried you were traumatized by the burglary. You didn't tell me the burglar was violent and knocked her down."

I managed to convince Sanjay I wasn't in imminent danger, and he agreed to go back to practicing his new act.

For once in my life, I couldn't get to sleep right away. Between the mess I'd left back home, the tension seeping through the walls of the inn, and the wind whistling outside, I didn't know what to do.

My last waking thought that night was that Lane had still not returned.

# CHAPTER 26

I awoke in the morning to a faint light streaming in through the window. Lane was asleep on the floor next to the bed. His glasses were on the windowsill. I had a completely unobstructed view of his face. His dark blond hair was brushed back, revealing his prominent cheekbones and the deep-set cheeks beneath. He breathed silently through his nose. His long eyelashes were a shade darker than the sandy hair on his head. They fluttered slightly as if he was dreaming. He looked so peaceful that I closed my eyes again.

I woke up for a second time to find Lane standing next to the bed. He was fully dressed, and back to wearing his glasses with his hair tumbling over his face. It took me a moment to remember he had disappeared the night before.

"Where did you go last night?" I asked. "And I'm a photographer now?"

"I was trying to solve this mystery," he said.

I sat up and ran my fingers through my hair to pull the tangles from my face.

"*That's* your excuse for spending the evening off somewhere with Fiona?" I said. "And you didn't answer my second question."

"I thought it was obvious. You heard that they need a photographer. I overheard them say as much. Malcolm is serious about his work. He might not have been so keen on letting you tag along on this dig without some function. The rest of them are archaeologists, and I've at least had some archaeological training."

"My camera's broken."

"I have one you can use."

"You—" I stopped myself. It's too bad I hadn't stuck with yoga. I really could have used the breathing techniques to keep me calm in the midst of Lane's vexing ideas.

"I have many talents," I said calmly. "All modesty aside, I'm aware of that fact."

The hint of a crooked smile crossed Lane's lips.

"One talent I do not happen to possess," I continued less calmly, "is photography. I'm not exaggerating when I say I might be one of the world's worst photographers. Why do you think I stuck the bracelet in my friend's hand before I took a picture of it? Otherwise you'd have probably thought it was a grapefruit."

"A grapefruit?"

"You know what I mean," I said, tossing the bed sheet aside and standing up. I was glad to see I had remembered to sleep in something sensible.

"The point is," I said, "what are we doing? I know, I know. I'm the one who led you here in the first place. But now I'm pretending to be a photographer on top of everything else? Coercing information from suspects isn't nearly as easy as it looks."

"Is anything?"

"Some things are."

We stood close in the small quarters. A hint of a smile popped onto Lane's face again. He cleared his throat, erasing all signs of it.

"And some things," I added, "aren't."

"Hurry up," Lane said. "We're going to be late. Breakfast is from seven to seven thirty, before everyone heads off for the dig."

"Tell them I have a hangover."

"You drink too much."

"And you smoke too much, but that's not what I meant. I want to fake a hangover so I can meet up with you all later. When everyone's gone, I'm going to try to search their rooms. Have you looked at these ancient locks?"

"Ah," Lane said, sitting down on the bed. "A girl after my own heart. You're not as bad at this as you think. I was wondering if you'd think of that, too."

"Then you could have made better use of your time last night and done it yourself," I snapped.

"I couldn't very well do it with everyone here," he said seriously. "People could have come up to their rooms at any time."

I couldn't tell if he was joking or if he would really have done it.

"I like your plan," he said. "These locks don't look like they'd stand up to much. It shouldn't be too difficult."

The idea hadn't seemed real until Lane began talking about it as if we were having a casual conversation about the weather.

"Be careful," he added. "You're not going to have much time."

"Why? I'm small, they'll believe I was feeling poorly for a while."

Lane looked at me thoughtfully for a moment before speaking.

"At least now I know that breaking and entering isn't how you provide for that enormous appetite of yours," he said. "You don't have much time because as soon as Mrs. Black finishes washing up after breakfast, she'll come upstairs to clean the two shared bathrooms. And by the time she's done, members of the dig will start returning intermittently to use the facilities. I thought it would be a good idea to have a talk with Mrs. Black to find out the schedule of the place."

"That's what you were doing last night?"

He stood up, bumping his head on the sloped ceiling. "We'll leave within twenty minutes," he said, "so you should wait a few more minutes and then go for it. Mr. or Mrs. Black can give you directions to the dig when you come down. You'll probably have over half an hour, but move quickly."

He took two steps and was at the door. He reached for the handle and then hesitated and turned back. He pulled a small object out of his pocket.

"This seems to work in the movies," he said, tossing me a Swiss army knife.

After Lane left, I threw on some clothes and my thick-soled platform boots. They'd be better than pointy heels for snooping without clacking on the floor, and afterward for walking through what I presumed might be a muddy dig. After donning the boots, I noticed something I hadn't spotted earlier. A tripod and camera had appeared on the small bureau.

The old-fashioned lock I stood in front of twenty minutes later didn't appear to need a Swiss army knife. At first glance I was sure my own key would fit into the lock. For a second I thought I almost had it. The key turned. But the door didn't open. It couldn't hurt to try the Swiss army knife. One of the gadgets was such a perfect size that seemed to be made for this. Well, what do you know.... That did it.

I stepped into the room closest to the stairway and closed the door gently. I could immediately tell this was Dr. Alpin's room. A fedora similar to the one he had been wearing the previous day hung over the bedpost.

As the organizer of the legitimate dig, he was my least likely suspect. But thinking back on the classic mysteries of my youth, the fact that he was the least likely suspect actually made him the most likely suspect.

I decided to stop thinking so much.

Malcolm Alpin was an average fellow. Socks on the floor. Old-fashioned shaving kit on the dresser. He had several academic books with him, which I leafed through in case he had hidden anything suspicious between the pages. He hadn't. I flipped over the pictures on the wall, felt along the floor boards, and looked inside the lighting fixture. I don't know what I was hoping to find, but whatever it was wasn't in this room.

In spite of my newfound ability to pick antiquated locks, I did not appear to be vastly improving my skills as a detective. I let myself out and moved on to the next room.

I found my groove on the second lock, twisting and pulling the key in a upward motion until the ruts fit firmly into the lock, then pushing on the pick until I heard a click.

Pull... twist... click....

The next room was much smaller, though not quite as small as the room Lane and I shared. It was immaculate. A journal sat upon the small bureau next to the bed, which confirmed my suspicion that this was Derwin's room. The journal was a scholarly record rather than a personal one, duplicating whatever he found most important from the dig log. A bureau drawer contained two blank notebooks and a volume of the *Journal of Scottish Antiquaries*. Neatly placed next to the notebooks and journal were two pencils, a case for binoculars, and a Swiss army knife. The knife wasn't as fully endowed of tools as the one Lane had given me. One of the tools was bent and didn't fit properly back into its slot. I picked it up suspiciously, seeing if I could spot traces of brake fluid on it. No luck. There were only traces of dirt and wood, as you'd expect on an archaeologist's Swiss army knife. The search of his room revealed nothing of interest either, except that Derwin kept his socks and underwear in separate little plastic baggies. I shuddered and left the room.

Pull... twist... click....

Knox's room. Men's clothing was strewn over most of the furniture. The only neat part of the room was the stack of photos of the dig placed on the windowsill. I flipped through the photos and got a sense of what I'd be headed toward later that morning. The photos were mostly close-ups of rocky land along the coast. He also had at least a dozen books in his room, more than the professor. The subjects included missing artifacts from Egyptian tombs, fraudulent illuminated manuscripts, and sunken ships rumored to contain treasures. A pamphlet stuck out of the edge of one of the books. The Gregor Estate.

In my excitement at finding the first concrete piece of evidence, I dropped the book. The pamphlet fell out and the book landed with a thud at an awkward angle. I scooped them both up, but the damage was done. I didn't know where the pamphlet had been placed, and several pages of the book were now crumpled.

I left the books and articles as close as I could to how I'd found them and departed.

Pull... twist... click....

A peculiar sensation came over me as I entered Fiona's room. The faded scent of perfume lingered in the air, mixed with the scent of cigarettes. A worn photo of her with Knox was wedged into a crack in the wood of the small dresser. A dried, flattened rose had been affixed to the side of the wall-hung mirror, and a light silk scarf was draped over the other top edge.

A loud creak echoed through the room. I froze. Someone was right outside the door.

# CHAPTER 27

Another sound followed from the hallway. Someone was definitely right outside the room. I must have taken longer than I meant to. Time flies when breaking and entering.

I scanned the room for a place to hide. In these small rooms, the only place remotely big enough was under the bed. A quick look told me the area was filthy enough that I would have needed a tetanus shot after hiding there. Although that presumably meant Mrs. Black wouldn't be cleaning under the bed, I didn't have the desire to give myself tetanus.

I looked under the bed one last time before it occurred to me that I was looking at this all wrong. Mrs. Black wouldn't be looking at Fiona's door as she cleaned the bathroom. I could simply step out into the hallway. I only had to act as if I was coming out of my own room.

I slipped out quickly and closed the door loudly. I waited a few seconds, then walked down the hall.

"Good morning dear," Mrs. Black said cheerily as I walked by. "Let me make you some breakfast."

In spite of my protests, she insisted on stopping her work and bringing me down to the kitchen. She wanted to give me a full breakfast, but I insisted that eggs and toast would be fine. She put a hot cup of tea in my hands. I took a sip, and the liquid nearly came out my nose.

"What the—?"

"It's thistle," Mrs. Black said. "It's good for the body."

"This is what you regularly serve since you're the Fog & Thistle Inn?" I looked into the cup. Sure enough, it was a real thistle, not a flower-infused tea bag.

"Oh, no." She laughed. "I've got a box of Tetley's. Thistle rejuvenates the body. Your gent said you were feeling unwell."

I put my nose over the steaming cup and breathed in. It smelled more potent than black tea. Never one to turn down anything potent, I tried another sip. It wasn't half bad when you were expecting it. Maybe this was what kept her and her husband young. Like her husband, Mrs. Black didn't look nearly as old as she must have been. Her round shape made her hobble slightly when she walked, but her face was youthful. Deep, dark blue eyes similar to Angus' dominated her face.

"This stuff is really good," I said after taking another sip. It was bitter and sweet and sour and salty all at the same time. This was my kind of drink.

"I know, dear. Drink up."

Mrs. Black placed a plate of runny fried eggs and a rack of toast in front of me and sat down on the chair across from mine.

"That's a nice gent you've got there," she said, as I scooped up some eggs. "I'm not sure about the others."

I stopped in mid-scoop.

"This group," Mrs. Black said. "They're not like guests we've had before."

"Have some of them been doing something disturbing? Something secretive?"

"I didnae mean to speak ill of the lot of them," Mrs. Black said, straightening her skirt even though it was already perfectly straight.

"It's all right. We're not close."

"Well...."

"Yes?"

"You'll not be knowin' about the local parts, but..." She paused and looked around, poking her head out of the kitchen before continuing. "My husband Dougie is none too pleased when I think there's something to the history o' these parts. 'Round the bend, right off the path to where those archaeologists are working, you'll be passing a fairy mound."

She looked at me expectantly.

"*Dunnae ye see?* That could explain the lot of it! The strange behavior. The creaking during the night."

"You saw a crew member sneaking around at night?" I asked. "Who—"

"The lot of 'em. They all went by the mound. It's close to Lammastide, when the fayrie power is strongest. It can drive ye mad."

"Something happened?"

"I'll tell ye," she said, her dark eyes boring into mine, "somethin' isnae right. Ach! Yer eggs'll get cold if you don't eat up."

"But you were saying—"

"Aye. I was sayin' ye'll want to take the long way round to the stones. Ye dunnae want to be settin' foot on a fairy mound."

# CHAPTER 28

I couldn't see the ocean as I set out on the path, but I could smell it. It was different from the smell of the Pacific Ocean in San Francisco, with the thick salty sensation blowing by with the fog, or the Arabian Sea along the coast of Goa, with its fruity scents wafting by in the warm breeze. Here along these remote cliffs was the crisp scent of untouched northern wind.

I wasn't sure exactly what I had expected—rolling fields of heather, dramatic Celtic crosses atop each hill, sheep running up to greet me—but none of those movie-studio realities came to pass. The winding dirt path led through a plain grassy field that was adjoined by numerous other grassy fields like the ones I passed on the train. Up close, the field had more mud and weeds than the far-off green fields the speeding train had suggested. I came upon a fence in the midst of the path, which had steps to assist people climbing over the barrier meant to keep animals in their place. A solitary sheep wandered along beside the fence, methodically chewing some weeds and looking singularly uninterested in my presence.

Past the sheep, the grassy land rose into a small hill. The fairy mound Mrs. Black had mentioned.

I walked around the sheep toward the mound. Enough people had warned me against it. What else could I do?

As I walked closer to the small hill, the sheep started baa-ing loudly. The sound was much louder than I expected. It stopped me in my tracks.

I took another step and the bleating grew louder again. Surely it was a coincidence. Or perhaps the sheep was domesticated and wanted some company. I turned and looked at it. The sheep stared back at me, calmly chewing some grass. I continued walking. The sheep's bleats began again. I didn't look back, but the sound followed me up the gentle incline.

I circled the mound more quickly than I might otherwise have done. It was a small, grassy hill. Nothing much distinctive about it.

Nothing except for a lone thorn tree at the top.

Back on the path, a burst of wind from the sea hit me as I reached the edge of the land. I stood high above the water, watching the frothy waves crash. The coastline below ran straight for a ways before curving outwards a mile or so to the north. I took out the camera and looked through its zoom lens. Small buildings in the distance came into focus. The landmass poking out into the sea held the ruins of Dunnottar castle. In the opposite direction, the inn was already out of sight, obscured by a slight slope in the land beyond a fence I had passed.

The path continued north toward the castle, but I turned south, following my directions. The wind was strong. If not for the fact that the current of air came from the sea rather than toward it, this coastal hike would have been a much more dangerous endeavor. With the natural curves and drops in the land it was necessary to pay close attention or risk spraining an ankle. Mr. Black's warning wasn't for naught.

Though the walkable grassy land ended abruptly, the drop-off to the sea wasn't sheer at all points. I passed a steep path heading down to a small alcove, next to some rocks stretching back up to high ground. Mixed with the sound of crashing waves, I heard faint voices. Following the voices, I spotted the top of another lone tree in the barren landscape. As its gnarled trunk came into view, so did the dig and crew.

Lane was facing me, his sleeves rolled up and a trowel nestled confidently in his hand, but it was Malcolm who spotted me first.

He set down a brush and walked up to me while Lane and Fiona spoke together over a pile of dirt.

"Sorry I'm late," I said.

"I trust you're feeling better?"

"Much. Mrs. Black gave me a wonderfully restorative tea."

Malcolm burst into a broad smile.

"Scottish drink takes a bit of getting used to, I'm afraid," he said.

I smiled meekly. At least I hoped my smile resembled meekness.

"You've brought your camera with you. Brilliant. You might want to borrow a hat as well. The chill is from the wind, but the sun will still do damage."

I don't usually sunburn, but I knew about the strength of the northern sun, so I accepted his offer. Malcolm led me over to the solitary tree, under which sat a large backpack with rain slickers sticking out of the open top. Clipped to the side of the pack was a fedora that matched the one Malcolm was wearing.

With my new hat, we proceeded to the pit where Lane and Fiona were working. Fiona drew broad strokes in a sketch pad while Lane cleared away debris. They were speaking quietly to each other but stopped as we approached.

"Nice hat, Dr. Jones," Lane said.

Fiona paused to glare at me, then went back to drawing.

"Here she is," Malcolm said.

It took me a moment to realize that "she" didn't mean Fiona. She was a rock. A two-foot-wide slab of gray stone, the edges rough but not quite jagged. Circling the rock, I could see that only about a foot of the rock poked out of the earth thus far. It looked solid, and I imagined it continued quite a bit further down into the ground.

"Well?" Malcolm said to me.

"Shall I get started taking photographs?"

"I can be out of the way in a few more minutes, Malcolm," Fiona said without looking up from her sketch.

"I think the light will be better for photos a little later anyway," I said. "Once the sun has passed overhead."

Malcolm nodded happily. At least I sounded like I knew what I was talking about. That's me, Jaya Jones. Undercover sleuth and bogus photographer. I hoped this whole thing would be settled before they had a chance to study my photographs.

I stepped back and took a better look at the rock, trying to guess what made it a Pictish stone. I noticed a few faint scratches, but they looked more like marks made by the trowel than deliberate writing.

As I examined the rock further, Knox and Derwin came into view, appearing out of thin air from behind the tree. They must have come up from a steep path down to the shore like the one I had passed earlier. Derwin carried a bag of equipment over his shoulder and a notebook in his breast pocket. A few steps behind Derwin, Knox was empty-handed but wheezing.

"It looks as if some kids have been down in the alcove cave drinking," Derwin said. "We should board up the entrance so they'll go elsewhere."

"They'll be harmless enough," said Knox, having caught his breath enough to speak.

Derwin shot him a dirty look. "Our nightly tarp," he said, "is a big welcome sign to a hooligan."

"That lot don't give a toss," Knox insisted. "It's not yobs round here. We don't need to take time away from our work—"

"Professor," Derwin said over Knox, "the cave full of beer cans is almost directly below us. This is of potential serious concern—"

"It's not like they'd come through this way," Fiona cut in. "How steep was that path you two walked down? You can't see our site from down there. Like you said, it's directly below us."

"Fiona is our voice of reason, as always," Malcolm said. "Good of you to realize the possible concern though, Derwin."

"It's not only that they might see our site," Derwin said.

"What's the problem?" Knox asked.

"Never mind," Derwin said, his thin cheeks flushing. He flung down the bag he was carrying and walked past us at a brisk pace. He nearly knocked into me, not seeming to care where he was going.

To get a better view of the cave they were talking about, I walked over to the tree that stood next to where Derwin and Knox had appeared. I stepped over the tree's imposing roots and walked around to the other side, which I had originally thought was the edge of the cliff. Instead, the tree roots grew into a slope of grass, with a steep, irregular dirt path zigzagging down to the shore.

"Why is she wearing those daft shoes?" Fiona said, not bothering to whisper. "Doesn't she realize this is a dig?"

I glanced over my shoulder and saw Lane grin at her. The rat. I looked down at my thick platform shoes. There was nothing wrong with my shoes. Didn't anyone understand what it was like to be short?

I could see the small alcove below, including something that appeared to be a rocky opening. This, I assumed, led to the cave where Knox and Derwin had found beer bottles or some other evidence of teenage fun. It looked like a perfect spot for a secret teenage rendezvous. It also looked like the perfect secret spot for something else. I took a step forward, trying to get a better look.

What if I had been wrong about Rupert and Knox's motive for joining the Pictish dig? What if they hadn't been either hiding out or after something at the Gregor Estate? What if *the dig itself* was their destination?

I had assumed the "treasure" Rupert was referring to was related to the Indian bracelet he sent me. That assumption was based on the fact that Lane knew the bracelet was part of a larger Mughal treasure, and that Rupert had mentioned "my research." What if that was the *wrong assumption*?

Just like all of those scholars I had berated, I had no proof. Only assumptions. I had no real evidence of what Rupert was up to, and he had been infuriatingly vague. What if the bracelet was related to an earlier scheme of Rupert and Knox's? All I really knew for sure was that there was a treasure out there. Somewhere.

A crazy idea hit me. As I thought it through, it didn't seem crazy at all.

Rupert had always said how pixie-like I was. Fergus was visibly shaken by how fairy-like he thought I looked. It wouldn't be a leap to assume that an old man wary of strangers would open up more to me than to Rupert or any of the others. The two old Scots knew about all of the local legends, including whatever fairy treasures were buried in the hills. Fiona was one of the original participants of the legitimate dig, and made it possible for Knox and Rupert to be there. She would have told Knox about Fergus and Angus during their phone conversations, and Knox would have told his good old friend and co-conspirator Rupert about the folklore that might be more than just stories. They didn't think they would need outside help at first, until Rupert thought of a clever way I could be of assistance. He needed to get me here to use me.

I didn't think Rupert was gullible or superstitious enough to believe in fairy treasure, but he would realize that most legends are based in fact. As students of history and archaeology know, lore about fairy treasures is often based on true stories of real ancient treasures. Treasures buried in hiding places such as the rocky cave in the alcove. It was all conjecture at this point, but it was possible things were finally starting to make sense.

I was so caught up in this thought that until a voice startled me out of my reverie, I didn't realize I was standing so close to the edge of the cliff.

# CHAPTER 29

"Hey," Lane said directly in my ear. "What do you think you're doing?"

He stepped up beside me, a fine layer of dust covering his clothing. He looked even taller than usual. He stood on a fat root of the tree, resting his hand on the trunk next to me.

"You're awfully close to the edge," he said. "Be careful, it looked like you were daydreaming or something. I don't need to remind you about other 'accidents' that have happened on these cliffs."

When I didn't answer immediately, he studied my face.

"What is it?"

"Not here," I said quietly.

"We're on a break now," he whispered. "We can go talk somewhere."

"It's not lunchtime yet, is it? It's only around eleven."

"We're in Britain. I thought you knew this place."

I looked over and saw Knox pouring tea out of a thermos.

"Honey," Lane said loudly, "let's go look around."

He took my hand in his and pulled me away from the edge of the precipice. His hand was warm and strong. He led me south of the dig. We walked in silence until we found a flat, wide-open space. We'd be sure to see anyone approaching long before they were within earshot. I realized my hand was still in Lane's even after we were long past the crew's field of view. Oddly, it felt so natural that I hadn't given it a second thought. I let go of his hand as we sat down on two relatively dry rocks. Lane looked at me and raised an eyebrow.

I opened my mouth, and then realized I had no idea where to start.

"You know how fictional detectives on TV always have their 'ah-ha!' moments," I blurted out, "where everything clicks into place?"

Lane waited for me to go on.

"Where the detective does something like dipping her spoon into the sugar tray," I said, "and the sugar sticks to the wet spoon, so she looks at the spoon and says 'Ah ha! Of course!' Because her subconscious has realized the fundamentally different way that things fit together when you do something differently."

"Jones," he said. "I hate to break it to you, but those moments are there to create a neat and tidy solution for the viewer."

"I'm trying to explain something important. Didn't you used to be a good listener? Just pretend I'm Fiona."

He was silent.

I took a breath. "We've been looking at this whole thing in the wrong way."

"Oh!" Lane said, sounding interested for the first time during the conversation. "You found a clue in someone's room?"

"What? Oh! Yes. I mean no. I mean, I thought so. Knox had a Gregor Estate pamphlet in his room."

"So you were right after all," Lane said. "I should have paid more attention while we were there. But we can go back—"

"No, let me finish. He had a lot of random items. No one had any dastardly plans tacked up on their walls. My idea doesn't have anything to do with something I found."

"Really? Then wouldn't a better analogy be that the detective looked at a clock through a water glass and the time was backwards? That way it's not a physical thing that has changed. Only her perception changed. The way she was looking at something."

"That's quite clever," I said through gritted teeth, "but right now I need you to be a little less pedantic. What I'm trying to say is that we've been assuming that the treasure Rupert is after is the same one you know about. But what if we misinterpreted his note? Or if he purposefully misled me to entice me here? It wasn't as if there was much to go on. Remember, even though he'd been at the British Library for days, he hadn't requested any information about the Mughals and their treasure. He was doing *something else*.

"I don't know what he's been up to for the past year. For all I know, he could have been involved in all sorts of crazy schemes with Knox—the bracelet having been just *one* of them. What if his motive wasn't to help him find some far-off Indian treasure? He wanted me to help him here. On this dig. When I saw him he kept talking about a treasure, but he didn't say *which* treasure.

"Think about what I told you he said to me on the train. He carefully omitted all references to what the treasure was. You weren't there for the whole evening last night, so you didn't see how Fergus and Angus reacted to me—"

"I saw enough."

"Then you understand my point. The way Fergus reacted to me was especially spooky. He seriously believed I was a fairy, one they called a *bean nighe*, who brings death. At least for a little while. But even after that he told me all sorts of fairy legends. They seemed wary of the other members of the dig, though. Remember when you entered the pub, they scurried off to their own separate table?"

"You think your ex wanted you to get Fergus and Angus to tell you the local legends that only they remember, leading him to a treasure."

"Exactly. Knox and Rupert had to have something specific to go on, something that would make them think there was real treasure here. Fiona was on this dig from the beginning, and she and Knox are going out. At least they were until you came along. Anyway, she could easily have told him about something that turned up at the dig. Looking down at the cave made me put it together. The cave would be a perfect place to bury a treasure. A folklore one and a real one. And did you notice how protective Knox was about not blocking off the cave?"

I pulled my knees against my body. The wind was getting crisper.

"That's a compelling idea," Lane said, "except that it's so far-fetched that it doesn't make sense."

"I knew it!" I said, standing up and jumping around to keep warm. "I knew you wouldn't want to let go of your apocryphal Indian treasure that will make your career."

"This has to be about the Rajasthan Rubies."

I stopped jumping and stared at him across the heather. "What did you say?"

"I was talking about the treasure."

My head spun as I realized what he was saying.

"You lied to me!" I yelled. "You've known what it was this whole time. What else have you lied to me about?"

# CHAPTER 30

"I didn't lie to you," Lane said.

"You called the treasure the Rajasthan Rubies." My voice shook as I spoke.

"I've been thinking about the treasure so much that I had to start calling it *something*."

"You make up pet names for all the mysterious treasures you come across?" I tried to raise an eyebrow skeptically. It looked so easy when he did it. I found I wasn't nearly as good. Especially when I was upset.

"This isn't just any treasure," Lane said. "The state of Rajasthan has a lot of Mughal jewelry of Persian influence like this. It has a nice ring to it."

"The Rajasthan Rubies," I repeated into the wind as I watched Lane. Did I believe him?

"Your ruby artifact and this bigger ruby treasure have to be what this is about," he said. "Your ex sent you a piece from the treasure that was clandestinely removed from a great Mughal court and hasn't been seen in centuries."

"It sounds to me like you need to get a life," I said, not quite sure I believed him, but not knowing what else to think. "You're starting to use words like 'clandestinely' in conversation. How did a Mughal treasure end up here? It makes much more sense for Rupert to be after a Scottish treasure, since we're in Scotland. But until we see Rupert again, we can't confirm anything. It's not like we can ask Knox outright, since not even Rupert trusted him. I need to find another way to talk to Knox."

"Even if I grant you your premise," Lane said, "if Fergus and Angus knew the details of some local treasure, why wouldn't they get it themselves?"

"Maybe they don't know some critical piece of information," I suggested.

"That your ex or Knox happened to stumble upon?"

I paced briskly around the heather. It wasn't nearly as bouncy as I had been led to believe.

"I didn't say I had everything figured out," I said.

"It's possible," Lane said, "but only in the grand sense that anything is possible, which renders any such assumption meaningless. More importantly, it doesn't help us figure out who would want to kill your ex, or where any treasure is. You're making me nervous, hopping around like that. Do you want my sweater?"

"No, I'm fine."

We stood there in silence for a few moments. Trust no one, Rupert had said.

"There's one more thing," Lane said. "Even if the other holes in your theory don't turn out to be actual problems, why would Knox and your ex risk their plan to excavate some part of the cave while a legitimate dig is going on nearby? This is only a summertime stint. Later they'd have the place to themselves and not have to work on the dig at the same time."

"Impatience?"

Lane raised an eyebrow.

"What?" I said. "It's the *start* of a theory. I know there's more to figure out. I'm going to try to talk to Fergus and Angus again this evening. We need to look at the alcove and cave as well."

"Not until nightfall, we don't. We don't know who will be suspicious if we do it during the day. You okay?"

"I thought things were finally starting to make sense. Don't you get the feeling that there's something strange going on here?

Mr. and Mrs. Black sense it. Fergus and Angus do, too. God, the atmosphere is even getting to me. I don't want to tell you what I thought I saw on my walk over here."

"Don't worry," he said. "We'll figure it out."

The sun was almost overhead when we returned. I walked to the standing stone, careful with my steps around the sifted dirt. Now that some direct light was hitting the rock face, I could make out some of the carvings. They were definitely man-made, intentional markings.

Derwin knelt next to me and spoke. "Remarkable, isn't it?" His breath smelled sweet from the lingering aroma of a clove cigarette. He looked almost happy. "My research was key in helping Malcolm make this discovery."

"I'll be sure to get good photos," I said. "I liked what you said last night about making sure the easiest theory isn't the accepted one just because it's easy."

"Thank you," he said stiffly.

"Oh good," Malcolm said, coming up behind me. "You're showing her what she needs to photograph. The faded lines right here, with the arrows at the ends."

Malcolm's eyes lit up as he pointed at the markings. How could these Pictish scholars care about a treasure if they were enthralled by the prevalence of rectangles and arrows in carved stones?

"If our theory is right," Malcolm said, "we should find even more standing stones here, somewhere near the rock face." He gestured as he spoke, his arm sweeping over the dramatic cliff-size excavation with pride.

The sun was in what looked like a good position, so I retrieved the camera and tripod. The crew were huddled around Malcolm. Luckily they weren't paying any attention to me as I fussed with the strange camera equipment.

Almost as soon as I was done capturing the various angles I imagined a real photographer would have thought of, the sun was swallowed up by a patch of clouds. Derwin and Knox got to work attaching metal poles around the square of the pit. Fiona held a tarp. I moved out of the pit and Fiona laid the tarp down on the earth.

The makeshift tent was up by the time it began to rain. Under the tarp, we ate a lunch of cold sandwiches and tepid tea. We wore rain slickers, because although the six of us fit easily under the covering, the sea wind blew the rain in sideways.

The sun peeked through the clouds as we finished our sandwiches, though the rain continued to fall relentlessly. I was wondering if they would call it a day, but the rain stopped as suddenly as it had begun, less than thirty minutes after it had started. Malcolm stuck his head out of the tarp, and then stood up and walked into the soppy grass.

"It's through," Malcolm said. He laughed when he saw my expression. "It's in my blood. Though I was raised in England, I'm a Scot. I can feel the Scottish weather."

"It doesn't hurt that he and Derwin live in St. Andrews," Fiona said.

"Fiona keeps me down to earth," Malcolm said with a wink.

Once the tarps were cleared, the rest of the crew fell into place, including Lane, doing their part to sift the dirt and clear the area around the embedded stone. I announced that I was going to walk up to the Dunnottar Castle ruins since they didn't need me. Everyone was focused on the stone. They barely looked as I left.

Lane's warning be damned, I was going to check out the alcove cave. He was far too careful for his own good. We'd never figure anything out if we stuck to his suggestion of waiting until the crew were asleep.

I headed north toward the castle. Once I reached the main pathway along the cliff, I walked for a few minutes before spotting a path that branched off downwards toward the ocean. The path wove back and forth, keeping it from being dangerously steep. This looked like more of a main path than the one under the dig. After I walked through dirt, grass, and rock, I found myself on a small strip of sand. I could see the rocky cave not far down the beach. The site above wasn't visible.

I wrapped my rain jacket more closely around me for warmth as I headed for the cave. The sky was clear but the crashing waves sprayed up a cold mist. Black rocks dominated the landscape. Where the land met the edge of the ocean, a chunk of rock jutted out into the water. I looked up and saw the steep path that led up to the dig. If one of the crew decided to poke his or her head over the edge, they would see me. I picked up my pace, hurrying the last few yards to the cave.

The opening to the cave wasn't more than six feet tall and three feet wide. It would have looked man-made, except that the edges were rocky and jagged.

I froze as soon as I stepped inside. A flickering light shone ahead of me. I was not alone in the cave.

# CHAPTER 31

I didn't think I had made any noise. Even if I had, the echo of the sea was more powerful than the sound of my rubber-soled footsteps. But there was a problem with my shoes. The heel of my boots wouldn't even garner a mild yelp when they made contact with the top of a foot. If I was careful, I could back out of the cave without being heard. I fished through my bag, searching for something that could act as a weapon, if it came to that.

I still had Lane's Swiss army knife. In spite of its many gadgets, I doubted the blade was sharp enough to cut anything firmer than a slice of cheese. At least it was something. I opened the blade, firmly planting the base of the knife in my palm. As quietly as I could, I crept back the way I'd come.

My mind raced as I retraced my steps to the front of the cave. Whoever was in the cave must have taken the path from the dig to beat me there. But how had they gotten away from the rest of the crew?

Even though my heart was pounding and my hand sweating as I gripped the knife, I knew I'd regret it if I didn't see who was in the cave. I took a deep breath and stepped forward.

I rounded the corner of the cavern with knife in hand. There she was.

Not someone from the dig. Not a mysterious offstage villain who had tried to kill Rupert. Not even a group of drunken teenagers. It was the sea.

A small, second opening in the rock face hadn't been visible from above or via my approach. It wasn't as big as the one I had come through, but big enough to allow in natural light. The clouds above were blowing by so quickly that the sun poked out for only moments at a time, creating the effect of flickering light.

This second door-like gap opened up directly onto the ocean. Shoving the knife back into my bag with shaking hands, I stepped onto the rocks.

The view was stunning. The sea crashed before me, filling my nostrils with the scent of salt, and spraying droplets of foam onto my face. Not a soul was in view. I might have stayed there longer had it not been so bitterly cold.

I stepped back into the cavern and spotted the crushed beer cans Derwin had mentioned. They were rusted with age. It didn't look like any teenagers had been there in years. Why had he been worried?

Patches of dirt and weeds covered the cave floor. The room was damp from ocean spray and rain. I felt a sudden urge to sneeze. I stifled it, still wary of company. Although the sea had tricked me, she had reminded me to stay on guard. Unlike the calm sea of Goa, this was a fierce body of water. If I were to fall—or be thrown—into the deep water, I knew I would not set foot on land again.

The cave consisted of two rooms, if you could call them that. I pulled out my key-ring flashlight and magnifying glass, and examined the walls. It had been worth lugging the piece of glass around.

Passing the beam of light over the wall of the larger room, I saw that part of the rock formed a smooth, bench-like seat. No wonder underage kids liked this place. I looked back at the rusty beer cans strewn opposite the natural bench.

I sat down on the rock seat and leaned back. The vertical part wasn't as smooth, and a pointy rock kept me from leaning back.

But not before I noticed that the pointy rock moved.

I half expected someone to jump out from behind the rock. They didn't. The rock had moved under my weight.

I turned and shone my flashlight on the edges of the large boulder. Someone had placed the large rock there. I rolled the rock aside and pointed the beam of my flashlight inside the hole. The opening led upwards. It was impossible to tell how far it stretched, but it was clear that no one could fit into this hole and climb up. I shone the light upward. That's when I saw the marks.

Someone had been digging in the cave.

Moss covered the rock, making it clear where someone had hacked into it. For the next few minutes I searched the cave carefully with my flashlight and magnifying glass. There was no pattern to the digging except for that the marks were in hidden, out-of-the-way corners. After one last sweep with the beam of my flashlight, I rolled the rock back into place.

As I stepped out onto the sand, a flash of blinding light struck my eyes. The sensation was unnerving, like a camera flash had just gone off. But there wasn't anyone else around. It must have been my imagination. After all, the cave had been dark compared to the bright sky outside. My eyes adjusted quickly, and I hurried back to the main path. The castle ruins loomed ahead as I ran. I didn't stop running until I was back on high ground.


I found Fiona and Malcolm in a heated discussion, both too caught up to notice me.

"It's a beastie," Fiona was saying.

"No," Malcolm said, "it's a fish—"

"Just because we're on the coast doesn't mean—"

"Regardless, that's the least important part," Malcolm said. "The lines in between the images—they're new symbolic shapes to supplement the V and the Z rods! It's an entirely new addition to their alphabet."

Derwin and Knox were a short distance away, but the discussion pulled them closer. I didn't see Lane.

"Mmm," said Derwin. "I see what you mean, professor."

Fiona squinted at the stone.

"I'm really not sure," Knox said.

"You aren't a Pictish scholar," Derwin said.

"I can spot natural damage to a rock—"

"Jaya!" Malcolm said, noticing me at last. He tipped his hat to me in greeting. "You must document this before we cover it for the day. I know the light isn't perfect right now, but Fiona won't have time to make a proper sketch before tomorrow, and I want to be sure to capture this stage. We might even be able to get our best reading of the rocks through the photographs. Sometimes changing the contrast reveals hidden features not visible under natural light."

I photographed the newly uncovered section of the stone and was able to make out some of the shapes that Malcolm was talking about. In spite of the tarp, dirt had turned to mud in some of the carvings.

"Can someone clear this out?" I asked.

Knox was the closest. I was surprised it hadn't been Derwin. Knox brought a brush and started sweeping out the mud.

"Not that brush!" a voice bellowed. It was Malcolm, though I wouldn't have recognized his voice if I hadn't seen that it came from his mouth.

"You *idiot*, how many times have I gone over the procedure for using the proper instruments!"

"Sorry, professor," Knox mumbled, looking around for a proper brush.

The color that had flushed Malcolm's cheeks returned to normal. "It's important to never use inappropriate tools for our work," he explained calmly. "I make sure each of the tools I bring to a project is suited to its task, to preserve our findings."

Knox cleared the dirt with a brush that looked nearly identical to the previous one. I snapped a few photos. Lane reappeared as I was finishing.

"We have to talk," I whispered.

"Now?"

"That would be good."

He slipped his hand around my waist. Suddenly, I felt myself falling.

Together we fell into a sloppy mess of mud created by the afternoon's rainfall. There was a splash as we hit the ground.

"Nice one," Knox said. Fiona stood next to him, stifling a laugh.

"You all right?" Malcolm asked, jogging up to us.

"Do you require assistance?" Derwin asked from a distance.

"I'm fine," I said. I set about disentangling myself from Lane and the weeds.

"I think we need to go back to the inn to change, though," Lane added. "We're awfully wet."

# CHAPTER 32

"Did you really have to do that?" I asked.

Lane and I were back in our cramped room. He insisted on waiting until we were here, behind thick walls, to have our big talk.

"It gave us an excuse to disappear together," he said. "I'll wash your clothes if you want."

"Turn around," I said.

"Why? Oh."

He turned and faced the window, and I left my clothes in a heap on the floor and pulled on some new ones.

"Couldn't you have just said you couldn't resist temptation any longer, and were taking me back to the room to ravish me?" I pulled his arm to turn him back around.

"The thought did occur to me," he said. He stood so close I could feel his breath. He didn't have much choice in the few feet of free space.

"Hey," I said, pulling my gaze from his. "How come only your pants got dirty?"

"Trousers, you mean. These Brits will think you have a filthy mouth if you talk like that in public."

"Fine, your *trousers* are muddy. How did you manage to spare your jumper?"

"Very nice," he said, with the hint of a suppressed smile on his lips. "I was the one who planned the fall. Now what was so urgent that I had to get muddy?"

"Someone has been digging up the cave," I said.

"I thought you must have found something," Lane said. "You were gone quite a while."

I swore.

"What?"

"If you knew where I was going, then someone else might've noticed as well. Do you think anyone guessed what I was doing?"

"If one of them is our guy, I'm sure he suspected something," Lane said. "But our guy's got to be suspicious of us already, regardless of where you went this afternoon."

"Or girl," I pointed out. "Although you seem to have forgotten, Fiona is high up on our list of suspects. She knows something."

"Tell me about the cave."

I told him about the digging, ending with how I wanted to be back at the bar before the dig crew returned so I could talk with Fergus and Angus alone.

"Good idea," he said, "but you know you won't really be alone. Every bar has a bartender, and every bartender has ears and eyes."

"Mr. Black?" I said, astonished. "You can't possibly think he.... Can you?"

A smile spread across Lane's whole face. It lit up the mixture of colors in his hazel eyes, which at the moment picked up the green from his sweater.

"Why are you smiling?"

"The way your mind works," Lane said in a soft voice. "I didn't think.... You're so cynical about your profession and people, but...."

"But what?"

"You're innocent."

I stared at him. "Douglas Black is not a murderer. Not because I'm naïve—which I'm not. He has no motive. It's not in his character. I'm only being sensible. Logically, it doesn't add up—"

"If you were as hardened by the world as you pretend to be," he said, "you wouldn't believe in character. You'd suspect everyone."

"Right. Whatever. I have to go meet Fergus and Angus. I hope Mr. Black has some bar snacks I can eat before dinner." I paused in the doorway on my way out. "There's a travel-size packet of laundry detergent in the front pocket of my backpack. You can wash my clothes in the bathroom sink."

When I arrived downstairs, the pub was cold and deserted.

"Mr. Black?" I called out.

He emerged from the back, whistling an ethereal tune. I ordered a scotch and a bag of chips. He poured the Scotch and was kind enough to start a fire in the fireplace early. After I assured him I was fine, he left me with my drink and the salty snack.

I felt better once Mr. Black was gone. I didn't think he was involved in anything sinister, yet I hadn't completely dismissed what Lane had said.

I tapped out a raga with my fingers on the wooden bar. Not quite the same as my drums, but I do love the way different materials feel to my fingertips and the varied sounds they create. This bar here wasn't as resonant as the skins of my tabla, but I liked the gentle, earthy patter I heard when I closed my eyes. I was much calmer when Fergus and Angus came through the door shortly after five o'clock.

"The wee lass," Fergus said, stopping as soon as he came through the door.

"Miss Jones," said Angus. He scratched his beard and sauntered over to the bar.

"It's my turn to buy you a drink," I said.

"Ach, no," Angus said.

"Why not, Angus?" Fergus said. "She's nae the *bean nighe*. I looked it up."

"You looked it up?" I asked.

"On the *In-ter-net*," he said, enunciating the syllables. "Angus was right. She'll nae be appearin' at half five."

Douglas Black appeared at the bar. "Right on time." He chuckled and poured them drinks without waiting for an order.

I followed Fergus and Angus to a table, and waited until Mr. Black disappeared to the back before I spoke.

"I wanted to ask you about some of those local legends you mentioned," I said.

"Ach, my fayrie ring, Angus, she wants to hear. Ye've got to look fer the thorn trees—"

"You'd be meaning the Tuatha De?" Angus asked.

"You said the archaeologists were digging for the wrong thing," I said.

"You dunnae want to be stealin' the treasure o' the fayries," Fergus said. "They'll curse ye."

"I don't want to steal it," I said. "I want to know about it."

"She's a trustworthy one, Fergus."

"Ach, Angus, ye'd be blabbin' treasures to all the lasses if I'd let ye. Never keepin' yer yap shut. I suppose there's no harm in telling ye, as ye will nae find it."

"What do you mean?" I asked.

"Fayrie treasure must reveal itself to ye," Angus explained. "Ye cannae see what they dunnae want ye to see."

"Unless I'm one of them."

"Ach, did ye hear, Angus?" Fergus's gray eyes grew large and his eyebrows shot up.

"I was joking," I said, laughing. "I didn't think you still thought I was a fairy."

Angus was already chuckling.

"I dunnae ken," Fergus said, shaking his head.

"I can tell the lass," Angus said.

"I suspected it," Fergus grumbled. "First opportunity ye goes 'n blabs it."

"We told ye about the Tuatha de Danann," Angus said, "who came from the clouds before the Picts 'n all the rest o' the inhabitants o' Scotland 'n Ireland."

I nodded.

"Lug's Spear is buried 'round these parts."

"Lug's Spear?"

"He who held it could not be defeated in battle."

"Ye left out the bits about the battle," Fergus said, his eyes widening wildly under his bushy eyebrows as if he was about to go into battle himself.

"Doesnae matter, Fergus."

"Ach."

"Where is it?" I asked.

"Ye cannae see it!" Fergus cried out in exasperation. "Only a fayrie—"

"If I could."

"If ye could," Fergus said, "ye wouldnae need to ask. But I'll tell ye, because ye cannae."

The ragged skin on his nose gave a twitch. His wild eyes darted around the room. Satisfied that we were alone, he spoke three words: "In the sea."

Out of nowhere, a burst of cold sea air whipped around us. Safely tucked inside the cozy pub, it was as if the phantom wind had appeared in response to the revelation. The fire flared up and crackled violently.

Angus was the only one who kept his head. Fergus' large white brows raised higher on his forehead in horror than when he first saw me. His wrinkled hands gripped the arms of his chair. I jumped in my seat, wondering if I might see anything appear out of the angrily hissing fire. Angus turned his head calmly toward the door.

"Ach," he said, shaking his head. "They dunnae ken to wait until the wind has passed before openin' the door."

"Sorry about that," Malcolm called out from the doorway. "I didn't expect such a big gust to follow me in."

# CHAPTER 33

The crew had packed up early because of the fierce winds, leaving the stone in the ground with a tarp they hoped would hold. In spite of the interruption, I now knew enough to realize why Mrs. Black heard late-night creaking. I knew why someone would be carrying out digging in the cave *at the edge of the sea*.

None of us were in a good mood that night. I doubted it was because of the overly salted bangers and mash. Fiona flirted with Lane, upsetting Knox, who in turn reacted by ordering pint after pint of beer, ignoring Malcolm's disapproving eye. Derwin ate even less than the night before, watching Malcolm pay more attention to Knox than to him.

As soon as plates were cleared, the crew went their separate ways. Malcolm and Derwin set out a series of notebooks to write up the day's work. Lane stood up to go outside for a smoke. Fiona followed. Knox headed for the bar and asked for a pint.

"You doing okay, Knox?" I asked, seizing my chance to talk with him alone.

"His dad didn't even tell me about the funeral, you know," he said. "Heard afterwards that it was a small private ceremony for the family. Since they didn't have his...you know, since they didn't find him." He wiped the back of his hand across his eyes. "I don't know what to do," he whispered.

"I can help."

"I'm not sure," Knox began softly, "about his accident."

I sat up straight and looked around. Nobody was paying attention to us. People never seemed to pay attention to Knox.

"What about it?" I asked.

"It's just...." He took a seemingly endless drink from his glass. When he set it down, the glass was empty.

He put his hand on my shoulder.

"You were good for him," he said.

"I don't know about that."

"You were. If you'd stuck around, I don't know if he'd have—"

"What?"

He shook his head. "Never mind. It doesn't matter now, does it?"

"It does."

"Well...."

The door of the pub creaked open and Fiona stepped inside.

"Knox," she said. "Fancy a pint?"

She shot me a glare of supernatural strength from her translucent eyes. If I'd been a more self-conscious woman I would have fled the room. Or at the very least, blushed. I did neither.

"Never mind," Knox said. "It was nothing."

Fiona linked her arm around Knox's. The two of them left the inn, the sound of a car engine following their departure. Apparently partaking in another pint would happen elsewhere. Damn.

Back in my room, I threw myself down on the bed. The clothes Lane had muddied were now clean and hanging to dry on the bureau. I stared up at the slanted ceiling, listening to gusts of wind and wondering when I'd have another chance to talk to Knox alone.

I rolled onto my stomach and sorted through my bag, looking for my cell phone. There were no messages on it. I threw it back in the bag. The door opened as the phone was in midair.

"Your ex still hasn't called?" Lane asked.

"My ex has a name. And no, Rupert hasn't called."

As curious as I was about what Rupert was doing, at this point I was more worried about his health. It had been too long since I'd heard from him. Had he made it to wherever he was heading? I pushed the thought out of my mind.

"We need to stake out the dig tonight," I said, sitting up and resting on my elbows. "I know there's a storm coming. I'm prepared."

"What did Angus and Fergus tell you?"

"Enough to suspect something," I said, "but not enough to know. They believe in these gods who supposedly came out of the clouds."

"The Tuatha de Danann?" Lane asked. He sat down on the opposite end of the bed, nearly brushing his head against the sloped ceiling.

"Do you really have to know absolutely everything?"

"I overheard part of your conversation," he said. "That first night in the pub."

"You have a remarkable talent for eavesdropping."

"I'm not sure if you mean that as a compliment. I didn't hear you tonight. What did they tell you?"

I told Lane about Lug's Spear, of the legend where the holder of the spear was guaranteed victory, and how Fergus and Angus thought it was in the sea around here.

Lane nodded. "You think it could be by the sea or at the sea, like the cave in the alcove."

"At least some spear that a real group of invaders did use, that would be attributed to this legend and thus considered a treasure. Hey, do you think this guy Lug is where the expression 'big lug' came from? If the real Lug was a really big guy, that would explain why he could never be defeated in battle."

"I like it," said Lane.

"You agree it sounds like we're finally onto something?"

"No."

"No?"

"You think your ex and Knox managed to find a specific enough reference without Angus and Fergus, leading them to the cave. But not specific enough to find it easily, so they're digging *by the sea.*"

"What's the matter with that theory?"

"Nothing," Lane said. "Absolutely nothing."

"Then what—?"

"It doesn't fit."

"You're stuck on your precious Rajasthan Rubies," I said. "I'm sorry you had to follow me all the way here on a wild goose chase from your point of view, but there's no sense in being stubborn when the evidence takes us elsewhere."

"Does it?"

"Of course it does. Haven't you been paying attention? Wait, why are you looking at me like that? You know something else!"

"Sort of."

I stared at him in disbelief.

"Why didn't you tell me?"

"I'm trying to."

Lane crouched down. I initially thought he was trying to avoid bumping his head on the slanted ceiling, but he remained kneeling on the floor.

"Hold on," he said. I felt the bed yank under me. "Look."

I looked over the side of the bed and saw what he was talking about.

The floorboards were as solid as they were everywhere else in the building, but directly behind one of the bedposts, where the floor and the wall joined, a crack was visible. I got up and looked more closely. It wasn't only a crack, but a crevice with room to put something inside of it.

"You realize," Lane said, "that this must have been your ex's room."

"I already thought of that, since it's the only one that was left. But since he's not really dead, he would have come back to get anything important he left behind. I know him. He would have risked it."

"He wasn't very thorough," Lane said. "While you were downstairs talking with Fergus and Angus, I searched the room. I found his hiding place."

"He left something inside?"

"Not on purpose. But look." He pointed to a small chunk of gold covered in dirt. "It would have been a tight fit to hide a thick bracelet. A piece broke off."

"He felt the need to hide it," I said.

"Meaning this treasure is the one that had to do with someone trying to kill him."

"What about the digging at the cave?" I asked.

Lane rummaged through his bag. He pulled out something that looked like a tiny tube of hair gel from a small bag of toiletries. I was about to roll my eyes in exasperation—although he did have very nice hair—when he moved not to the mirror but to the door frame. Taking off the cap, he stood, held it up to the top hinge of the door, and squeezed out a few drops.

"You've heard the doors creaking," he said. "We don't want to alert anyone when we go find out."

# CHAPTER 34

I wasn't cut out for Scottish weather. Bundled in three layers of clothing, I shivered as we stood inside the cave. The storm hadn't yet materialized, but strong winds toyed with the clouds. A large moon hovered above us, lighting up the coast. At first this seemed fortunate, because it meant we could see better. Then we realized it also meant someone approaching wouldn't need a flashlight. They would be more difficult to spot. The crashing waves would also drown out the sound of approaching footsteps. Lane and I had to pay close attention.

Earlier that night I'd asked Douglas Black for a flask of whisky. I helped myself to it in an attempt to take the edge off.

"You do realize that doesn't actually make your body any warmer," Lane whispered.

"I thought summer in San Francisco was cold," I whispered back through chattering teeth, slipping the flask back into my bag. "I don't think my body temperature ever adjusted to leaving Goa."

Lane's face was partially hidden in shadow from our concealed position, but my eyes had adjusted and I could see him clearly. Our eyes met.

"This will work better," he said, unbuttoning his coat.

He pulled me toward him, but in a way that was completely different than I imagined—rather, completely differently than I would have imagined if I had imagined any such thing. Which I certainly hadn't.

He spun me around and pulled me backwards against the open coat so that my back rested against the sweater on his chest. He wrapped the coat around me, and his arms curled around my midsection. His chin rested on top of my head.

"You should feel warmer in a minute," he said quietly.

His breath was warm against my hair. We stood in silence, looking out at the sand and the sea. I never saw a thing before I heard the noise.

I had been paying attention. I truly had been. I didn't see anyone approaching from the stretch of shore in front of us. The noise came from behind.

Lane heard it, too. He let go of me instantly. The motion was so quick that I nearly lost my balance. He hurried around the corner and vanished into the back of the cave. I rushed after him. When I got there, Lane was already on his way through the back opening of the cavern.

I heard him swear above the sound of the crashing waves. His voice was faint in the midst of the other sounds at the water's edge. I didn't think he would rush headlong into darkness without knowing what was beyond. But if he'd acted without thinking....

I climbed through the hole. I expected to find Lane at the same lookout point. But he was nowhere to be seen.

I scrambled to the edge, fearing he had been swept out to sea. There was no sign of him. The sea was pitch black under the night sky, and the waves pounded fiercely. He could have been right below me but I wouldn't be able to see or hear him.

I was about to call out when he appeared.

"There's a hidden path," he said, stepping onto the rock from what I had thought was a sheer drop below it.

"But—"

"It blends into the rock face," he said, "before it hits the coast on the other side. There's no way you could have seen it when you were exploring before."

"How did you find it then?"

Lane didn't answer. Instead, he took my hand and pulled me sharply away from the edge, into the small opening and back into the cave.

"I thought I saw—" he began, but then stopped. He stood looking out through the jagged rock opening.

"You thought you saw *who*?"

"Not *who*," Lane said. "*What*."

I could barely make out his face in the shadow of the cave, but his voice was slightly unsteady. He shook it off with a forced laugh.

"The stories of the locals must be getting to me," he said, shaking his head. "And this Gothic setting. At the base of a cliff in the moonlight with the crashing waves...it's ridiculous, really. I saw a person running away. That's all. Whoever our mysterious cave digger is."

"But what did you *think* you saw?"

"The figure. It was small and pale. Almost familiar." He shook his head. "For a second, I thought it was the *bean nighe*."

I almost laughed. One look at Lane's face and I thought better of it. Instead I did what I should have done in the first place. I broke into a run. Lane followed.

In the darkness, the seaside path was too dark to follow. We hurried along the main path, hoping we might reach the top of the cliff with him—or her? or it?—in sight.

We scrambled up the steep path. Once we reached high ground, we kept up our pace for a few minutes. But the landscape was empty. Whoever had been there was gone.


We let ourselves into the inn. I insisted on waiting downstairs with the weak hope that the person had taken a roundabout way back to their lodgings—if these were indeed their lodgings. We decided the best place to wait would be the middle of the stairs, where we would be hidden from both the upstairs rooms and the main door, but could see and hear both.

"Why didn't we think of doing this in the first place?" Lane whispered after several minutes of silent waiting.

"People could be doing all sorts of things in the night."

"Let's go," he said. "We didn't beat him back here."

"Whoever it was didn't necessarily beat us back here," I said once we were safely inside the room. "We were assuming it was someone on the dig. But Rupert said he was going to go after the treasure, too."

Lane swore under his breath.

"This whole thing is a complete farce," he said.

"I thought he was too injured to do much of anything," I said, "but if he was doing better, he could be here."

"And not contacting you?" Lane tore off his jacket angrily, and instinctively reached for his pack of cigarettes. "I don't know how you could have ever been involved with such a—"

"What?"

"No one should be able to do that to you."

"No one has *done* anything to me," I said crossly. "I can handle myself."

Lane threw down his cigarettes and scooped me up in his arms. "Jones," he said, "I know you can. What I wonder is if you can handle me, too." He lifted me onto my tiptoes before tilting my head back and enveloping me in a kiss.

I wasn't sure if my feet left the ground or if it only felt as if they did. He lowered me onto the small, lumpy bed. At that moment, nothing had ever felt so soft.

My head hit my bag, so I pushed it over—right as my phone buzzed in my ear. I'd turned the ringer to vibrate while we were on our stakeout, but next to my ear the noise was jarring. Lane swore under his breath and let go of me.

"You better get it," he said. "It might finally be your ex."

"Sanjay," I said into the receiver, out of breath from Lane's kiss. "Now isn't really a good time." A light on my phone was blinking, indicating other messages. "Sorry I didn't call you back earlier."

"I never should have let you go on your own," Sanjay said.

Lane frowned as he watched me. From the volume of Sanjay's voice, Lane could hear him.

"He's not—" I began to whisper to Lane with my hand over the receiver.

"Are you talking to someone else?" Sanjay asked. "Isn't it almost midnight there?"

"Television."

Lane gave me a sharp look before slipping out of the room. Great. Lane was jealous of Sanjay, the person who was more like a brother than my own brother.

"Was that a door slamming?" Sanjay asked. "What's going on over there?"

I was alone and wide awake in the closet-size room, so I took the time to fill in Sanjay about what was going on with Rupert not being killed after all, and everything going on at the dig and the inn. Well, not quite everything. But I hoped Sanjay might catch something I was missing. He was good at that sort of thing.

"It sounds like you need to force Knox to tell you what he knows," Sanjay said.

"That's what I was thinking, but it's not easy to get him alone."

Sanjay grumbled something under his breath. "You don't want him alone. He might have tried to kill his friend, remember? You need him to give you information in a way that isn't dangerous. Is he in his own room, or with his girlfriend?"

"His own room."

"That's easy, then. Leave him a note under his door. Tell him you know what's going on and he better stay late after breakfast to talk to you if he knows what's good for him. The innkeepers will be there. You'll be safe."

In spite of Sanjay's melodramatic framing, his suggestion was better than any of the ideas I'd had that day. After I hung up with Sanjay, I slipped a note under Knox's door.

\* \* \*

When I woke up in the morning after a fitful night's sleep, I was alone. My cell phone light was still blinking. I was about to delete the messages, since I was sure they were from Sanjay, when I saw that two new phone numbers also appeared on my call log, both from the UK. My body tensed. How could I have been so stupid to assume all my missed calls were from Sanjay?

"Christ, Jaya," Rupert's voicemail began. "Don't you ever answer your bloody phone? I didn't want to tell you this in a message, but since you're not picking up, you've got to believe what I'm going to tell you. I'm so sorry to have gotten you involved in this, love. You have to get out of there. You're in danger. Lane is one of them."

# CHAPTER 35

I shivered with panic as I listened to the rest of Rupert's message.

"I'm sorry I didn't listen to you about that burglary," he continued. "I know I said it couldn't be related to all this. I was wrong. But I couldn't have known, could I? Forget about keeping an eye on that lot for me. I don't care if you hate me, but do it later. I can be back in London in a day or so, and I can meet up with you then if you're still speaking to me. For Christ's sake, get away from him."

This could not be happening.

It absolutely *could not* be happening.

Lane couldn't be one of them—whoever "they" turned out to be. It didn't make any sense. I had been the one who approached *him*. I couldn't believe that he would do anything to hurt me. Especially after that kiss.

Yet at the same time I didn't believe Rupert would be cruel enough to make something like that up. He was manipulative sometimes, yes, but he had his limits. At least, he always had with me.

I couldn't bear to listen to the message again. I looked at the call log. The call had come in after I turned my ringer off while Lane and I were hiking out to the cave.

Even if I believed he would stoop so low, the calls couldn't have been a reaction to Rupert being at the cave and having seen Lane and me together. This was no jealous reaction. He believed what he was telling me.

There was another message on my phone. After the news in the first message, I didn't think I wanted to hear what I'd learn in the next one.

I cursed my sound sleeping when I saw that the call had arrived this morning. But this news wasn't bad. A library assistant at the British Library was calling to inform me that they had found information pertaining to my query. The documents were waiting for me, but they could only keep the hold until closing that day since it was so busy that summer. The connection was fuzzy, so I listened to the message a second time to make sure I'd heard everything.

That was my out. I was almost a full day's drive from London, but who the hell cared. I didn't know if I needed anything else from the British Library, but I definitely needed to get out of the Fog & Thistle Inn and think. I think well when I'm driving. Especially if it's a Jaguar.

I hesitated briefly before gathering my things. I'd left that note under Knox's door. There was no way to get it back before he saw it. But at that moment, I didn't care. All I knew was that I had to leave that inn.

Reaching for my sweater, I accidentally picked up one of Lane's shirts along with it. The scent of cigarette smoke triggered something in my mind. When I had searched Fiona's room, I had smelled cigarette smoke. There hadn't been any smoker's paraphernalia in her room, though. Because Fiona didn't smoke.

Knox didn't smoke either. Derwin was the only smoker of that group, and he smoked those distinctly scented cloves. So Lane had been spending time in Fiona's room. Either he was up to no good like Rupert's message had said, or he had another type of interest in Fiona. I didn't like either scenario.

I dropped Lane's shirt and rushed downstairs, my head spinning.

Malcolm, Derwin, and Lane sat at a table in the pub, drinking tea and eating sausages and eggs.

"I'm sorry," I said to no one in particular, "but something has come up and I need to go out of town for a day or so."

"Lane didn't mention—" Malcolm said.

"He doesn't know yet."

"I spoke with my brother," I lied with the first thing I could think of, "and one of my cousins is visiting England from India. It would be terribly rude of me if I didn't see him while he was here."

"Oh," Lane said, standing up. "I'll go pack—"

"He's very old-fashioned," I said. "I'm afraid he wouldn't approve of you. I'm going to take the car."

Malcolm opened his mouth.

"I'll be back as soon as I can to finish up the photography," I said.

Mrs. Black emerged from the back with a plate of kippers.

"Pull up a seat!" she said.

"Sorry," I said. "I'm afraid I've got to get going." I pushed open the door.

"Trouble in paradise, eh?" I heard Derwin ask Lane. Before Lane could answer, the door shut.

I didn't care what my excuse sounded like. My thoughts blurred into the background as I shifted gears and accelerated the Jaguar onto the highway headed to London.

I turned up the car stereo loudly, trying to blast out every thought from my mind. It ended up giving me a headache instead. My temples throbbed as I hit the clutch and the gas, but the ache was better than being alone with my thoughts.

I stopped in Perth for gas and some lunch. My plan was to console myself with pre-packaged sandwiches, heavy on the mayonnaise, but when I got to the supermarket, all the food only made me think of Rupert and Lane. I passed the wine section and thought about what Rupert would have picked out for a dinner party. Going through the produce aisle, I wondered what Lane would have bought to cook. Or did he even cook? Maybe he was lying about that, too. I left the supermarket and picked up a kebab instead.

Back in the car I threw my bag onto the passenger seat. The contents spilled onto the seat and the floor. My old phone tumbled under the seat. My cell phone. The realization hit me that I hadn't gotten the new number until *after* I had been to the British Library for assistance.

I had told Jeremy that I would check in with him directly, as I had later that day. There was no way anyone at the British Library could have known my number. *Only Rupert and the people at the inn would have access to the new number.*

One of them had set me up.

I reached Jeremy right away. "Sorry I haven't been able to narrow down your search yet," he said.

"That's not why I'm calling." I told him about my voicemail.

"That's impossible," he said. "You were working with *me*. It's crazy here this summer. I'd like to see you back, so I've got your project on my list to look into. But I most certainly did not ask any underlings to call you on my behalf. Why would I?"

I think Jeremy liked to hear himself talk. He had a beautiful voice, but I didn't have the energy to listen endlessly. "I believe you, Jeremy," I said. "I didn't even give you this phone number, remember? It must have been an impostor."

Jeremy didn't reply for a moment. "Who would want to impersonate a librarian?"

"That's the question."

After assuring Jeremy that he didn't have to worry about librarian fraud on a grand scale, I turned the car back around. Biting into my kebab, I headed back toward Aberdeenshire. I had no idea what was going on, but I was going to find out.

I would have made it back by the late afternoon except I was so upset that I turned onto the wrong road and spent some time being lost. It was early evening by the time I turned into the parking lot in front of the Fog & Thistle Inn.

I eased the Jaguar into the dirt lot in front of the inn, knowing I had no choice but to confront Lane. I hadn't worked out what exactly to say, and I didn't have a chance to. All my half-formed ideas vanished when I saw what was up ahead.

I pulled up next to a police car.

# CHAPTER 36

As I came through the door, my ears were assaulted by raised voices. Fergus and Angus were gathered with the crew, as were Mr. and Mrs. Black. A young police officer with a bright red face was trying to keep order, but everyone was talking at once. Knox and Fiona held hands and spoke excitedly to the policeman. Mr. Black's boisterous voice joined in. Mrs. Black wrung her hands. Fergus ranted and gesticulated to no one in particular. Angus shook his head and mumbled what I assumed were meant to be soothing words. Malcolm, in his attempts at calming the group, was shouting himself hoarse. The group fell silent when they saw me.

It was Derwin who broke the silence. "Your gentleman friend has evidently been up to no good," he said. A smug expression seeped across his face.

"Ye know Mr. Peters, miss?" The young officer asked me. I realized that Lane was the only person missing. This was really happening. Rupert's message had been true.

"Is he all right?" I asked. "Where is he?"

"Up in 'is room, with Constable Kincade."

I headed up the stairs.

"Hang on a moment, miss!" he called, but before he could follow, chaos had broken out again, and the group demanded his complete attention.

The door to the room I had been sharing with Lane stood open, and a second police officer, one who didn't look quite as young or as red-faced as the first, searched the room. Lane sat handcuffed to the radiator.

"What are you doing?" I asked, entering the room.

"Please step back, miss," he said. "Who might you be?"

"This is my room," I said. "What's going on?"

"He's a thief who nicked some jewels from an important gent," the police officer answered for him, and went back to searching the room.

I watched the officer for a few stunned moments without speaking. Of all the things Lane could have done, that was the one thing he couldn't possibly have been involved in.

Lane looked pleadingly at me. His face was pale.

"We don't have any jewels," I said. "You won't find what you're looking for." The ruby bracelet was safely tucked away in my safe deposit box. Wasn't it?

"He's got a picture of stolen property, miss, and the word of the gent he stole from."

"This has got to be a mistake," I said. "Who called you?"

"That's police business. Now if you could please follow us down to the station, miss."

"Am I in any sort of trouble?"

"There was no mention of you, miss. But we'll be wantin' to talk with you as well."

The police station was several miles away. Dusk fell as we wended our way through the small roads leading to the village. The station was small and the jail even smaller.

I paced in the waiting room for half an hour before the younger officer told me I was free to talk with Lane. He led me back to where they were holding Lane, in a clean, windowless stone cell, and left. It was difficult to believe my surroundings. How had I ended up outside a jail cell in a foreign country, looking through the bars at a man who had kissed me so passionately the previous night?

"What the hell is going on?" I asked.

"I was hoping you could tell me." His voice was steady, but it was a forced calmness. His hands were less steady. I saw the quiver of the cigarette he held.

"Why aren't they interrogating you?" I asked.

"They tried for a few minutes," Lane said. "I told them I didn't know anything. The younger one, Brown, convinced Kincade to let you talk to me. They didn't know what else to do with me. I bet these two haven't seen anything worse than a bar fight."

"Who called the police? Do you think it was really the person Rupert stole the bracelet from? But how would they even know we had it?"

He shook his head, taking a drag of his cigarette and not meeting my gaze. "They wouldn't tell me anything. It doesn't make any sense. Unless...."

"What's the matter with you, Lane?"

"In case you hadn't noticed," he snapped, "I'm in jail."

"I know they're saying you're a jewel thief, but there's no way they can prove you stole something you don't have. It'll be straightened out in the morning."

"That's not it."

"What then?"

"Jones," he said softly, "what happened this morning? And last night? Why didn't you tell me that you had a—"

"Sanjay isn't my boyfriend. But I can't imagine why that matters now. This morning I got a phone call from Rupert. He told me."

"Told you *what*? Let me guess. He wants to get back together with you, so all of a sudden it's meaningless what we—"

"It has nothing to do with that," I snapped back.

"Then please tell me what you're talking about."

"He told me that you're involved," I said. "With *them*. The bad guys. The burglary at my apartment. You're why I'm in danger."

He kicked the bench in the cell. "That's why you ran off this morning."

"He wouldn't make up something like that," I said.

Lane breathed deeply, trying to steady his voice. "I don't know what your ex's motives are," he said with a forced calmness, "but I swear to you I don't know what's going on any more than you do."

"Why have you been sneaking around with Fiona?" I blurted.

A shadow passed over his face for a fraction of a second before he answered. "She's the only one who won't talk to you," he said. "I was trying to get information. She knows as much as Knox about this secret plan of theirs. You know, you two would really be great friends if you didn't hate each other."

"Gee, thanks for being so *helpful.*"

"It doesn't look like you've figured out any more than I have." He spat out the words, but I heard the shakiness in his voice.

"Maybe I have," I said, "if I believe Rupert."

"Jaya, I swear to you."

I searched his eyes, trying to find the truth. "What am I supposed to think?"

"I would never hurt you."

It wasn't the words. Or even the way he said them. It was the way he looked at me. I saw it with frightening clarity. A jail was a strange place to feel safe, but I knew Lane would never harm me. I felt he would, in fact, do everything in his power to make sure nobody else did.

"I know," I said.

"I need you to trust me."

"God help me," I said, "but I do."

"I need you to get me out of here," he said, flicking out his cigarette and bringing his hands up to the bars that separated us.

"You mean *tonight?*"

He nodded. "They think I stole the jewels."

"So what?" I said. "It's just some stupid ploy. The evidence will wash out by morning, and then they'll let you go. They can't hold you indefinitely. I mean, come on, it's not like you're some internationally famous jewel thief."

"That's the thing," Lane said. "I am."

# CHAPTER 37

"I'm not *anymore*," Lane said. "I swear to you, I wasn't lying when I said I have nothing to do with this situation."

I took him in, my eyes not wavering from his. My pulse quickened as the pieces clicked together in my mind.

"The overly complex tools on your knife I used as a lock pick," I said. "Knowing to figure out Mrs. Black's schedule. Thinking to check the floorboards. Realizing the significance of my burglary even before you knew what I did. Even your hair gel that fixes creaky doors."

He nodded slowly.

"Jaya, you have to believe me. It's all in the past—"

"*What*—I mean *how*?" I didn't know how to complete any of my thoughts. There was too much I wanted to say next.

"I promise I'll tell you everything once I'm out of here," Lane said. "But I have to get out of here *tonight*. They wouldn't have my prints here in the UK, but there was a little incident on the Continent. I'm not sure if they actually got my prints, but in case they did....These night shift guys don't know what to do with me, but the day shift might think to run things by Interpol."

"This is why you were so suspicious of me when we met!"

"But I didn't stick with my skepticism, in spite of my better judgment. The problem was I had the exact opposite feeling. I knew I could trust you."

"You really don't have anything to do with any of this?"

"I swear, Jaya."

In spite of my better judgment, I knew what I had to do. After a last look at Lane, I headed to the front of the police station. I took a deep breath, strode up to the front desk with confidence, and hoped my plan would work.

"You realize who he is, don't you?" I said to Constable Brown.

"Uh...Mr. Peters?" he answered, confused.

"You do realize what an important person he is back in the States."

"He is?" Constable Brown said.

"What's this, Ben?" said Constable Kincade, emerging from the next room with a cup of coffee in his hand.

"The young miss, she ah, was tellin' me about Mr. Peters."

Constable Kincade looked at me. "What's this?"

"This is a false charge," I said, "made up against Mr. Peters because he's a prominent individual. There's no evidence against him whatsoever. If you would check into the evidence, we could straighten this out tonight. If you keep an innocent American in jail overnight just because you fail to check up on the facts, the consequences will not be pleasant."

Constable Kincade was not impressed.

"We local constables aren't as daft as Sherlock Holmes mysteries on the telly would have ye believe."

"Of course not," I said. "Which is exactly why I know you'll do the right thing. Mr. Peters didn't do anything wrong, and there are people out to accuse him."

"Who's accusin' him?" the wide-eyed Constable Brown asked.

"Only the victim," Constable Kincade answered firmly.

"The accusation is completely false," I said. "If you could take a few minutes to check into it...."

"I've been very courteous under the circumstances—"

"Ach, better safe than sorry, eh, Nick?" Constable Brown cut in with a grin. "I could phone Sir Edward Gregor, followin' up on the fax he sent to tell us about the theft. It's early yet."

"Gregor?" I said.

"You know him?"

"Gregor, like that nearby estate?"

"Same family, yes," Constable Brown said.

"Wait here," Constable Kincade said.

I sat in a small waiting area, generously supplied with tea bags and hot water, and I took advantage of the hot beverage as I waited.

Two cups of tea later, the policemen came to greet me together.

"Sorry for the mix-up," Constable Kincade said solemnly. "Please accept our apologies."

"It was a hoax!" said Constable Brown. "The fax of the jewelry appraisal wasn't really from the owner!"

"We don't usually get false allegations of this kind 'round here," Constable Kincade added. "We had no reason to doubt the information. Well then." He cleared his throat. "I'll go release Mr. Peters." He left the room hastily, leaving me with the grinning Constable Brown.

"Who falsely accused him?" I asked Constable Brown once the superior officer was out of earshot.

"Someone here in the Grampians," he said happily. "I spotted the number on the top o' the fax. It wasn't from London, where Sir Edward Gregor lives. It was a local phone code."

"Sir Edward Gregor lives in London? Not here?"

"Nobody *lives* in those old family tourist centers. The current Sir Edward Gregor lives in London. He's Sir Edward, so we weren't going to ignore it, were we?"

"Thank you for following up tonight."

He smiled back at me and poured himself a cup of tea.

"Hope he's not too upset 'bout us bringin' him in."

"I'm sure he'll be fine," I said, smiling back at him. "Like I said, he's used to this kind of thing, being so famous and all."

"Ach, o'course."

"I'm still confused about this allegation, though," I said. "What did it say?"

"We were faxed an appraisal of Sir Edward's fancy jewelry," Constable Brown said. "The jewelry looked like it was from the same set as the one in the photo we found in Mr. Peters' possession. But it wasn't really Sir Edward Gregor who faxed us. We spoke with him. He still 'as his necklace. It wasn't even stolen by anyone."

"*Necklace*?" That wasn't what I was expecting. That meant there was another piece from the treasure out there somewhere. "Could I see the fax?"

Constable Kincade walked into the room and interrupted. "Mr. Peters is waiting outside for you," he said. "Work to do, Ben. Good evening, Miss Jones."

Dark had descended completely while we were inside. The night air was crisp. Clouds flitted across the night sky. The weather in Scotland was very good at obliging my mood. Lane stood in the shadows, away from the light in front of the police station.

"You're amazing," Lane said. He moved his hand as if he was about to grab mine. I moved away from him to avoid the touch and walked toward the car.

"The car is this way," I said. "I need full concentration to drive on the left side of the road at night. No more talking until we get out of here. Then you can tell me everything." My voice was steady. The emotions bubbling inside me weren't.

"You're not going back to the inn, are you?"

"No. I don't know where we're going yet. Somewhere away from here."

My mind raced as I drove through the night. I'm sure my driving matched the speed of my thoughts but Lane obliged me by not saying a word. An idea was forming in my mind. It almost fit. A member of the Gregor family had a piece of the treasure, but not the whole thing. Pictish standing stones and a Pictish archaeological dig were close to the Gregor Estate, which was built by a man who made his fortune during the time of the British Empire in India. Something connected the Pictish dig and the Rajasthan Rubies to the Gregor family.

I drove to the empty parking lot of the nearby Dunnottar Castle ruins. The ruins can only be accessed on foot, via the steep path that leads down to sea level and then back up the sea-bound cliff to the fortress.

The parking lot is across the abyss, giving a view of the castle in all its ruinous glory atop the treacherous cliffs overlooking the ocean. In the faint moonlight, the stones appeared as a black silhouette in front of the sea.

I pulled into the dirt lot, with the sliver of moon high above the ruins. I put the car into park and turned to face Lane, looking at the now-familiar shadows beneath his smooth hair on his angular face.

I reached over and pulled him toward me, kissing him deeply. His lips were cold and smoky. And more than anything, wonderful. He didn't resist or question me. His tension melted away as the powerful kiss lingered.

My phone buzzed. Lane pulled away.

It was a text message from Sanjay. *You okay? Did it work?*

I couldn't believe that less than twenty-four hours had passed since he suggested I leave a note under Knox's door. A note that I hadn't yet been able to follow up on.

"My friend has the worst timing," I said. "One second."

*Worked great,* I typed back. *All is well!* No sense in worrying Sanjay for no reason.

"Are you sure he's just a friend?" Lane asked.

"Sanjay?" I laughed at the ridiculous idea that Sanjay was anything other than like a brother to me. "Yes."

I threw my phone back into my bag.

"It's time for you to tell me what you were talking about at the police station," I said.

"I know," he said. "I owe you an explanation."

With the dramatic castle as a backdrop, a small night animal scampered across the field, too small to spook me into thinking it was my *bean nighe* fairy.

The *bean nighe*. The spirit of a dark-haired young woman who died in childbirth.

The answer clicked into place.

It was so simple. The British East India Company was the key all along. Just not in the way I thought it was.

"Jaya?" Lane said. "Are you listening to me?"

"I've got it," I said. "I know what this is all about."

Lane might be up to no good. But I also knew I was safe with him. And that I wanted to be there with him. That was enough. I had a million questions, but there would be time for him to answer them later. We had something more pressing to attend to.

"I trust you," I said. "I need you to trust me now."

# CHAPTER 38

I started the car and pulled onto the small road leading to the inn for the second time that evening. I hoped Fergus and Angus hadn't already started on their walk back home.

"What are you doing?" Lane asked. "It looks like you're headed back to the inn."

"That's exactly what I'm doing. I need to ask Fergus and Angus one question. Then I'll know if I'm right."

"You can't be serious."

"Don't worry, I don't think this is about Lug's Spear instead of your Indian treasure. You were right."

"That's not what I'm getting at," Lane said. "You can't expect me to walk in there. Someone set me up for a reason. It'll be better if they don't know I'm out of jail. I don't know that it's such a great idea for you to go back in there, either."

I swore.

"Pull over," Lane said.

"We're not close enough to the inn yet," I said. "I'll leave you with the car, but I'm still going back in. I have to ask them—"

"No, that's not what I meant. Look."

Sure enough, at a slight bend in the road the headlights bounced off Fergus and Angus, who were walking down the side of the road.

I pulled over and turned to Lane. "You don't think Fergus and Angus are involved, do you?"

"Well, it's too late anyway." He pointed. "They've seen us."

I stepped out of the car. With the headlights off, the night was dark. Fergus and Angus walked without a flashlight. Without heavy coats either. Lane leaned up against the car and lit a cigarette as Fergus and Angus approached. He glanced at me with an inquisitive look, but didn't speak. My eyes adjusted to the faint moonlight as the two dark figures drew near.

"Break out then, did ye?" Fergus said to Lane with a crooked smile as the two men reached us.

"Ye dunnae say," Angus said. He took his pipe out from between his lips and looked Lane up and down.

"All a misunderstanding," Lane replied.

"Told ye, Fergus," Angus said.

"Ach, ye'll be winnin' the wager."

"Can we give you a lift?" I asked.

"Suppose it's a bit nippy this evenin'," Fergus said.

Angus nodded, and we all climbed into the car. Fergus told me where to go.

"I need to ask you a question," I said.

"Aye?" Fergus said from the backseat.

"Fergus, when you thought I was a dark fairy when you first saw me, was it a specific *bean nighe* fairy you thought I was?"

"O'course. Ye think I'm daft 'n go 'round seein' fayries everywhere?"

"Tell me about her," I said.

"Ach, it was the local lass down the way who died givin' birth to a child. Makin' her a *bean nighe*. A wee lass, lookin' like ye."

"She means the story o' the lass," Angus said.

"Ach, I ken. Ye think I'll be daft as well, Angus?"

"Well, yer not tellin' the story to the lass, Fergus, are ye?"

"Ach."

"Ye'll need to turn off the road here," Angus directed me. "Ye see," he added, "it was a local lass, is why we have our local *bean nighe* legend."

"*Legend*," Fergus scoffed.

"Let me guess," I said, stopping the car in front of a cottage that Angus indicated was his. "Was this shortly after 1857?"

I turned toward the backseat and saw Fergus' wild white eyebrows go up in consternation. "Ach," he exclaimed, "it's how I said. She's one of 'em! How else would she have figured the year?"

"'Tis an interestin' question, Fergus," Angus said thoughtfully.

"Why did you think Jaya looked like her?" Lane cut in.

"The portrait," Fergus said.

"A portrait of the lass was at the Rat & Parrot pub down the way," Angus added. "They'll be havin' the *details*, Fergus."

"Ach."

"Jaya looks like the local woman in this portrait from a hundred and fifty years ago?" Lane asked.

The two men nodded in agreement.

"What was her surname?" I asked.

"Was it McDonald, Angus?" Fergus asked his friend.

"McDonnah."

"Close enough, eh?"

My heart sank. I had been so sure. But neither McDonnah or McDonald fit my theory. It felt even worse to be let down after feeling as if I had figured it out.

I pulled over where Angus indicated. Both of them stepped out. Fergus was grumbling about Americans not making any sense. He assured me his own home was close by, so there was no need for me to go to the bother of taking him a few yards down the road. I suspected he wasn't sure he wanted to be in the car with me any longer.

Angus walked up to the door of the charming small cottage, and Fergus started down the dirt road. Angus was turning his doorknob when the idea struck me.

"Angus," I called out, scrambling out of the car and running up to him. "She died giving birth to a child. So she was married?"

"Aye," he nodded.

"So McDonnah was her *married* name."

Angus scratched his beard and looked me over.

"Do you know her maiden name?" I continued.

"That one I can be sure of. She was a Gregor. That's why they took back her portrait from the pub, once they opened up that Gregor Estate."

That settled it. I was right. I rushed back to the car.

"You're driving," I said to Lane, pushing him over to the driver's side.

"I don't suppose it would do any good to ask why it matters that Fergus thinks you look like one of the Gregors from one hundred and fifty years ago who became part of a fairy legend?"

"One hundred fifty years ago," I said. "Don't you see? 1857 was the Sepoy Uprising. *That's* how the Rajasthan Rubies made it out of India undetected, and why the treasure hasn't resurfaced. One of the Gregors *did* get his hands on the treasure and smuggle it out of the country. The one who built the estate. I know what we're looking for now: *An Indian treasure wrapped up in a Scottish legend.*"

# CHAPTER 39

The Gregor Estate was desolate in the dark night. A harsh wind rippled through the smattering of trees. The ravine that ran along one side of the large house was black in the darkness of the night, creating the ominous sensation that we were at the edge of a dark void.

"It was Gregor family jewels that were supposedly stolen by you," I said. "The police officers told me they received a fax from Sir Edward Gregor of London. This family is the key to the treasure after all."

I broke off. "I don't suppose you can break us in?" I wasn't sure if I was joking.

Lane turned toward me with a mischievous glimmer in his eye.

"Not without research," he said. "There could be dogs, alarms, who knows what. You'll have to wait until it opens. Now, are you going to tell me exactly what you've pieced together?"

"I suppose you're right that it doesn't make sense to break in," I consented. "But it doesn't matter. I can tell you what's going on. Think about what we learned when we first came here. Willoughby Gregor, the man who built this estate, was a Company man. His son Connor worked for the British Raj, not the Company. It was much more organized by then. Connor wasn't the one who made the fortune that created this estate. His father did. And I know how he did it. *By stealing the Rajasthan Rubies.* Connor is portrayed in the role of patriarch in those portraits we saw at the estate because he was the one to make a big deal of the family's wealth. His father

Willoughby wouldn't have wanted to show off his wealth because of how he created his fortune. We didn't pay enough attention to the timing."

"But it wasn't easy for the British to steal treasures of such significance just because they were in power," Lane said.

"I know," I said. "But there was one period of time where it would have been possible. I cannot believe that I was so blind before. This estate was built in the late 1850s. That's right after the Sepoy Uprising, India's first battle for independence from Britain, in 1857. Rupert didn't get the scope of my research wrong after all. This uprising was a huge deal in its implications, and led to the end of control of the British East India Company and the creation of the British Raj.

"Sepoys were the Indian soldiers employed by the Company, and some foolish moves on the part of the British led to an uprising in Delhi. The British were entirely unprepared. The Sepoy soldiers were both Hindu and Muslim, and rumors began circulating that the new rifle cartridges, that had to be bitten before being inserted into the rifles, were greased with cow and pig fat, which was obviously unacceptable to the Hindus and Muslims. This was going on amidst the backdrop of rumors of forced conversion to Christianity, and the Doctrine of Lapse was in full swing—" I broke off as I noticed Lane's face displayed a combination of amusement and impatience.

"The history lesson is important," I said. "Mass chaos broke out, too many people died, and property was destroyed and stolen. At the end of the uprising—also called The Great Mutiny, for obvious reasons—the Mughal Empire was finished, and the East India Company was abolished in favor of rule directly from the British Crown."

"A time of chaos," Lane said. "A perfect time for looting a treasure."

"Exactly. You can see the importance of the turmoil. All sorts of people were displaced and treasures of all kinds were looted.

That whole year, while the power structure was established, the meticulous record-keeping of the British fell apart."

"But what does that have to do with the *bean nighe*?" Lane asked.

"The answer is inside the estate," I said, "along with the answer to where the treasure is hidden."

"You're not going to tell me how you suspect it was done and how it tells us where the rest of the treasure is?"

"It sounds silly if I don't show you. I can show you as soon as the estate opens. Relax. I know now that no one is going to break through the car window and yank me out—"

"I really wish you would stop saying things like that." Lane ran his fingers though his hair, looking nervously out of the car.

"I got you out of jail," I said. "You've been holding out on me a lot longer than I have on you. Now tell. And start at the beginning. I know it must be a long story. We have time. Talk."

Lane sighed, and though his face remained stoic his eyes smiled at me.

"Jones, you have got to be the most exceptional woman I have ever met."

"Don't you dare get sentimental on me, I liked you just fine before. And that's not the beginning."

"Shall I start with my father?" Lane said. "Isn't that where one is supposed to start?"

"Only if I was going to psychoanalyze you."

"Please don't. But it makes sense anyway. My father did business overseas, so I spent most of my childhood in the American schools in too many European and Asian countries to count."

"Your foreign languages," I said. "And the cigarettes Nadia liked."

"That's why I understand that feeling of yours about not quite fitting in, not like you're supposed to." He tapped an unlit cigarette against his leg nervously. "It's strange, telling the story of my life— the real one, I mean—to anyone."

A gust of wind shook the car. The night sky was clear above us, but clouds loomed in the distance.

"I had a natural aptitude for linguistics," Lane continued, "along with a natural skepticism of everything my father did. All of his wealthy associates cared more about their vacation homes and mistresses than their wives and children."

He paused and looked out into the night instead of facing me, seeming to search for what he wanted to say.

"Superficially, I fit in everywhere I went," he said, "picking up the language easily. You'd think it was something I should have been happy about. But I wasn't. They were so contented to play by their rules, using morally questionable business practices to keep their yachts and their caviar coming. No one even likes caviar. They think they're supposed to savor it, so they buy it and pretend to.

"It was a game. Imitating their mannerisms, their accents, their speech patterns. By the time I left for college in England, I didn't have any grand dreams of what to do with my life. All I had was bitterness."

"So you just decided to become a jewel thief?"

"It wasn't a conscious choice." He rubbed his eyes, his lean fingers bumping up against the thick frames of his glasses in the process. "This isn't easy for me, you know. For all I know you could turn me in."

"Why would I do that?"

"Do I have any right to think that you wouldn't?" He cast his eyes downward. When I squeezed his hand, he looked back up at me.

"It wasn't a conscious choice," he said. "I flitted around to various groups, always pretending to be someone I wasn't. Then I met a man. John. I guess you could call him my mentor. He showed me something more productive I could do with my talents.

"I'm not going to lie to you and say I was altruistic—fighting the system to change the world, or being Robin Hood, or any nonsense like that. But I never stole from anyone who couldn't afford it, and I never used a weapon—John taught me that—so I never hurt anyone, either monetarily or physically. I just helped myself. And got even with them."

It all made perfect sense from everything that I had seen in him. I didn't want to forgive him, or make excuses for him. But I didn't want to judge him either.

"It happened without me realizing how far I'd come," he said. "I was good. Good enough that I wasn't afraid of getting caught. I assumed a different persona and was a completely different person in every city.

"You know what it feels like," he said. "Fitting in on the surface, but wanting something more, even if you can't grasp what that something is."

"What did you steal?" I asked him. But I thought I already knew the answer.

"Mostly jewelry. Sometimes art. But jewelry is easiest to sneak out of the country."

"That's why you knew about this treasure—and what it was called!"

"I'm afraid so. It's not quite as bad as you make it sound, though. I hadn't put it together until you brought me the photograph. No one had. Not scholars, and not people with, ah, other ideas in mind, either. There were vague rumors in certain circles of a piece of the Rajasthan Rubies existing, like there was speculation in academic circles that artwork showing the jewels might have depicted real jewelry, but nothing concrete—no proof—so I had to piece things together."

"But how did I find you in that office at Berkeley?"

"My tiny little art history graduate student office? That really is my office."

"You really are a graduate student?"

"Of course. I wasn't faking that. I merely didn't tell you how I came by the knowledge of jewelry and art that got me there." He paused and tried to gauge my expression in the dim light.

"You're wondering why I gave it all up for the luxurious offerings of my thirty-five-square-foot graduate student office?"

"It does make one wonder."

"France," he said. "A few years ago.What happened in France is what made me get out."

He paused, struggling with himself again. "It's a miserable story. What I was involved in was no longer so clear-cut. I had enough money by that point that I didn't really need to—"

"What did you do with all the money?"

"I have it. It's tucked away."

"You still *have* it?"

"You'll notice it comes in handy." He indicated our rather extravagant car. "What, you didn't think I was going to say I gave it all away to charity, did you? I'm not Robin Hood, remember?"

"But you...."

He waited for me to finish, but I didn't know what I wanted to say. I wanted to kick him and comfort him, turn him in and protect him, watch him rot in jail alone and never stop holding him. None of these contradictory things could be expressed in words. Not by me at any rate.

"I didn't turn myself in or give the money back to people who in effect stole it in the first place," he said. "That wouldn't have set things right. Those people didn't deserve the things I took from them. But I needed to find my own peace with the world. I'm not happy about some of the art and jewels that ended up in private collections. So here I am, giving something back to the world."

"Saving history," I said, "one artifact at a time."

"Well, now that you've made my life sound like a Hallmark card for art historians, I really have no choice but to return to a life of crime."

I swore.

"Nervous humor," he said, misinterpreting my outburst.

"That's not it," I said. "That's why you wanted to find the treasure!"

"You don't have to yell. I'm right here."

"You don't want this to make your career," I said, the truth hitting me. "You lied to me when you said that's why you wanted to come to the UK. You don't want to be famous, not even in your field. You want to hide. Your hair and thick glasses covering your memorable face, your clothes that blend into whatever environment you're in. You don't want to be remembered. You don't want to find the treasure for yourself. You want to save it from them."

"I thought that was rather obvious at this point."

"*Nothing* is obvious at this point. And yes, I am aware that I'm yelling, thank you. You want to save the treasure from Rupert and Knox because they're treasure hunters. You don't know what the two of them will do with it, and you want to make sure the knowledge isn't lost."

"Did you hear something?" Lane asked, whipping his head around. I supposed he was used to listening for faint noises in his line of work.

"It's my stomach," I groaned. "I'm starving. We must have been here half the night."

"At least."

Sifting through my bag, I found a squished chocolate bar near the bottom. I offered Lane half. He declined, so I ate it myself.

"Now that you're done with your psychoanalysis and your candy, you can tell me what you think we'll find inside the estate. I know you need to see something to be sure, but I won't hold it against you if you're wrong. I promise."

"Sorry," I said. "There's too damn much going on to keep my head straight to tell this right. All these distractions...."

I trailed off.

"Jaya?"

"The distractions."

"You already said that."

"He wouldn't, would he?" I mumbled.

I couldn't believe I didn't think of it before now.

"Lane, were you wondering why we were both sent on such pointless diversions today?"

"To get us out of the way, obviously. Divide and conquer."

"That's what I was thinking," I said, "but with all that's going on, I didn't have time to think it through. Think about it. Even if you were stuck in jail for a few days, I would have realized the library was a fake errand soon enough."

"The library? What library? I thought you took off because you said your ex made up some story about me being in on trying to kill him."

"No," I said. "That's why I was mad, but that wasn't the diversion. I received a fake call from a librarian at the British Library in London saying they had some information for me, so I used it as a way to get away from here. I didn't think Rupert would have made up something like that, but I didn't want to believe that you were...that you could have...I needed to think."

"You mean there was another ploy meant specifically to get you out of the way?"

"Exactly."

"That means the timing—"

"I know," I said. "That means the timing is important. But why now?"

Lane swore. "I wasn't arrested to keep me away from you and this situation," he said. "Both of our diversions must have been meant to keep us away from something happening *tonight*."

"Tonight? Why tonight? They've been here for ages."

"But your ex hasn't," Lane answered, shaking his head. "You said he told you he was recuperating from the failed attempt on his life, but as soon as he was up to it he was going after the treasure. He knows he doesn't have a lot of time since someone else is after it. He tried *last night*, but we were there and stopped him. So he had to make sure we'd be out of the way tonight."

"But he doesn't know where it is," I insisted. Then I groaned. "Oh, God. He *thinks* he does, though. We've got to get back to the dig. Lane, we haven't been seeing what's right in front of us this whole time."

"The cave," Lane said.

I nodded. "There's something at the site of this dig that has nothing to do with any of the ancient inhabitants of Scotland. Not the Picts. Not fairies. Not the gods of legends. I had half of the explanation of the treasure figured out, but our diversions gave us the answer to another piece of the puzzle. Our Indian treasure, the Rajasthan Rubies, it's not only here in Scotland or on the grounds of this estate, but *hidden at the site of the dig*."

"That's why they've been digging at the cave right underneath the dig."

"We've already wasted too much of the night. We've got to get to the dig before it's too late."

# CHAPTER 40

Lane drove to the dig. Fast. And to think he thought I had endangered our lives with my driving earlier that night. He wasn't even attempting to drive on the road. We did pretty well until one of the tires skidded in a puddle of mud so deep I was sure we wouldn't make it out. Lane knew how to handle a car. We eased out of the hole with only a minor lurch, but the engine stalled.

"We can walk from here," Lane said.

I found a spot that didn't look like it would be a precipitous climb down to the alcove. Though clouds had again covered the moon, the rain held off. I turned on my flashlight and we started the descent.

"I don't know if this is such a good idea," Lane said from right behind me. "The original path we went down before is better."

"Don't be silly," I said. Right before my foot hit a patch of gravel.

The flashlight flew out of my hand as I stuck out my hand to steady my fall, in an attempt to stop the tumble turning into a full-blown slide down the rocky slope. My other foot left the ground. A strong hand grabbed my wrist.

The action prevented me from slipping down the steep hillside, but Lane had taken hold of me with such force that he lost his balance and fell. He fell backwards, but he didn't plunge down the steep path. His hand remained locked on my wrist, and he grunted as I fell on top of him.

I tried to turn around to face him, leading to another groaning sound.

I turned around carefully. "Your glasses!"

"That's okay," he said. "I don't need them."

"You don't?"

"I need *something* for my vision. I thought glasses were a nice scholarly touch—ouch—but I have contact lenses in my pocket."

I tried to stand up, but he held me there.

"Please be careful, okay?" he said. Then without warning he pulled me closer to him in a sweeping motion, and brought my lips to his for an intense moment. He believed me about the urgency of the situation, though. He let me go quickly and stood up.

"I lost the flashlight," I said.

"I don't think it matters. Look."

He was right. The faintest rays of light were already starting to appear on the horizon.

"The sun comes up early here in the summer," he said.

"We wasted that much time? Come on, we need to hurry. Do you need your contacts in to climb down?"

Lane shook his head, and we moved quickly. As the sun began to peek more strongly over the horizon above the sea and below the layer of clouds, we entered the cave.

Rock debris made it immediately clear that someone had been here since the night before. We made a quick inspection of the cave and determined that whoever it had been wasn't there now. We were too late.

What would I have done if I had encountered someone? I was fairly certain Rupert had been there digging, but what if I'd been wrong?

I took a closer look around the inside of the cave while Lane was putting in his contacts. The only sign of activity was a gaping hole in the rock directly next to the entrance. With his vision restored, Lane came up to me and more thoroughly inspected the crudely dug hole.

"He didn't find anything," he said.

"How can you tell?"

"From the way the rock is cut," he said. "Nothing has previously been carved out as a hiding place. He'd know that if he knew what he was doing. You said he finished a PhD in archaeology? It's possible something may have been wedged into the natural formation, but he couldn't have found much."

I stepped back and looked him over. He was a whole new man without his glasses. He ran his fingers over the rock's surface.

"What would you have done if we'd found someone here?" I asked.

Lane turned and looked up from the shattered rock face.

"Played it by ear," he said, shrugging. "That's all you can do in a situation like this."

I wandered toward the smaller entrance of the cave as Lane continued to inspect the freshly dug hole. I stepped through the small second opening, out onto the sunlight on the rock. I discovered to my horror that we were wrong about no one else being there. I called out as I rushed forward.

Knox's body lay askew on the jagged black rocks. His head was bashed in, and blood trickled onto the rock, wet with seawater beneath him.

# CHAPTER 41

I ran as far forward as I could without slipping and bashing my own head. I stopped at the edge of the large flat rock, then carefully stepped onto the smaller uneven rocks at the water's edge, so I could reach Knox. I knelt at his side and felt for a pulse at his neck. If the gash on his head or the vacant expression in his open blue-gray eyes hadn't been enough, the lack of a pulse gave me the definitive answer that he was dead.

I couldn't pull my eyes from Knox's face. His hair was streaked across his forehead, wet with a combination of water from the misty sea air and blood. He looked so familiar, like he should open his eyes at any moment. I don't know what I had expected—that he would look like a mannequin once his breath had left him? In a way it was even more upsetting than when I had thought Rupert was dead. Even worse was my feeling that I might have been able to prevent this. If I had stayed and talked to Knox, he might not have come out here. He might not be dead. *Why had I acted so rashly?*

I didn't realize I was grasping Knox's shirt collar until I felt Lane's hands pulling me back.

"You've got blood on you," he said after he dragged me back onto the stable flat rock.

I looked down at the thick red substance on my hands and the sleeves of my coat. "I know."

"This won't look good."

"I know that, too."

"We can't go to the police." He said it matter-of-factly, but his voice wasn't callous. It could have been the wind, but I thought I detected a slight unsteadiness. I found myself shaking as I looked down at Knox. It wasn't from the chilled air swirling around us.

"They'd figure it out eventually," I said. "Since I didn't do anything."

"There's nothing we can do for him now. All it would do is get you tied up while we could be straightening out the last of this mess."

I sat down on the rock. Lane pulled me back up. "Not here," he said. "We have to get out of here."

"But—" I began, gesturing toward Knox's lifeless body.

"High tide is receding now," he said. "The water won't have a chance of reaching him for half a day. We'll come back if no one has found him by then."

I stared up at him.

"It's one of those things you learn to pay attention to," he said. "It came in very handy during one job."

I snapped out of my stupor with this detailed reminder of Lane's past. The recurring unsettling thought crept back into my mind. How could anything like that be completely left behind? He had been paying attention to all sorts of details in the past few days.

"We should go," he said.

"Finding that bastard Rupert would be a start," I said.

"The police will do that later."

"What?" I stared up at Lane. "That's not what I meant. You can't really think Rupert did this to Knox. Now that I've almost figured it out, with the missing pieces we each have, if we found Rupert, the three of us could figure it out together."

"Who else is there? Your ex had to be the one who was here digging last night. You admitted that. He got rid of us for that very purpose. He must have tried to do the same thing to Knox. That diversion misfired, and now Knox is dead."

"He wouldn't do that."

"Will you *stop* sticking up for him!" Lane yelled. A vein bulged on the side of his temple. He wasn't any calmer than I was.

I knelt at the edge of the water and washed the blood off my hands. I felt queasy as the lapping water rinsed the blood away.

"Let's go," I said. I started back through the cave. Lane fell in step beside me. I could see him seething, but he didn't speak.

When we reached the opening of the cave, Lane jogged ahead of me. I saw why as I caught up with him. He had located his glasses. He tucked them into a pocket and we kept walking.

Back at the car I tossed my coat into the trunk with shaking hands. I'd gotten Knox alone, but not in the way I ever intended. I tried to suppress the urge to scream. The urge to cry. The urge to throw up.

"We should go back to the Gregor Estate," Lane said. "It should be opening soon, so we can get those last answers we need."

I knew he was right. I had to focus. That was the only way I was going to get through this. I got into the driver's seat and started the car.

The estate wasn't open yet. Although the sun was now strong in the sky, it was still quite early. The early morning wind whipped around the car. Lane silently removed his coat and handed it to me.

"Chivalry again?" I asked. "I like this better." I lifted myself out of my seat and onto his lap, and buried my head on his chest. He wrapped his strong arms around me and held me there. Neither of us spoke. Lane's long fingers stroked my hair as he held me close. I couldn't push the vivid image of Knox's lifeless body from my mind, but I no longer felt like throwing up.

Wheels crunched on the gravel drive. The man from our last visit pulled long legs out of a miniature car. I hopped out of our car.

"I'm sorry," he said, "but we're not open until—"

"We're catching a train in a little over an hour," I said.

He smiled down at me. "You're the lass from the other day. Found our military history interesting after all then?" He winked and beckoned for us to follow him as he unlocked the double doors.

"Ye'll still need to pay the admission tariff," he said.

After paying, Lane followed on my heels as I hurried to the great hall. This time, instead of being drawn to the portrait of Connor Gregor that dominated the room, I went straight to dark-haired Elspeth Gregor.

Young Elspeth couldn't have been more than twenty years old. The fashionable gown she wore suited her petite frame. Her black hair was pulled back from her face, revealing delicate features slightly resembling those of the man next to her.

"She's Willoughby Gregor's daughter," I said, reading from the panel next to the portrait. "Born in 1840. No mother listed."

"He was in India at that time," Lane said.

"A merchant for the East India Company—before European women went over to India."

"Elspeth's mother was Indian," Lane said. "That's why Fergus and Angus saw a slight resemblance to you when they remembered this portrait."

"Angus confirmed what I suspected," I said. "This is the portrait that started the local *bean nighe* legend. Willoughby Gregor fathered a child in India, and brought her home with him when he returned to Britain. She married a local man, and when she died in childbirth, a local legend that she was a *bean nighe* fairy began— probably because of her small and distinctive looks, since it wasn't uncommon for a woman to die in childbirth back then. She'd have had a slightly different accent, too. Not quite Indian but not quite English or Scottish either. Adding to her mystique with the locals."

"You were thinking it was a part-Indian woman who Fergus knew to be a fairy," Lane said. "That's why you looked so familiar to him, and why you asked about her name to confirm your theory."

"When I looked at the timing in history, their actions make perfect sense. With the chaos of the Sepoy Rebellion, the societal rules of the British in India changed. The British Crown didn't want their men marrying the natives anymore. It was one thing for unorganized merchant sailors to do so, but now they were directly representing the British Crown. Willoughby needed to get his family out. Interracial children were in a bad spot.

"It was the perfect mix for opportunity. A poor British merchant with no ties back at home and no future in India. He could take advantage of the chaos and both save his family and make off with the treasure that you traced to Delhi."

"But he didn't save his wife," Lane said.

"What do you want to bet she told him about the treasure in the first place? The Mughals still had the treasure, Lane. Someone hid the treasure, or at least made very sure it was kept out of the public eye. You said it disappeared not long after 1611. I didn't put it together at the time, but 1616 was the year Jahangir gave a charter to the East India Company. Someone knew, even then, that a treasure like this needed to be protected.

"But," I continued, "how could someone get such a treasure out of the country? Even with the bureaucracy less stringent, it wouldn't be easy."

"It was his daughter," Lane cut in. "She could pass as white if she assumed the right dress and mannerisms, and could have dressed up in an appropriately voluminous dress, as was the style. That's a great way to smuggle jewels."

Nodding, I continued. "I don't know what happened to her mother, but it was a time of war. Countless people died. Especially those who took risks, such as removing a treasure. Willoughby Gregor managed to get the treasure and his daughter back to Britain. He needed to come to this bleak region of Scotland to keep his treasure a secret, rather than somewhere like London where people would question his wealth."

"And because gold is an easy metal to melt down," Lane said, "he could easily sell as many of the stones and gold as he needed to in order to get set up here, but he'd need to hide the rest somewhere. He didn't have a fortified castle, so he'd want to hide his treasure somewhere that only he knew about. Like a unique site along the coast, near where he was building his estate."

"The same type of distinct coastline," I said, "where people hundreds of years before him thought to put their stone-carved messages as well. So it's not remarkable that the Pictish stones would be around there, too."

"Not bad, Jones."

He paused. "But how did your ex find out about this?"

"As I was starting to explain earlier, Knox...." I faltered. I swallowed and pushed the scene from my mind.

"Knox worked at an auction house in London," I said, "and that's the documentation that our trickster used to get you arrested—an appraisal of a necklace with a similar stone—which must be the one in this painting. Sir Gregor had this old family piece of jewelry appraised but didn't sell it. He didn't take it to a museum or a scholar, so they wouldn't have realized its historical significance. You said how obscure it was. But Knox, with all his interest in treasure hunting and his archaeological training, would have spotted the significance.

"What I'm not sure about," I added, "is how Rupert and Knox put it together with the cave next to the site of this dig Fiona was on. Even if she mentioned the Gregor Estate nearby and they put it together with Sir Gregor, how did they get the bracelet Rupert sent me, but not the rest of the treasure?"

"The dirt," Lane said. "There was soil in the bracelet when you showed it to me."

"Soil like on a dig." I groaned. "That's why Rupert called it an *artifact*. Not a *treasure* or a *bracelet*, either of which would have made more sense. They must have found it buried like an artifact."

"In this region," Lane said, "the weather is strong enough to reshape stone cliffs. So the bracelet wouldn't necessarily have been found with the rest of the treasure that was buried for safekeeping."

"This estate would have used up some of the treasure," I said, looking around at the heavily adorned walls. "But if what we're speculating about the treasure is true, there was a lot, so he wouldn't have had to use much of it."

"Then why doesn't the family have more than one piece?" Lane asked. "And where is the rest? It's not in the cave where Knox and your ex were digging. I don't know why they thought it was there, but there's nothing buried in that rock face."

"Knox and Rupert were digging in the wrong place because they didn't realize it was *Willoughby's* treasure," I said. "They were only focused on Connor, the son Willoughby had with his second wife. He's the one who finished building this estate and left his mark."

I pointed first to the portrait of Willoughby's sullen-looking Scottish wife Mary, then to Connor's massive portrait that dominated the room. The artist knew how to capture a personality; I caught a glimpse of a spoiled boy in his large blue eyes. Between those two, I could imagine why Willoughby hadn't wanted to share his treasure with his new family.

The only other painting close to the size of Connor's was the landscape painting of seaside cliffs directly opposite the portrait. I walked over to get a closer look.

"It's our cave," I said. "It doesn't look the same, but that's it, isn't it?"

"They were looking for a clue from the wrong man," Lane said. "They assumed it was Connor's treasure and Connor's hiding place, for the superficial reasons here in this room. They didn't realize the significance of the periods when the father and son were in India."

"Rupert thought he was missing something in a clue left behind from Connor, who worked for the British Crown in India. That's what he thought I could help him with. But we need to find what *Willoughby* left behind that points to the treasure."

Lane began the search in the gun room, where many of the pieces were listed as having belonged to Willoughby. I was drawn back to the room full of haunting portraits. I spent so long examining the rows of portraits that Lane joined me before I was done.

Past the professional portraits, I found something I hadn't noticed before. An illustration. It wasn't very large, or even very good.

It was a crudely drawn picture of a tree with a young girl sitting in front of it. As a piece of art it was awful. But at the same time, there was care in the charcoal pencil markings. It was a loving piece of work. The lines were carefully drawn if not skillful. She was a girl, not yet a woman, but I recognized her. Elspeth. The landscape was shapeless, but the tree was drawn in detail. It was the early formation of a tree, but already its roots were strong and knotted. Elspeth's hand was pointing at one of the roots.

I don't know how long I stared at the sketch. "He meant it to be for her," I said. "But she died. That's why the treasure was never dug up."

"Willoughby's daughter?"

"This was his own sketch," I said, pointing at the small illustration. "That's where it is. *Not in the cave. Under the tree.*"

"I guess I was wrong," a voice said from across the room.

A voice I knew.

Rupert stood in the doorway.

# CHAPTER 42

"Jaya, why don't you come over here," Rupert said, glaring in Lane's direction.

In one graceful motion, Lane moved in front of me, blocking Rupert.

"Stay away from her," Lane said.

Rupert laughed. "Jaya," he said, and rolled his eyes in the direction of the door. "Didn't you get my *message*?"

"Oh, get over it," I said. "Both of you."

I stepped out from behind Lane.

"Neither of you is trying to hurt me," I said, trying to push Lane's arm aside so I could easily see them both. "Really."

"But Jaya," Rupert said through a nervous laugh, "didn't you listen to—?"

"Jaya, I know you think you know what you're doing," Lane said, "but don't go over there. He's a murderer."

"A *murderer*?" Rupert said. "I know we haven't officially met yet, but you've got your signals a bit crossed. I'm the person who's supposed to have been murdered."

"He's talking about Knox," I said.

A look of confusion spread across Rupert's face. "What are you talking about?"

Lane's muscles tensed as Rupert stepped further into the room.

"Like you don't know he's dead," Lane said.

Rupert looked between me and Lane, then collapsed into a chair. He put his head in his hands and swore. I tried to go over to him, but at my first sign of movement Lane reached out and grabbed my arm too firmly for me to move.

"He's a good actor, Jaya," Lane said.

"Ow, you're hurting me," I said, even though he wasn't.

He released his grip immediately, as I knew he would. I went to Rupert.

Lane swore, but I was already kneeling next to Rupert. He put his head on my shoulder and I ran my fingers through his soft, unkempt hair. He needed a moment to compose himself. I wasn't going to deny him that.

"How did it happen?" he asked, looking up. His face was even more hollow than before. His eyes were moist, but he held himself together.

"Down at the cave," I said. "He'd been hit with something. Or against something."

Rupert looked at me, confused. "The cave? But I was there last night." He put his head in his hands again.

I didn't look up, but I felt Lane right behind me.

"I told you it was him," Lane said. "He was the one at the cave. The night before, too. He was the short pale person I saw, who looked familiar because I had caught a glimpse of him following me in London. And that was why he made sure to get rid of us last night, so he could do his digging in peace. Locking me up in a jail cell."

"Oh, that," Rupert said dismissively. He wasn't his usual flip self, though. "It would have been sorted soon enough." He looked at me. "I didn't get you arrested, love. You always loved libraries, so it wasn't such a big deal for me to send you—"

Lane scoffed. Rupert looked up at him. "Like you have any right to complain," Rupert said to him. "Using Jaya to go after the treasure for yourself."

"That's not what he's doing," I said.

"You didn't used to doubt my word," Rupert said, attempting a smile but failing. "He's involved in the break-in at your apartment. I swear to you—"

"As if that means anything to you," Lane cut in.

"I know what I'm talking about, Jaya," Rupert said. "I spoke with his University's department secretary. I know what his advisor has been doing with him."

Silence filled the air.

"Son of a bitch," Lane said slowly. "I know Michael had been down on his luck, but I never would have suspected—"

"Professor Wells," Rupert said, "has been having his students make inquiries in the UK about a missing Indian bracelet."

I looked over at Lane. "You told him?" I asked.

"He's my advisor. The one whom one asks to advise," Lane said with obvious annoyance. "We ran into him right when you were leaving, remember? I didn't think he'd do anything crazy like break into your apartment to try to retrieve it. I mean, I knew he was going through a bad divorce, but I didn't really think—"

"That explains one big mystery," I said.

"You don't actually believe the wanker, do you?" Rupert asked.

"Will you both grow up!" I shouted, stepping away from them both. "Rupert did not kill anyone, and Lane is not involved in a plot against me. I don't care if you don't trust each other, but trust *me*."

"I know you must feel the need to—"

"Shut up, Rupert," I said. He looked crestfallen. "I'm truly sorry about Knox. He didn't deserve to die like that. But Lane didn't kill him."

Lane opened his mouth.

"And neither did Rupert," I said. "Now that that's settled, Rupert, you're going to pull yourself together and fill in the remaining missing pieces that only you can answer."

"What—*now*?" he asked.

"This whole thing would have been much easier to figure out," I said, not bothering to hide my anger, "and we could even have saved Knox's life if you'd just told me everything from the beginning."

Rupert slumped back down into the chair. I might have been a bit too harsh to blame him for his best friend's death, though it was very possibly true that Knox needn't have died.

"I'm sorry," I said. I really was. "But we need to figure out who killed Knox, and also make sure it doesn't happen to us."

Rupert looked at me, a hollow version of a smile forming on his lips.

"Well...." he said. He glanced at Lane skeptically before turning back to me. "I suppose—" His voice broke off as two elderly tourists entered the room. I should have figured the estate was now open since Rupert had gotten in. The tourists nodded and smiled at our strange, disheveled group, and proceeded to study the paintings on the walls.

I grabbed Lane and Rupert and dragged them outside to the garden. I believe it was a grand garden with a variety of rare roses, but even if I had been inclined to notice such things, I was in no condition to pay attention to them. I barely noticed the cold wind whipping around us.

"Sit," I said, indicating a stone bench. They glanced at each other, then back at me. They sat. "You're going to tell me exactly what is going on."

# CHAPTER 43

Lane cupped his hand against the wind and lit a cigarette. He blew the smoke out of the corner of his mouth directly onto Rupert's face. Rupert was too distraught to notice.

"Knox was working at that big auction house," Rupert began. "Sir Edward Gregor came in to get a piece of jewelry appraised to see if he wanted to sell it. It was the only piece like it in his possession, some family heirloom, so he didn't know if he could get much for it beyond the value of the gemstone itself. It was appraised at the value of the ruby, since no one had any idea where the piece might have come from. Sir Edward decided not to sell it, but Knox saved one of the photographs of the necklace.

"You know the type of things Knox always read instead of working on his dissertation. He'd seen references to some old treasure called the Rajasthan Rubies. When he saw Sir Edward's ruby necklace, he thought it might be a part of that bigger set because of the unique size and shape. What is it, Jaya?"

My face must have shown recognition of the name of the treasure Lane had mentioned. Lane's face was impassive.

"Oh, the *Rajasthan Rubies*?" Rupert said derisively. "Daft name, I know. It wasn't in any of the literature I found at the library, I can tell you that."

"Then where—?"

"I didn't ask Knox." His face again clouded over. He shook his head sadly. "We knew there had to be something sketchy about the treasure," he continued, "since this bloke only had one piece of it. But of course it wasn't enough to go on, was it? We didn't do anything else at the time. That was over a year ago. But then, a few weeks back—"

He broke off as another set of tourists wandered into the garden.

"Bloody summertime crowds," he grumbled.

"I suppose we should find somewhere more private," I said, though I hated to interrupt Rupert's story. "Come on."

The two men stood up from the bench, glaring at each other once more before they followed me. We walked in unfriendly silence toward the front of the estate and the car park. We were about to reach the front of the main house when Lane dropped his cigarette and threw me up against the hard stone wall.

"Police," he said in a loud whisper, pinning Rupert against the wall with his other arm.

I looked around the side of the wall quickly before Lane pulled us back. Two policemen were standing over our rental car, inspecting the license plate.

"Your coat?" Lane asked as soon as we were further down the side of the house.

I groaned, closed my eyes, and nodded. "It's in the trunk."

Lane swore. "Someone must have seen us leaving the dig," he said. "We've got to get out of here."

"And do what?" I asked.

"Knox's blood is all over your coat," Lane said. "Whatever we decide to do, I'd rather it not be from inside a jail cell again." He shot Rupert a spiteful look.

"Look, I'm sorry about that," Rupert said. "All the evidence told me you were in on it, didn't it? Let's get out of here. I've got a car."

"We can't very well walk up—"

"It's not in the car park," Rupert said exasperatedly. "I've been trying to stay out of sight, remember?"

Rupert led the way through the side of the garden, toward a sloping hillside. We followed a path along the edge of the mound until Lane held back.

"It looks like part of the path up ahead is in plain view from the car park," he said.

"Not much of it."

Lane did not look pleased. "Trying to hide from the police is completely different from blending in and keeping away from people who think you're dead. They're looking for us."

"Then it's equally imbecilic," Rupert said, "to stand here arguing instead of heading to my car."

"We'll have to go this way," Lane said, walking off the path.

I followed.

"Where the hell is he going?" Rupert said.

The small ravine that had looked ominous during the night was now a welcome sight. Lane walked quickly, not slowing when he reached the edge of what I saw was a small stream with high banks. There wasn't much water in the ravine, but there was mud. Lane jumped in without hesitation. I could barely see the top of his head from where I stood. He turned and put his arms up to help me down.

"It's better than the alternative," he said softly, lifting me down. "You're on your own," he added to Rupert.

"It's my car," Rupert pointed out.

"You're welcome to take the main path and explain to the police officers who spot you why you happen to not be dead. I'm sure Jaya and I will have plenty of time to get away by some other means while they work out your story."

Rupert jumped down behind us, splashing in the mucky water.

Lane led the way, walking sure-footedly in the gummy mud. We emerged on a dirt road with a Peugeot parked along the shoulder.

Safely inside the car, we sat in silence as Rupert headed toward the highway. Rupert handed me a knit cap. I didn't need to ask why he wanted me to put it on. We sat tensely as he tried to keep an inconspicuous, casual pace on the smaller roads on the way to the A90.

Once we were heading south on the highway, blending in with the other small cars and trucks, I broke the silence.

"Lane Peters, meet Rupert Chadwick."

# CHAPTER 44

"Charmed, I'm sure," Rupert said into the rear view mirror.

"Where are we heading?" Lane asked. His knees were almost even with his chin in the cramped back seat. Now that we were out of immediate danger he kicked over a bundle on the seat next to him and stretched out his legs.

"Hey, watch it with your mucky feet," Rupert said, looking into the rearview mirror.

"It's only a little mud."

"I've been staying at a flat in Edinburgh," Rupert said. "It's a couple hours' drive, but it'll give us a place to sort things out."

"Keep talking while you drive," I said.

"Where was I?" Rupert said.

"Three weeks ago."

"Nothing had come of Knox thinking there might be something to Sir Edward's ruby necklace—until this summer. Fiona rang up Knox from this dig she'd arrived at. She mentioned that during their initial survey, they found a ruby in the earth. They assumed it had fallen off a piece of jewelry from some wealthy hiker, so they turned it in to the local police station. Since the Gregor Estate was next to the dig site, and since the stone was a ruby, that got Knox thinking. The dig was understaffed, so Malcolm was happy to have extra help. Knox was able to search around at night, and he found that ruby bracelet I sent you. It was shallowly buried in a sandy area along the cliff.

"Knox rang me up, since now that we had a location, we had more to go on. Since the Rajasthan Rubies hadn't been seen in ages, except for the necklace that Sir Edward Gregor had, we thought the treasure must still be hidden. We guessed that Connor Gregor got lucky and succeeded in getting the treasure out of India, and he brought it back to Britain. He'd been in India under the Raj, and Sir Edward Gregor was his descendant. It all fit. We thought Connor must have left a clue somewhere. But as much as we searched, both at the Gregor Estate and around the site where we found the bracelet, we didn't find anything else. That's when I thought you could help. We never stopped to think it might have been someone else in the family. I was right that I needed you."

Rupert paused as he passed a truck on the road.

"We were exhausted from digging at night and exploring and helping on the dig during the day," he said. "At the time, I thought it was sleep deprivation making me paranoid, but something seemed strange on the dig. A mood. Something was off. I was sure someone had found out what we were doing. I hid the bracelet in my room, and when I went to check on it one night, I could tell someone else had moved it. That's when I decided to send it to you. It seemed like your specialty. Plus you were always so clever. You told me how easily you'd figured out the clues left in that company man's diary. I knew you'd be able to find something we missed."

He glanced over at me fondly before turning his eyes back to the road.

"And I was right," Rupert said, smiling as he drove. "How did you put it together with the girl?"

I explained briefly about Rupert having the historical timing wrong, that it was Willoughby and Elspeth who left India during the Sepoy Rebellion, and how I put it together when Fergus and Angus thought I looked like the *bean nighe* fairy of the local woman who died in childbirth.

"The girl in that painting looks nothing like you," Rupert said once I was done with my explanation. "Half the girls in London look more like her. You're much more striking. Hmm. I wonder if he loved her because she was his daughter or because she got the jewels out of India for him. She made him a very rich man."

"That's horrible," I said.

"What? Like you didn't wonder?"

"No," I said. "He took her with him at a time when it was clear being the child of an interracial marriage in India wasn't going to be easy. You only needed to look at that loving sketch he made to know I'm right."

We drove along for a few minutes before I persuaded Rupert to continue with his narrative.

"How did you end up with the bracelet?" I asked. "Why didn't Knox have it?"

He gave a raspy laugh that I didn't like the sound of.

"Knox was nervous," Rupert said. "Felt like someone was watching him. He never saw anyone, but you should have seen how jittery he was. But you know where my skepticism got me. I thought he was paranoid before he gave it to me, but once I had it, I thought I might go mad myself. I needed to get it away from the dig.

"Right after I drove to a village to mail you the package, I had the accident. I knew for certain that it hadn't been my imagination after that. Someone was serious enough about having the treasure that he was willing to kill for it. I had the upper hand with him thinking I was dead, so I took advantage of that and thought I could quickly find the rest of the treasure while no one was watching me. I needed a few days to rest up, as I told you. I hadn't had any luck at the Gregor Estate yet, so I thought I'd at least try my luck at the British Library. You always seemed to find such helpful information there, like the diary that gave me the idea about the treasure being from a Company man in the first place." He glanced at me fondly again. "But library research is always so dull, and I didn't find anything.

"I nearly had a heart attack when I saw you at the library," he continued. "I'd left you messages telling you not to worry about getting in touch. I didn't want you getting involved in the mess that nearly got me killed."

He explained how he came back to look for more clues at the Gregor Estate. He thought he had figured out where the treasure was buried. He wanted to get everyone out of the way for what he assumed would be his last night of digging, but he again came up empty-handed.

"I knew I'd lost my one big chance at doing such blatant digging without arousing suspicion," he concluded, "but I was so *sure* I'd find it. I didn't see Knox before I left. Someone else is after the treasure."

I stared out the window, watching the landscape around us rush by in a blur.

"Maybe we got the motive wrong," I said.

"What?" he asked distractedly, passing a slow-moving car on the highway.

"What if it wasn't about the treasure," I said, thinking out loud. "You admitted to completely destroying the cave right underneath the dig. Malcolm Alpin wouldn't let anything compromise his dig."

Rupert looked at me incredulously.

"Malcolm?" he said. "It's not possible."

"I know he seems like a perfectly likable man most of the time, but I've seen him when he has one of his fits of anger about his dig—"

"He thinks the knowledge to be gained from the dig is enormous," Lane said from the backseat. "His scholarly expedition is too precious to let anyone ruin it with a fanciful treasure."

"And his fanatical devotion to proving his ideas in place of mainstream accepted theories," I said.

"Don't you two ever stop finishing each other's sentences and shut up?" Rupert said. "That's not it. You two can collaborate about theoretically brilliant motives all you like, but Malcolm couldn't have killed Knox. I sent him on a wild goose chase last night as well.

I was worried about his habit of checking up on his beloved dig. After your friend here was arrested, I called up the inn and left a message for Malcolm that there was some paperwork back at his university he needed to sign first thing in the morning to assure his grant for this dig was processed properly. He needed to head back to St. Andrews that night to assure being prompt for the morning meeting."

My hands gripped the dashboard as I took in what he was saying.

"You see," Rupert said, "there's no way Malcolm could have done it. Thanks to me, he has an alibi."

# CHAPTER 45

"You can kill him later," Lane said, correctly guessing my desire to reach across the car and strangle Rupert. He put his hand firmly on my shoulder, preventing the accident I was in danger of causing.

"For now," Lane said, "we need to deal with the fact that Malcolm isn't the killer."

"It made so much sense," I said. "I really thought I had it."

"Yes," Rupert said, "but greed is a better motive, isn't it?"

I didn't like the angry look in his eyes, or the way his fingers gripped the steering wheel so tightly that the veins on the back of his hands looked as if they might pop.

"If we're done questioning each other now," Rupert said, "maybe it's time we got down to figuring out what happened to *my best friend.*" He swallowed hard. "Jaya, you may have identified where the treasure is, but that doesn't tell us who's after it or who killed Knox."

I didn't know what to say. I watched the road fly by, listening to the strained hum of the engine as Rupert drove as fast as the Peugeot would take us. I closed my eyes to rest for a moment.

"Where are we?" I asked, rubbing my eyes.

"We're here."

In the flat at the outskirts of Edinburgh, Lane cooked up a big pan of thick bacon he found in the fridge. I paced the kitchen with a cup of strong coffee, watching Rupert sleep on the couch in the adjoining living room.

"No eggs?" I asked as Lane slid the bacon and a piece of stale toast onto a plate. "I thought you were a master chef."

"The eggs were on the counter. If you want to risk eating them, be my guest." He set down the pan and rested his hands on my shoulders. "What do you want to do?"

"I don't know," I said, glancing over at Rupert. He was snoring lightly, but it was a shallow sound. His lips were cracked. They hadn't been on the train. His bandaged arm rested on his side, and his sleeve was pulled up enough for me to see it was bleeding again. He was getting worse, not better.

"He's not faking it," Lane said quietly, following my gaze.

"Should we drop him off at the doctor?" I asked.

"Only if you want to get arrested."

"Maybe it's worth it. Look at him."

"No doctor," Rupert called out from the couch. "I'm fine. Just need sleep," he mumbled before falling back asleep.

"I should go back," Lane said. "We need to find out more about what's going on."

"Hang on," I said. "I'm sure you're implicated almost as much as I am."

"I don't mean go back as *me*," he said quietly. He took my hand in his and led me to the kitchen table. "You know that stuff I told you, about my being good at pretending to be other people?"

"They'd recognize you. They know you. You're tall. You have distinctive cheek bones. Your hair."

"I'd need to pick up a few things first."

"This is how you—?"

He nodded slowly, his eyes fixed on mine. I saw fear in his eyes. Not the panic of being caught, but the dread of being judged by me.

I reached across the table. I took his hand in mine and squeezed. A forced cough from the kitchen door pulled my eyes away from Lane's.

"All right there?" Rupert said.

"You should be sleeping," I said. "Are you sure we can't take you to the doctor? You don't look good."

"Thanks for the concern," Rupert snapped, rubbing his temple.

Lane handed Rupert a plate of cold bacon.

"Cheers," Rupert grumbled, out of habit more than courtesy I was sure.

"We were discussing what we should do," I said.

"Come up with anything?"

"I need to borrow your car," Lane said.

Rupert stopped chewing. "Not bloody likely. Jaya, I told you this tosser—"

"You're supposed to be dead," Lane said, "and the police have Jaya's coat covered with Knox's blood. I'm the only one who can do anything."

I looked expectantly at Lane. He clearly didn't want Rupert to know that disguise was one of the skills he possessed.

"What do you want to do?" Rupert asked, then resumed chewing the cold bacon.

Out of habit, I went to the cabinets in search of the HP sauce I knew Rupert liked on his bacon.

"Where's your HP sauce?" I asked Rupert.

"I don't think there is any," he said through a mouthful. "Knox doesn't like it."

"Knox?" My mug of coffee slipped from my fingers. Ceramic pieces shattered on the kitchen floor as I stared at Rupert. "Please tell me I'm wrong about what I think you're saying."

"What's the matter?" Rupert asked. "I'll survive without HP sauce. It's hardly worth smashing Knox's dishes."

"You can't be that stupid," Lane said. "You brought us to Knox's apartment?"

"You don't really think the police would...." Rupert began. "I've been staying here since I knew he'd be gone at the dig."

"Of course they would, you idiot," Lane said. "He's a murder victim now. Jaya, tell me everything you've touched in the kitchen."

"You can't be serious," Rupert said. "Jaya, where did you *find* this—"

"She's the prime suspect in a murder investigation," Lane growled at him, rubbing a dish towel over the counter tops and cabinets. "Now are you going to sit there acting jealous and let her go to jail, or are you going to start being helpful?"

# CHAPTER 46

Lane maneuvered Rupert's car from the Edinburgh suburb of Leith into the crowded center of the city.

"I'll come check into the hotel with you," he said, "but then I should take off before it gets to be much later."

"You never told us what the bleeding hell you intend to do!" Rupert said.

"I have a friend in Aberdeen," Lane said coolly. "I'm not going to get him mixed up in this, but he would gladly go to the inn and get some information about what's going on."

"Oh. Well why didn't you say so in the first place?"

Lane did the talking at the front desk, and we went up to our two adjoining rooms.

"Two rooms," Rupert commented. "I wonder who's sharing."

We didn't enter the second room. Lane and I didn't have any luggage to unpack. Besides my messenger bag, our belongings were still at the Fog & Thistle Inn. Rupert tossed his bag on the floor and lay down on one of the beds on top of the covers. He crossed his arms behind his head and closed his eyes.

I stepped out into the hallway with Lane. I looked down the empty corridor with checkered carpeting and cream-colored walls, and then into Lane's face. He looked so different without his glasses, even with his hair falling over his face in the same manner. The same intense hazel eyes gazed at me. How could anyone mistake those eyes?

"You sure you know what you're doing?" I asked.

He smiled confidently, but sadly, and kissed my forehead. I watched him disappear down the hallway. If he was as good at disguising himself as he claimed, I also had to accept another possibility. How easy would it be for him to walk away? I wasn't sure I would ever see him again.

I took a few deep breaths before returning to the room, then closed the door softly behind me so as not to disturb Rupert. God knew he needed the rest.

"Are you in love with him?" Rupert said from the bed. I walked over to him. His eyes were still closed, and his face was more drawn than before.

"You need to sleep," I said. "Do you want me to get some supplies to change the bandage on your arm again?"

He opened his eyes and sat up, moving the pillows so he could lean against the headboard. His blue-gray eyes had all but lost their bright blue vigor, and the gray stood out next to the grayish tint of his sunken sockets.

"We know each other too well for that," he said.

"For me to buy you disinfectant?"

He smiled weakly.

"For you to get away with ignoring me," he said.

I sat down on the edge of the bed. "The answer is, I don't know," I said.

He smiled again, and took my hand in his. I didn't object.

"Your fingernails," he said. "They're still short. How are those drums of yours?"

"Still got them," I said. "Transatlantic flights are no match for my tabla."

"Why did we ever break up?" he asked.

"I left the country, remember?"

"Yes, I know that part. Long-distance relationships are way too romantic and impractical for either of us. But you could have stayed."

"You never asked me to."

"What if I'm asking?"

"You're a little late."

He held my hand, looking at me in silence for a few moments before his eyelids drooped. He sank down onto the pillows. I covered him with the blanket from the other bed.

"Don't go," he mumbled, before falling into a restless sleep.

I sat on the other bed for what seemed like hours. I had my headphones with me in my messenger bag, so I listened to music as I scribbled notes on the hotel stationery about who could possibly have killed Knox and left Rupert in such bad shape. I think the bhangra beats I was listening to must have been overly complex, because I ended up with two lists. One that included everyone at the inn as a suspect, and one that excluded everyone because it didn't seem possible for them to have done it. I wadded up the sheets of paper and quietly left the room to get some food. I returned a short time later with some new clothes, including a new pair of heels, fish and chips, and refreshment.

The scent of the fried fish and pungent condiments woke Rupert, but only long enough for him to eat a piece of fish and wash it down with a lager I'd picked up at the off-license down the street along with a bottle of Macallan whisky for me. I was momentarily worried that I shouldn't have given alcohol to someone with an injury, but then I remembered that bit of advice concerned head injuries rather than infections. The alcohol would probably do him good.

I turned on the television at a low volume and flipped among the five channels of reception while drinking the whisky before I fell asleep to news about the dental crisis in Scotland.


I woke to the smell of kippers under my nose. I'm told that most non-Brits can't stand the smoked fish that's saltier than anchovies, especially as a breakfast food. I love it. It took me a moment to remember where I was, before sitting up in my clothes from the day before to find the room full of daylight and Rupert standing next to me. He looked somewhat better than he had the night before. His eyes were no longer as sunken and dark, and his smile approximated a hearty one.

"Hungry?" he asked.

"Always." I looked across the room. "Room service?"

"You really do sleep through everything, love."

For a few moments I could almost imagine life was back to normal. The familiar smells and the familiar sight of the man in front of me brought me back to a time when life made sense. The illusion quickly faded as I looked at Rupert's sickly pallor. He and Knox would never again be able to go on a crazy adventure together.

"Where's Lane?" I asked.

"He didn't come back."

"You checked the other room?" I asked.

He nodded. "He probably stayed over at his friend's house in Aberdeen," he said, taking a bite of eggs from the tray. His eyes watched me intently.

I forced myself to speak. "I'm sure you're right."

After eating far too many kippers, I took a long shower and got dressed in my new clothes. Lane still wasn't there when I came back into the room.

As I stood at the window, looking out at a view of a cobblestone alley, Rupert came up beside me.

"It'll be okay," he said.

"You used to be a better liar."

"Right now I feel like I used to be better at a lot of things."

"I know what you mean."

"What the bloody hell has happened to our lives?" he said. He held me tightly with his good arm around my waist, but didn't attempt to do more than that. That made it all the more difficult to push him away.

# CHAPTER 47

I was desperate for a decent cup of coffee, and probably even more desperate to do something other than sit helplessly in that hotel room. I left the hotel and walked down the narrow street, with cars somehow managing to whiz by in two directions. I found a coffee house almost immediately, but took my time sipping the strong coffee before heading back to the hotel.

"See, she's *fine*," Rupert was saying as I opened the door.

Lane stood a few feet away from Rupert, his appearance showing no signs of whatever disguise he had assumed. He had fixed his thick black glasses and was wearing them again. A small locked bag lay at his feet.

"What did you learn?" I asked.

"Malcolm is back," Lane said. "And he isn't happy that some joker is wreaking havoc on his dig. They're all there, so that isn't going to help us narrow things down."

"That's a really insightful friend you've got there, Lane," said Rupert.

"Both Jaya and I are under suspicion," Lane said. "Mostly Jaya. Her blood-stained coat, and a note from Jaya the police found in Knox's pocket."

"Bloody hell," Rupert mumbled, sitting down on the edge of his bed.

"The police aren't watching the dig around the clock," Lane said. "They don't have that kind of manpower to spare, since they're not positive what's going on. All of the people on the dig have been instructed not to leave. Mr. and Mrs. Black were asked not to take any unexpected trips as well, which they found rather amusing."

"That's great," Rupert said. "We're in exactly the same place as we were yesterday. If only we all had such helpful friends we'd be out of this in no time."

Lane looked ready to throttle Rupert. My turn to intervene.

"We needed that information," I said, "but now we need to figure out who is behind everything. Lane is right. I'd rather not be figuring out the bad guy from a jail cell. Or wait until something happens to another one of us. I'd rather figure out who is the homicidal maniac."

"Your language has become a bit overwrought in your old age, Jaya," Rupert commented.

"Damn it, Rupert. When are you going to realize life is not a game?"

"When are you going to grow up and realize that perhaps it is?"

Rupert and I glared at each other.

"Let's make a list," Lane suggested.

"I already tried it," I said. "Last night. After you left and Rupert fell asleep. I thought it might help. But it doesn't. Don't make me fish it out of the trash."

"It's really not such a bad idea," Lane insisted.

"He's right," Rupert said.

"Fine," I said. "I'll summarize."

They both looked at me imploringly. I got up and fished the crumpled pages out of the trash.

"We can rule out Knox," I said, "for obvious reasons. Next there's Professor of Scottish archaeology Malcolm Alpin, who, if we are to believe Rupert's statement, we can also rule out. It's too bad, since it really was such a good theory."

They agreed we had to rule him out, though Lane only admitted it grudgingly, eyeing Rupert.

"No one else has an alibi that we know of," I said, "so let's go through motives. Fiona Murdoch, who has never been known for her good judgment and is taking a hell of a long time to complete her dissertation—though I'll agree she's on a better path than Knox took—was the instigator of this whole mess when she told Knox about the ruby. She could have finally gotten fed up with Knox and with you, Rupert, but why not leave you out of the whole thing if that was her intent? It seems easier not to put yourself in a position where you're going to need to kill someone. Leaving us with her motive, which makes no sense.

"Moving on to Derwin McVicar, the pompous graduate student of archaeology—"

"You're in Britain, love," Rupert cut in. "So the proper terminology is post-graduate student."

"Two to one non-Brits in the room, so the proper terminology is simply 'graduate'," I countered. "Getting back to the point, Derwin is a pretentious man who is too busy kissing up to the professor to do much else besides write methodical notes. He certainly wouldn't be distracted by an Indian treasure. Anyone disagree? No?

"Moving on to the others who aren't a part of the dig, Mr. and Mrs. Black have full run of the inn since it's their establishment, so they could have found out what you were up to, Rupert, but why would they care? They seem quite content running their little inn.

"Lastly, Fergus and Angus. They're a bit eccentric, and they thought you should be digging for fairy treasure rather than Pictish history, so I grant that they're a bit of a wild card, but I still don't see them bumping off members of the crew one by one to prevent the dig from moving forward. If the purpose was to stop the dig, there are easier ways and, at the very least, better people to target."

Silence followed my exhaustive list.

"You're not thinking badly enough of people, Jaya," Lane said finally. "How do we know the Blacks don't have more motive than you think? What if one of them secretly wants to run off to a Caribbean island if only they had the money?"

"But that doesn't make any sense," I insisted. "We can't go inventing motives we don't know exist. That won't get us anywhere. By that logic, anyone could develop a greedy streak."

"All right," Rupert said. "Brainstorming, then. I say...Derwin McVicar did it. With a name like that, he's got to be messed up in the head. Traumatized since childhood and all that."

I stared angrily at Rupert. I saw Lane looking intently in his direction as well.

"That's not a bad idea," Lane said slowly.

It was Rupert's turn to look incredulously at Lane. "I was joking, old boy," he said.

"No, no," Lane said, shaking his head. "But his name. Derwin McVicar. It's far too good to be true, isn't it?"

Rupert and I stared at him.

"I mean that it could be an alias," Lane said. "Did anybody know Derwin before he came to the dig?"

Rupert and I were silent for a moment.

"I think he worked with Professor Alpin before coming here," Rupert said.

"It was a recent connection," Lane said, "not long before he found some research that got him to the dig."

"But nobody knew about the treasure until Knox found the bracelet," I added.

"How do we know that?" Lane said simply. "For all we know, it could have been Derwin who dropped the bracelet when he found the treasure."

"The bracelet wasn't dropped recently," Rupert said. "Knox wasn't daft. He could tell the difference."

"I think my head may explode," I said, throwing myself down onto one of the beds.

"Then what do you propose?"

I looked up to find them both looking at me expectantly. Rupert's chest moved up and down with effort. Although he would never say it, it was clear how labored his breathing had become.

We needed to get Rupert to a doctor soon. He'd never go willingly until this was settled.

We didn't have much time.

"It's your turn to act," I said to Rupert. "These speculations are getting us nowhere. Your 'amnesia' has come to an end. You're going to appear at the pub and flush out the killer."

# CHAPTER 48

The storm that had been teasing us with cold winds finally broke that night. I sat alone in the car as the rain beat down on the windows.

One of the items in Lane's new bag had been a warmer coat for me, much more appropriate for the Scottish weather than anything I had brought for the summertime trip. I was still chilled, but at least my teeth weren't chattering.

Since Lane and I were wanted by the police, Rupert was the only one who could safely reveal himself at the inn. Even more importantly, someone in that inn thought they had killed Rupert, so they should have some sort of reaction when they saw him alive.

Lane didn't trust Rupert at all, so he wanted to be there, too. I didn't trust Rupert's health, so I agreed Lane should be there to help Rupert with the murderer.

We couldn't tell this to Rupert, of course, so Lane made up an excuse to go off with his friend in Aberdeen to get some more help, when in truth he would be applying his disguise and appearing back at the inn as a traveler at the same time Rupert went to the inn.

I was waiting in the car a short distance away. It had been close to an hour. What was taking so long?

We decided the best time to go would be around dinner, so everyone would be gathered together. But that time was long past now. Where *were* they?

I was almost fed up enough to walk over to the inn myself, taking whatever consequences came with that decision, when I heard a noise. It wasn't the storm. It was a branch breaking under a foot. I jerked my head around, unsure of which direction the noise had come from. It was impossible to see anything through the storm.

The passenger-side door yanked open. Before I could move, a man lunged into the car and pulled the door shut.

The unfamiliar, dark features came close to my face as he grabbed me and wrapped his hands around my arms. The grip was tight. I shifted my lower body and lifted up my left foot to bring it down on that of the attacker. Before I struck, I realized I knew the touch of those long fingers.

"Where is he?" a familiar voice asked frantically. "And why wasn't your door locked? There's a murderer on the loose, you know."

I looked into his face and didn't recognize Lane except for his touch and the sound of his undisguised voice. It was especially dark that night with the rain falling steadily, but I could see the outline of his features, and it didn't seem possible that this was the shape of his face. Even the scent of his breath was different.

"What do you mean *where is he*?" I asked, in shock.

"Your ex," Lane said.

"Rupert's at the inn. Why aren't you?"

"No, he's not. That's where I've been. He never came inside."

"That can't be."

Lane swore.

"Where did you leave him?" he asked. "And when?"

"Almost an hour ago, right here. I saw him walking toward the inn."

"But not going inside?"

"I closed the car door before he got all the way there. The rain was coming down sideways."

Lane ran his fingers through his wet—now brown and frightfully curly—hair, and I got a better look at his face. It was rounder, less angular, than the face I knew. And his eyebrows...they were bushier. In place of his usual glasses he wore circular wire-rimmed spectacles. He noticed me staring.

"Later," he said.

I looked away from his face so I could focus on the matter at hand. My gaze wandered to his midsection, which was somehow different as well.

"I don't know how anyone could have gotten him," I said.

"That's what worries me. I think he couldn't face them. He ran."

A fist banged on the window next to Lane. He covered my mouth with his hand before I could make a sound.

The knock came again.

Lane motioned for me to stay quiet, then rolled down the window of the car.

"All right?" said a Scottish voice coming from Lane's mouth. "Right fierce storm."

"Ye've no need to pretend to me," Angus said.

"Surely I don't know what ye—"

"Ach," Angus said. "There's no time for that, man! I mean ye no harm. Somethin' is amiss." He pulled open the door behind Lane.

"Wot are ye—" Scottish Lane asked.

"Ach," Angus said again, slipping into the back seat "The others cannae see. No one *looks*, do they? It's in the eyes."

I wondered if it was the first time Lane had ever been found out. And by an eccentric old man, no less.

"Evenin', Miss Jones," Angus said, leaning over the seat to see me. A flash of lightning lit up the sky, illuminating his grave face.

"What's wrong, Angus?" I asked. A clap of thunder sounded, and the rain beat down against the car more furiously.

"Is nae right."

"What are you talking about?" I asked. I almost had to yell to be heard over the torrent.

"Didnae yer gentleman notice when he was in the pub?"

"I wasn't sure if it was only my imagination," Lane said. "I was most concerned about watching out for your ex through the front door."

"Wait, Angus, *did* Rupert go inside?" I asked.

"Rupert?" Angus repeated, pausing from adjusting his rain-soaked coat collar. "The young man who went 'n crashed his car?"

"The crash injured him," I said. "But didn't kill him."

"Aye," Angus said slowly, comprehension dawning on him. "No, I havnae seen the boy."

"You're talking about how tense the mood was?" Lane said. "I felt it, too. Malcolm and Derwin didn't seem to pay attention to anyone else, huddled over some charts to figure out how to remove their stone."

"Their obsession," Angus said, shaking his head. "When a man is dead, and the two of them is still there calmly talkin' on and on about gettin' at their Pictish stones in the ground. Is nae right. Is nae right at all."

I stared at Angus.

"What did you say?" I asked.

"Wot did I say?" Angus asked, startled, looking over at Lane.

"You said the two of them," I said, answering my own question. "*Their* obsession, not *his* obsession."

"Aye," said Angus.

"Jaya," Lane said, "we don't have time to stand around debating theories with Angus right now. It's more important that we find your ex." He turned to Angus. "He was with us tonight, but he's missing. And I don't think he ran off. I think I know where he went."

"I'm not wasting time theorizing," I said. "We were right about the motive, but not the *person*. Derwin is just as obsessed. He's the one who was spying on people who weren't where they were supposed to be on the dig. The blinding lights we saw. It was his binoculars. He's been watching us. And remember he was so concerned about sealing off the cave? That wasn't so he could prevent someone else finding a treasure he wanted for himself. He was worried the dig wouldn't be stable if someone was digging in the cave underneath it. Derwin killed Knox and tried to kill Rupert to protect the dig."

"Wot are ye sittin' here fer?" Angus said. "Yer friend is in danger. Stay here, Miss Jones. We'll be back."

I was too startled to disobey. The sound of the rain filled my ears as they opened the door and jumped out, slamming it behind them. This time I remembered to lock the door.

Sitting alone as the torrential downpour surrounded me, I felt the car sway beneath me. Lightning flashed again, leaving me exposed to whoever might be watching.

In less time than I would have thought possible, they were back. I unlocked the door and they piled in.

"Derwin is gone," Lane said.

"But you said he was there when you were in the pub," I said.

"He was," Lane said. "But he's not in the pub now, and he's not in his room."

"Where's he gone?" I asked

"To check on his obsession," Angus said. "On this of all nights, it might not be safe. He'll need to be sure."

"And your ex has gone to get the treasure," Lane said. "If Derwin finds him...button your coat, Jones. We're going out there."

Angus was spry, and also well prepared. He had his own flashlight in his jacket pocket, which he no doubt used when he and Fergus walked the long path home on stormy nights. In spite of the harsh rain, he kept even pace with Lane, with me a few steps behind them in my inappropriate shoes for the slippery path, as they hurried to the site of the dig—and the tree with the treasure buried beneath. The frequent lightning helped our search for the path—if not our nerves—and we found our way.

I was out of breath and soaking wet by the time we came upon the site. Not a soul was in view. But a small tarp had been sloppily erected, and the tree had been massacred. Lane swore. Angus followed suit. Loose earth had been dug up from around the roots of the tree in an attempt to gain access beneath them. The digging was haphazard, but had not gone far. A trowel lay at the edge of the tarp a few feet from the tree. Lane went over to it.

"Dunnae touch it!" Angus shouted. "Cannae ye see there's blood?"

# CHAPTER 49

Lane stopped before he picked up the bloody trowel. Under the edge of the tarp, the rain hadn't been able to wash away a liquid thicker than water visible on the base of the tool. It wasn't the pointy edge, though. Thank God it wasn't the pointy edge.

"There's naebody," Angus said. "Wot's been done?"

"I think Rupert tried to dig up a treasure," I said, looking frantically around while I spoke. "Right here under this tree, and Derwin found him and tried to stop him."

Lane looked down over the side of the cliff near the steep walkway.

"He didn't kill him here with the trowel," Lane said.

"The tide," Angus said. "He's goin' to set him out in the tide."

Lane and I stared at Angus.

"He's supposed to be dead in the sea already," Angus said sagely.

"Oh God, he's right," I said. "His car went over a cliff and they thought he was dead because they never found the body but his car was on the rocks. If Derwin means to kill him for real, then he'll want to make it look like the way Rupert was thought to have died."

"We won't be able to sneak up on him," Lane said. "Even in the storm, they'll see us coming."

"Not if ye follow me," Angus said, a wicked smile on his face.

Of course. He knew about the hidden path where Lane had seen the *bean nighe.*

Angus led us south a few yards to a path we hadn't noticed before. It was indeed the hidden path that Rupert had previously used to evade us. It was easy to miss, and difficult to traverse, especially in the rain. I didn't want to go barefoot, but it wasn't going to be easy to climb down in my heels. Lane took my hand.

"Stay with me," he said.

Instead of following the path all the way down along the rocks to the edge of the sea, Angus led us down to where the rocks met the cliff's edge. As I stepped forward, my foot gave way, slipping on the rock. Lane's hand still held mine. He pulled me back and set me on my feet.

Angus looked back at us. I could see him more clearly now. The storm was letting up. We continued on.

We were still heading downward, though our movements were more up and down as we silently scrambled across the rock formation. Angus held up his hand once we had reached a flat spot directly above the entrances to the cave. Lane and I stopped in our tracks.

The rain stopped. The only sound was the crashing sea.

Angus motioned for us to move forward, and we stopped even with him, near the edge of the small landing above the cave.

We had come down so far that we were almost at sea level. The rocks below us were being swallowed by the lapping tide, and I slowly made my way toward the edge. They came into view right below us.

I saw Rupert first. He was lying on a rock, being splashed by the sea water. A red gash was visible on the side of his head.

He wasn't moving.

I rushed forward without thinking, but Angus pulled me back. Yet I had gone forward enough to catch a glimpse of Derwin standing on a rock next to Rupert. The sea was crashing loudly enough that he hadn't heard us.

"Lane," I hissed. "You're the hero. Don't you have a gun or something we can use to stop him?"

"I don't use guns. They get you into more trouble than they're worth."

"Thanks a lot, MacGyver."

I wrenched my arm out of Angus's grasp and crawled to the very end the ledge. My hair whipped around me as I looked over the edge. Derwin was close. Only a few feet below me. He stood on a rock much higher than the one Rupert was on. I swung my legs around so they were hanging over the side. Derwin still hadn't seen me, and the roaring waves muffled our movements. He was standing in the doorway of the second opening to the cave, looking between Rupert and the opening, so that no one on his level could sneak up on him.

"Don't do it, Jones," Lane's voice whispered into my ear.

Neither of them would ever let me act if I hesitated and gave them time to stop me. I needed to do it now.

I jumped.

I landed right behind Derwin, bending my knees to cushion the jump. It actually worked. There was no hiding my presence any more, but I had a couple seconds of confusion in which to act. I hadn't counted on the fact that my legs were momentarily unsteady from the big leap. As I tried to steady myself, I saw something I hadn't noticed before. Derwin was holding a sharp metal hook in his hand.

I wasn't the only one who had seen the weapon. Lane jumped down on the other side of Derwin, pulling Derwin's attention away from me. It was a gallant effort. If the rock he landed on hadn't been slick from the rain, and if he hadn't been wearing so much extra weight in the padding of his disguise, he might have been even more effective by landing upright. As Derwin turned to face Lane's fallen form, his arm flew up and I saw the metal gleam. I had only a second to act.

My first kick hit Derwin's thigh, and he cried out in pain. With my adrenaline so high I hadn't been aware of how hard I had kicked him.

When I drew my leg back, my foot pulled loose of my shoe. The heel was stuck in Derwin's leg.

He bent over in pain. Balancing on the ball of my now-bare foot, I swung my other foot around and clipped him in the cheek, slicing the tip of my remaining heel across the fleshy part of his face like a knife. A red line of blood spread out and ran down his face, and he staggered to the edge of the rock.

Toward me.

"You've ruined everything!" he yelled. "Why? Why didn't you let me stop them? You said you understood. You understood that what I was doing wasn't easy. But it was right."

His voice made me shiver. He lunged at me with the hook. The motion of his attack brought back the jiu-jitsu class drills of my youth. I jumped away, and from the unexpected angle I was able to pull his weight onto my shoulder from behind. Because of the center of gravity, the move is one of the few things easier for a short person than a tall one. Barely feeling his weight, my body lifted his. His tall form rolled over my shoulder and flipped onto the hard rock below.

As he hit the ground, the sharp hook fell from his grasp and landed a few feet away. Derwin was conscious but stunned. He groped around in a daze. As he grasped for the hook, he slid on the slick surface and slipped off the edge of the rock.

I thought I heard him yell, but the sound was swallowed up by a wave. Lane was standing now, and rushed forward toward the spot where Derwin had gone over the edge. I ran over to where Rupert had lain.

He wasn't there.

It was this rock, wasn't it?

I stepped forward, dreading seeing Rupert underwater on another rock that was now swallowed up by the tide.

Two figures came into view. Angus had heaved Rupert onto a different rock on higher ground. They were both soaking wet with sea water.

Rupert moaned.

"He needs to be taken to hospital," Angus said.

"Derwin needs to go, too," Lane said, out of breath, coming up behind me.

"Did I—"

"No," Lane said. "He fell onto a sharp rock below. But he's alive."

Lane looked at me earnestly. I had the strangest foreboding.

"Can you two manage—?" he began.

"Go, man!" Angus said, more quickly than I could get a word in. "We'll met ye at the hospital, looking like yerself. Ye might bring an extra pair of shoes for Miss Jones. I dunnae think she'll be wantin' these."

# CHAPTER 50

Lane didn't meet us at the hospital. A pair of new shoes had been dropped off with "Jones" printed in thick black marker on the box, though, so I knew he had been there. They were heels in my size.

He didn't return to the Fog & Thistle Inn, either. His luggage was gone from the room, and an envelope had been left for Douglas Black with double the amount of money needed to pay for our room. I heard that the local police station had also "misplaced" his arrest file.

I can't say I blamed him. There were bound to be lots of questions, and if he could avoid them...well, who in his position would have done any differently? The last thing people at the inn had observed about the two of us was that we'd had a fight, so he had a legitimate, unsuspicious reason for being gone.

I savored the strong peaty flavor of yet another local Scotch on my tongue and enjoyed the warm fire on my toes. I was finally thawing out.

It was the following evening, and I was sitting in front of the fireplace at the inn with a blanket on my lap and a single malt Scotch whisky in my hand.

The police were quick to grasp the situation, and I had only spent a couple hours at the station. That left me the rest of the day to visit Rupert at the hospital, have a long phone conversation with Sanjay and a short one with Nadia, and to properly dig for a treasure beneath the tree.

Malcolm had a bit of a shock when he saw the initial damage done to his site, but once the situation was explained, he agreed to excavate the tree in search of the lost Indian jewels.

Perhaps he wasn't completely altruistic. There are complicated laws governing treasure trove, and as the person with official government permission to be digging up that stretch of the coast, Malcolm might have thought he could fund more Pictish digs with the windfall from locating a lost treasure. He sorely needed it. Fiona had decided to leave, and I couldn't blame her.

Douglas Black came over to where I sat with Malcolm, Fergus, and Angus, and asked if we needed another round.

Our drinks were quite full, but he soon got down to the real reason he was hovering.

"The missus was wonderin'," he said. "How did you realize it was Derwin that was tryin' to do the harm?"

"I didn't know until the last minute," I admitted.

"She thought it was me!" Malcolm said heartily, not trying to keep his voice down. The pub was so full with locals who had heard about the adventure that there weren't enough tables to go around, and Malcolm was enjoying being a minor celebrity. "I'll take that as a compliment, Jaya. I do love my stones."

"I did have the right motive," I said to Mr. Black, "but the wrong person. If going after the treasure wasn't the motive, then I realized the digging for treasure could seriously disrupt the dig. Malcolm had put so much time and energy into his obses—I mean, into his passion, that it made sense for him to be passionate enough to kill to protect it.

"When I learned Malcolm had an alibi, I realized that Derwin had the same interest. And having studied geology, he was worried about what digging in the cave underneath the dig would do to the structural integrity of the site. Once Derwin was suspicious of Rupert's activities, he used his knife to get at the hidden bracelet in the floorboards of Rupert's room. That's why he tried to kill him. He also had binoculars that he used to spy on all of us. When I saw him walking back up to the crew after I found the cave, I thought he was returning from using the facilities at the inn. If I'd been more suspicious, I might have noticed then that he was watching me."

"He's claiming to the police that he never meant to kill Rupert," Malcolm said. "Only injure him so he'd leave the dig. He can't claim that about Knox. Such a shame. I thought he had real potential." Malcolm looked down into the fire.

Douglas Black shook his head incredulously.

"Never trust a fellow who dusnae smoke real cigarettes," he said.

"Daft," Fergus mumbled. "A treasure worth a fortune in 'is hands, 'n he puts it back, 'n goes 'n kills instead."

"He'll be in hospital for a time," Angus said. "Nae pretty recovery for tha' one."

"And Rupert's finally getting the medical attention he needs," I added. "He should be out of the hospital soon, as long as his father doesn't kill him."

"Dougie!" a female voice called from the back. "Yer not askin' about the treasure!"

Angus stifled a smile. Malcolm laughed out loud. "Ach," Fergus mumbled.

"I'm gettin' there, woman!" Mr. Black grimaced.

"The treasure Jaya found is safe under guard at the police station until it can be transferred to a museum," Malcolm said. "My treasures are still in the ground."

"Miss Jones found her fayrie treasure," Fergus said approvingly, grinning broadly and revealing his gray teeth.

The British and Indian authorities would no doubt take ages to sort out what would happen to the Rajasthan Rubies. I still had the original artifact that had set off this whole adventure, but even if I had been tempted to forget to mention the bracelet to the authorities, I doubted Rupert would let me. Not now that I was heading back to San Francisco and close proximity to Lane, rather than staying in Britain with him.

Rupert hadn't been able to sneak off with the treasure, so the jewels were all safely at the police station. At least I had every reason to believe they had all of the jewels....There was only a slight possibility it wasn't the storm that had disturbed the spot at the edge of the tree after we left in search of Rupert. And it was most likely only our overactive imaginations that made it look like the antique box we found so close to the surface had been opened recently. Just because some of the dirt around the hinges looked a little disturbed....

Could a reformed jewel thief resist?

There was still a king's ransom of treasure left. Ruby-laden gold ornaments for all kinds of adornment, in the same beautifully ornate style as the bracelet I had first seen only a week ago. And more importantly, the diary of Willoughby Gregor. The history, and the knowledge, had been left for the world.

I had a few minutes with the diary before the police confiscated it for safekeeping for the proper authorities, whoever they were determined to be. The story we had pieced together was true. And it wasn't only a story. It was a life. Many lives. Their loves, losses, successes, risks, and beginnings. Willoughby Gregor, a merchant with the East India Company, who married Ameena Bashir, an adventurous young woman who knew of a rumored treasure that had been hidden away. She didn't survive the Sepoy Rebellion or make it out of India alive, but the fortune she found for her beloved husband and daughter did. The first page of Willoughby's diary said more than anything else: For Elspeth. His daughter.

Willoughby hadn't revealed the treasure to anyone else, even though Elspeth had died first. He had removed some of the pieces for his estate and family, dropping one piece during a fierce Scottish storm, but not the vast majority of riches. But I had to wonder....

Willoughby didn't destroy that sketch showing the location of the treasure after Elspeth's death. He wanted someone who understood to find it.

As for me, the one who found the treasure? I'd found something much more than I was expecting. The one item Lane had left behind was a piece of paper with the address of an apartment in Berkeley. I didn't know what I'd find there, but I knew who I'd find. And I could hardly wait.

# Author's Note

Though *Artifact* is a work of fiction and the characters and treasure in the book came from my imagination, the historical details about Scotland and India are true.

In Scotland, the story of the Picts is presented as scholars have pieced it together. Though this particular archaeological site does not exist, Pictish standing stones are being unearthed to this day. The cliff-side setting is an accurate portrayal of that region of the Highlands of Scotland and the nearby Dunnottar Castle is a dramatic site to visit. The legends of the Tuatha de Danann and the *bean nighe* are alive and well in Irish and Scottish folklore.

In India, the styles of Mughal artwork described are real, as are the challenges art historians face in separating factual depictions from artistic license. The battles and social norms of the British East India Company also existed as they are described in the book. The British East India Company transformed itself from a trading company into a military power, assuming a greater military and political role after the 1757 Battle of Plassey, with the British Crown taking over direct rule of India a century later, after the Sepoy Rebellion of 1857. Indian independence was achieved in 1947. There were many violent conflicts leading to lives and treasures being lost, but during certain periods of time there were also marriages between British men and Indian women. It's entirely possible that the story in *Artifact* may have played out in unrecorded history...

# Reader's Discussion Guide

1. Written in first person, the reader only sees what Jaya sees. Was she a reliable narrator, or did she have blind spots you could see?

2. Would you make the same choices as Jaya? Would you have hopped on a plane to Scotland if you were the only person who believed someone dear to you was murdered? Would you have bailed Lane out of jail after he revealed his secret?

3. *Artifact* is a fair-play "puzzle" mystery where the reader is given clues to solve the mystery. Did you solve it? What types of misdirection obscured the truth about the treasure and the killer?

4. What was the most surprising plot twist? Did you find the plot twists the most memorable parts of the book, or were you more drawn to the characters and their relationships?

5. Superstition is used to reveal non-supernatural truths. How did Scottish legends and folklore shed light on the secrets of the buried treasure? Were you familiar with any Scottish folklore before reading *Artifact*?

6. Being part of two cultures and spending parts of her life in each, Jaya describes feeling like an outsider. Do you think that's one of the reasons she and Lane have a connection? And is that why her music is such an important part of her life?

See the scenic settings of the Jaya Jones Treasure Hunt Mysteries on Gigi's Pinterest boards: http://pinterest.com/GigiPandian

Learn more about the history of British India and Scotland at the British Library's online gallery: http://www.bl.uk/onlinegallery

# GIGI PANDIAN

Gigi Pandian is the child of cultural anthropologists from New Mexico and the southern tip of India. After being dragged around the world during her childhood, she tried to escape her fate when she left a PhD program for art school. But adventurous academic characters wouldn't stay out of her head. Thus was born the Jaya Jones Treasure Hunt Mystery Series. The first book in the series, *Artifact*, was awarded a Malice Domestic Grant.

**Don't miss the next book in**
**The Jaya Jones Treasure Hunt Mystery Series**

# PIRATE VISHNU

Gigi Pandian

## A Jaya Jones Treasure Hunt Mystery (#2)

A century-old treasure map of San Francisco's Barbary Coast. Sacred riches from India. Two murders, one hundred years apart. And a love triangle. Historian Jaya Jones has her work cut out for her.

1906. Shortly before the Great San Francisco Earthquake, Pirate Vishnu strikes the San Francisco Bay. An ancestor of Jaya's who immigrated to the U.S. from India draws a treasure map...

Present Day. Over a century later, the cryptic treasure map remains undeciphererd. From San Francisco to the southern tip of India, Jaya pieces together her ancestor's secrets, maneuvers a complicated love life she didn't anticipate, and puts herself in the path of a killer to restore a revered treasure.

Available February 2014

Visit www.henerypress.com for details

**Be sure to check out Jaya's prequel novella**
**FOOL'S GOLD featured in**

# OTHER PEOPLE'S BAGGAGE

### Kendel Lynn, Gigi Pandian, Diane Vallere

Baggage claim can be terminal. These are the stories of what happened after three women with a knack for solving mysteries each grabbed the wrong bag.

**MIDNIGHT ICE by Diane Vallere:** When interior decorator Madison Night crosses the country to distance herself from a recent breakup, she learns it's harder to escape her past than she thought, and diamonds are rarely a girl's best friend.

**SWITCH BACK by Kendel Lynn:** Ballantyne Foundation director Elliott Lisbon travels to Texas after inheriting an entire town, but when she learns the benefactor was murdered, she must unlock the small town's big secrets or she'll never get out alive.

**FOOL'S GOLD by Gigi Pandian:** When a world-famous chess set is stolen from a locked room during the Edinburgh Fringe Festival, historian Jaya Jones and her magician best friend must outwit actresses and alchemists to solve the baffling crime.

Available at booksellers nationwide and online

Visit www.henerypress.com for details

## Henery Press Mystery Books

And finally, before you go...
Here are a few other mysteries
you might enjoy:

# LOWCOUNTRY BOIL

Susan M. Boyer

## A Liz Talbot Mystery (#1)

Private Investigator Liz Talbot is a modern Southern belle: she blesses hearts and takes names. She carries her Sig 9 in her Kate Spade handbag, and her golden retriever, Rhett, rides shotgun in her hybrid Escape. When her grandmother is murdered, Liz high-tails it back to her South Carolina island home to find the killer.

She's fit to be tied when her police-chief brother shuts her out of the investigation, so she opens her own. Then her long-dead best friend pops in and things really get complicated. When more folks start turning up dead in this small seaside town, Liz must use more than just her wits and charm to keep her family safe, chase down clues from the hereafter, and catch a psychopath before he catches her.

Available at booksellers nationwide and online

Visit www.henerypress.com for details

# DOUBLE WHAMMY

Gretchen Archer

## A Davis Way Crime Caper (#1)

Davis Way thinks she's hit the jackpot when she lands a job as the fifth wheel on an elite security team at the fabulous Bellissimo Resort and Casino in Biloxi, Mississippi. But once there, she runs straight into her ex-ex husband, a rigged slot machine, her evil twin, and a trail of dead bodies. Davis learns the truth and it does not set her free—in fact, it lands her in the pokey.

Buried under a mistaken identity, unable to seek help from her family, her hot streak runs cold until her landlord Bradley Cole steps in. Make that her landlord, lawyer, and love interest. With his help, Davis must win this high stakes game before her luck runs out.

Available at booksellers nationwide and online

Visit www.henerypress.com for details

# BOARD STIFF

Kendel Lynn

## An Elliott Lisbon Mystery (#1)

As director of the Ballantyne Foundation on Sea Pine Island, SC, Elliott Lisbon scratches her detective itch by performing discreet inquiries for Foundation donors. Usually nothing more serious than retrieving a pilfered Pomeranian. Until Jane Hatting, Ballantyne board chair, is accused of murder. The Ballantyne's reputation tanks, Jane's headed to a jail cell, and Elliott's sexy ex is the new lieutenant in town.

Armed with moxie and her Mini Coop, Elliott uncovers a trail of blackmail schemes, gambling debts, illicit affairs, and investment scams. But the deeper she digs to clear Jane's name, the guiltier Jane looks. The closer she gets to the truth, the more treacherous her investigation becomes. With victims piling up faster than shells at a clambake, Elliott realizes she's next on the killer's list.

Available at booksellers nationwide and online

Visit www.henerypress.com for details

# DINERS, DIVES & DEAD ENDS

Terri L. Austin

## A Rose Strickland Mystery (#1)

As a struggling waitress and part-time college student, Rose Strickland's life is stalled in the slow lane. But when her close friend, Axton, disappears, Rose suddenly finds herself serving up more than hot coffee and flapjacks. Now she's hashing it out with sexy bad guys and scrambling to find clues in a race to save Axton before his time runs out.

With her anime-loving bestie, her septuagenarian boss, and a pair of IT wise men along for the ride, Rose discovers political corruption, illegal gambling, and shady corporations. She's gone from zero to sixty and quickly learns when you're speeding down the fast lane, it's easy to crash and burn.

Available at booksellers nationwide and online

Visit www.henerypress.com for details

# THE AMBITIOUS CARD

John Gaspard

## An Eli Marks Mystery (#1)

The life of a magician isn't all kiddie shows and card tricks. Sometimes it's murder. Especially when magician Eli Marks very publicly debunks a famed psychic, and said psychic ends up dead. The evidence, including a bloody King of Diamonds playing card (one from Eli's own Ambitious Card routine), directs the police right to Eli.

As more psychics are slain, and more King cards rise to the top, Eli can't escape suspicion. Things get really complicated when romance blooms with a beautiful psychic, and Eli discovers she's the next target for murder, and he's scheduled to die with her. Now Eli must use every trick he knows to keep them both alive and reveal the true killer.

Available at booksellers nationwide and online

Visit www.henerypress.com for details

# PORTRAIT OF A DEAD GUY

Larissa Reinhart

## A Cherry Tucker Mystery (#1)

In Halo, Georgia, folks know Cherry Tucker as big in mouth, small in stature, and able to sketch a portrait faster than buck-shot rips from a ten gauge -- but commissions are scarce. So when the well-heeled Branson family wants to memorialize their murdered son in a coffin portrait, Cherry scrambles to win their patronage from her small town rival.

As the clock ticks toward the deadline, Cherry faces more trouble than just a controversial subject. Between ex-boyfriends, her flaky family, an illegal gambling ring, and outwitting a killer on a spree, Cherry finds herself painted into a corner she'll be lucky to survive.

Available at booksellers nationwide and online

Visit www.henerypress.com for details

# FRONT PAGE FATALITY

LynDee Walker

## A Headlines in High Heels Mystery (#1)

Crime reporter Nichelle Clarke's days can flip from macabre to comical with a beep of her police scanner. Then an ordinary accident story turns extraordinary when evidence goes missing, a prosecutor vanishes, and a sexy Mafia boss shows up with the headline tip of a lifetime.

As Nichelle gets closer to the truth, her story gets more dangerous. Armed with a notebook, a hunch, and her favorite stilettos, Nichelle races to splash these shady dealings across the front page before this deadline becomes her last.

Available at booksellers nationwide and online

Visit www.henerypress.com for details

Made in the USA
San Bernardino, CA
04 March 2015